Meadows Taylor

Tara

A Mahratta tale

Meadows Taylor

Tara
A Mahratta tale

ISBN/EAN: 9783337137151

Printed in Europe, USA, Canada, Australia, Japan

Cover: Foto ©Andreas Hilbeck / pixelio.de

More available books at **www.hansebooks.com**

TARA

A MAHRATTA TALE

BY

CAPTAIN MEADOWS TAYLOR, M.R.I.A.

AUTHOR OF 'CONFESSIONS OF A THUG,' ETC. ETC.

IN THREE VOLUMES

VOL. III.

WILLIAM BLACKWOOD AND SONS
EDINBURGH AND LONDON
MDCCCLXIII

TARA:

A MAHRATTA TALE.

———◆———

CHAPTER I.

THERE is nothing, perhaps, more effectual to deaden, if not to relieve recent misery, than the sensation of rapid motion. Leaning back in the palankeen, with the doors now shut, and the fresh breeze blowing refreshingly through the open blinds, Tara felt herself hurried swiftly and smoothly along, while her attention was at once occupied and distracted by the occurrences of the journey. Sindphul, its temple and trees: the lane which was the bed of the rivulet, through which the bearers plashed rapidly: the village gate now shut, and its bastions manned with men to keep out marauders: the long shady narrow lane, overhung with trees;—then, beyond, the plain, covered with rich crops of grain now ripening: the shouts of the men and boys, perched upon their stages in the fields,

slinging stones at birds: the song, drawling and
monotonous, of the bullock-drivers at the wells,—were
all familiar objects and sounds to the desolate girl
being carried rapidly by them. Would she ever see
them again?

As they passed their own garden, she looked among
the trees—perchance she might see Sudba, the old
bullock-driver, or Puréshram, the gardener; but there
was no one visible, else she had cried out to them.
Were they dead, too? Ah! how often had she wandered among the trees there with her mother, and
watched the butterflies among the flowers! The
bearers stopped to change opposite the wicket gate,
and she could see the bright beds of white jessamine,
unpicked as yet, and large marigolds, and white and
yellow chrysanthemums, which the men were saving
for the Dusséra. Who would gather them now? Over
them, the same bright yellow and white butterflies were
hovering in hundreds, and the fierce green and blue
dragonflies chasing each other, or darting here and
there, quick as thought, and glistening in the sun.
Then she remembered the omen in her garden as she
sat spinning, and fell back on the pillow shuddering.
It was true. She remembered too that the bird had
sat for a while, and twittered a sweet low song. Was
he that bird, that noble, gracious youth, who had spoken
to her so gently, so kindly? She tried to follow the
thread of this thought back, but failed. Her mind
was sadly confused and wandering, now reverting to
the omen, now to the objects she was passing, and the

people they met:—who were they? what doing? whither going?—to the horsemen, the monotonous tramp of whose horses never ceased, some behind, some before, some around her,—fierce, dark-bearded fellows, whose very proximity she would have dreaded before,—who were now guarding her respectfully by his order; while the kind old man, to whose charge she had been specially committed, rode close to the side of the litter, and where the path was narrow, asked her, through the blinds, if she were well, and wanted anything.

Fazil, son of Afzool; she remembered the name. It was strange to Hindu lips, but had a musical cadence, which her memory retained as she repeated it to herself. Fazil, son of Afzool; and he had a sister Zyna. What would she be like? Would she be kind and loving to her? like Radha? Was he not beautiful, and very fair, almost ruddy.

Into all these channels, confused, and whirling her mind hither and thither like dust and straws before the wind, her thoughts wandered dreamily, apparently avoiding the bare, hideous fact that all were dead whom she loved—all who had protected her up to last night. But this would not long be denied its place. It was a horrible reality not as yet fully understood: —which her gentle mind could not grasp.

Dead! who saw them die? They were alive last night,—who had killed them? If she had seen them die, that, indeed, would be surety. No, it was not true. They could not be dead,—they could not have

left her so helpless. It was some fraud, some deception. She had not gone far: Sindphul was close by:
she would run and sit in the garden, and wait for her
mother; and she half-opened the door of the litter.
Shêre Khan rode by it, erect and stern, but bowed down
to her as the door moved. " Do you want anything,
lady?" he said. " Go to sleep; it will rest you."

The voice, kind as it was, dispelled the other thought,
and brought back the bitter reality of desolation and
the events of the night. How she had been lifted up—
and the girl Gunga's laugh of triumph and mockery
rang in her ears, and was before her eyes now, as she
pressed her hands against them; the rude men who
carried her down the steps: the fearful shrieks and din
in the temple: the shots and blows, growing fainter
as they carried her away: and, above all, the voice
of Moro Trimmul, exulting with Gunga that they
were safe from death, and had Tara captive. " To
Rutunjun first," he had said, " and then——"

" From that worse than death he saved me," she
thought, with a shudder. " Fazil saved me—Fazil, son
of Afzool—else I were helpless with Moro now. And
they were dead—her people, all dead? Yes, the
detail Fazil had related was brief and circumstantial.
The Bhópeys would not lie—why should they? They
were weeping, and had taken him up dead. Her father,
a negro had killed him, they said. She felt no hope
could come out of this detail. They had lifted him
up and put him . . . No, she could not follow that.
That beloved father, dead — disfigured with ghastly

wounds !—mother, whom Janoo had seen dead, and
Radha . . . . all ? He had said so. How could he
—Fazil—know of Janoo, or the Bhópeys, her father's
dependants, so as to deceive her with names ?".

So, round and round, whirling, dashing hither and
thither like the motes in a sunbeam, staying nowhere,
sometimes utterly blank, the girl's thoughts ministered
to her fast growing misery. The hot dry eyes, red
and swollen, looked out sometimes vacantly as the
bearers changed shoulders. She felt powerless to move,
careless as to what became of her. As the reality of
the death of all, pressed on her mind occasionally with
greater force, she sat up and gasped for breath, and
again fell back upon the cushions ; then the monotonous cries of the bearers as they shuffled along rapidly,
and the dull tramp of the horses, with the sense of
motion, were relief from mental agony : and, after a
time, she slept.

The action of setting down the litter, awoke her
with a start. Under some trees not far from a village
gate, there was the small hut of a Fakeer. Shêre
Khan was speaking to the old man, and the troopers
were dismounting from their horses. Shêre Khan
came to her.

" I have sent for the Josee's wife," he said. " The
Syn here says she is a kind woman. She will bring
you water and something to eat. We rest here while
the men get their breakfasts, and the horses are fed.
Fear nothing. Open the litter,—it is cool and pleasant
in the shade under the trees," and then he left her.

So it was. She opened the door and looked out.
A small grove of mango trees, with a smooth green
sward below them, and some cattle and goats grazing
there in the cool shade ; a boy and a girl tending
them looked inquisitively at her, and the girl came up
shyly and sat down by her.

"Do you want water, lady?" she said. "I am the
Josee's daughter, and those are my goats. I will go
and tell my mother you want water. You are a Bramhun, are you not?"

Tara patted her head in assent—she could not speak ;
and the girl ran away, crying to the lad not to let her
goats stray.

By-and-by the child and mother returned, and the
latter brought a copper vessel of water and a drinking-
cup.

"Here is water, lady," she said ; "will you get out
and wash your face? Surely, I know you," she continued quickly, as Tara turned her face to her. "Where
have I seen you?"

"No matter," said Tara, "I do not know you."

"Perhaps not," said the dame drearily. "So many
travellers come and go, and . . . but no matter. Shall
I cook anything for you? will you come to our house
and bathe?"

"No," said Tara ; "they will go on presently; I will
stay here."

"Come hither, Ooma," she said to the girl, who was
standing apart, and she whispered to her ; "Go, and
come quickly," she added aloud.

" Do not send for any one else," said Tara ; " I am well."

" Are you not ill ? " said the woman. " Ah, your eyes are red and swollen."

" I have a headache," replied Tara ; " it is so hot."

" Yes," said the woman, sitting down, and putting her arm kindly round Tara, and pressing her head against her own bosom—" yes, you look tired and weary, but it will pass away. Wash your face and hands, and your feet—it will do you good, and refresh you. Put out your feet—so—I will wash them."

The cool water was refreshing as it was poured over her hands and feet ; and after the woman had dried them with the end of her saree, she again laid Tara's head against her breast, and patted her as though she were her own child.

" You look so weary," she said ; " have you travelled far ? "

" From Tooljapoor," Tara replied.

" Is all well there ? " asked the woman. It was a common question with no meaning to the asker, but of how much to Tara !

She could not answer, but clung, almost convulsively, to the kind breast on which she had laid her head.

" I see," said the woman ; " so young and rich, and yet thou art in sorrow, lady—rest here." And she drew her the more closely to her, and patted her as before. So they sat till the child came back, who brought upon a plate, covered with a handkerchief, a few simple sweetmeats and some parched rice. " Eat,"

she said, "if ever so little ; eat a bit of ' Luddoo,' *
and drink some water." Tara shook her head, and only
nestled the closer to the soft bosom : it was strangely
like her mother's.

"Poor thing, poor thing," thought the woman to
herself, "what can ail her? Perhaps her husband is
unkind. Eat, my rose," she said aloud, "eat this."
And she broke off a piece of the cake and put it to
Tara's mouth. "I made it myself, and it is quite pure
and clean. Eat it; open your mouth." Tara did so
mechanically, and she put it in.

Tara tried to eat, but her mouth was dry and hot;
she could not swallow, and felt choking. The woman
saw it, and rubbed her throat gently. The hardness
and constriction seemed to relax, and she was able to
swallow what she had taken, and to eat a little more,
the woman feeding her.

"Good," she said kindly, "try again by-and-by. O
lady, what heavy grief is on you that no tears come?
Can I do aught for you?"

"Nothing," said Tara; "only do not leave me while
they are absent."

So they sat silently. If Tara could have wept, it
had been well; but that blessed relief was not to come
yet. She was quiet, however, sitting there, almost
stupified, resting her head against the woman's breast,
who still patted her. Every now and then the great,
sore, hot eyes looked out drearily. Some of the goats
and cattle browsed under the trees, others had lain

* A sweetmeat made of milk, flour, and sugar, rolled into balls.

down resting in the shade. There was no sound but a faint rustle of the breeze among the leaves, the dim buzz of flies, and the droning song of a man, at a well in a garden near, singing to his bullocks, and the distant plashing rush of the water as it was emptied from the bag into the cistern.

And so they sat, till one by one the bearers gathered near them, and tied up their hookas on the palankeen as before. Then the horsemen came up, and she heard Shêre Khan asking her if she were ready, and telling the bearers to take up the palankeen. Tara had put the gifts she had received at the shrine under her waistband, and remembered them. As the palankeen was taken up she took them out and put them into the woman's hand, who, expecting perhaps a few copper coins, stood looking at them in amazement.

"May your grief pass from you, and may God be merciful unto you, my child," said the woman. Ere Tara could reply, a bearer had shut the door, and the men ran on with renewed vigour.

Yes, the little change had refreshed her, and she again fell asleep, mercifully; and it was evening, and the shadows were lengthening fast, when she became aware that they approached a large town, passed through a busy bazar crowded with people, then emerged from it; crossed over a bridge, from which a large piece of water was visible on the left hand, and the towers and bastions of a fort washed by it; then the gloom of a deep-arched gateway, and light beyond. A respectably dressed elderly woman, in Mahomedan costume, took hold of the side of the palankeen, and ran along with it a short distance.

"Stop," she cried to the bearers,—"this is the place; put it down, and go away."

Then Tara saw several other women advance and hold up a heavy sheet so as to screen her as she got out, and the door was opened; and Goolab, for she it was, speaking a rough dialect of Mahratta, bid her come forth. As she did so, and stood there, Goolab "took the evil off her," as was her custom;* and other women coming forward with plates, on which were coriander and mustard seed, waved them over her. Thus welcomed, Tara now stood waiting a signal to advance; and Goolab, seeing her trembling violently, put her arm round her, looking with wonder at the richness of her apparel and the heavy gold ornaments she wore, her exceeding beauty causing respect and silence even from the loquacious and privileged nurse.

"Enter," said a low sweet voice from within a curtain hanging across a doorway, which was slightly opened.

* Women pass their hands over the person on whom the ceremony is performed from head to foot; then turning the backs of their hands against their temples, make all their knuckles and finger-joints crack loudly. This is done to avert consequences of Evil Eye.

CHAPTER II.

TARA advanced, still trembling, and clinging to Goolab, and trying to hide her face in the end of her garment; she was only sensible of the same sweet voice, as a girl of great, and to her strange, beauty, took her in her arms, embraced her, and said gently, "Peace be unto you! you are welcome, with the peace and blessing of Alla upon you!" and that another taller and older lady embraced her in like manner, and said the same. After that for a long while she remembered nothing.

When she recovered, she was lying upon a soft bedding in a small room, near an open window which looked out upon the lake that encircled the fort, glowing with the reflection of piles of sunset-clouds. On what seemed an island in the lake was a Hindu temple, with a high pyramidical roof, around which hung the rich foliage of several magnificent trees, and temple and trees were reflected double in the still water. These were the first objects that met her sight.

Then, turning round, the same young face that she had seen on entering the apartment bent over her, and a soft warm hand was passed over her face, and the

ends of the fingers kissed in loving greeting; but the
girl did not speak, though a sweet smile spread over
her features, and she seemed to beckon with her left
hand to another person behind her, whom Tara could
not see. Another moment and her deliverer advanced,
saluting her respectfully.

Fazil had ridden fast to overtake Tara, but had not
succeeded. Twenty men, a light palankeen, and the
hope of a liberal reward, had induced the bearers to
put out their utmost speed, and they had well re-
deemed their promise of reaching their destination
before sunset; but he had arrived soon after.

"Go away, brother," said Zyna, " do not speak to her
now ; you have seen that she is safe—that is enough."

"My sister," he replied in Persian, that Tara might
not understand, "not so.   It will grieve her, and thee
too, sorely, but she must know the truth.   Do not go
away.   I will speak to her in her own tongue, and
show her these sad memorials which I have brought.
It is mercy not to delay in such cases.—Can you
listen to me, lady, a few moments?" he continued to
Tara; " what I have to tell you is not worse than what
you have already heard, but it will confirm it; and
truth and reality are ever better than doubt."

"If you please to say it, sir," said Tara, who had
arisen directly she saw Fazil approaching, and stood
by the window.

"If—if—you saw anything that had belonged to
them you would know it, perhaps," said Fazil hesitatingly.

Tara's bosom heaved so that she could not speak. She appeared as if gasping for breath, with the same distressing symptoms as when, in the morning, he had told her first of her bereavement,—and she trembled violently. She could not stand, and crouched down against the wall.

"O not now brother! not now," pleaded Zyna, who put her arm round Tara, and was supporting her.

But Fazil was merciless. "It must be," he said. "And now lady, listen. If you had any doubt, these will remove it. After I left you the second time I went to the Cucherri for what Janoo Näik told me he had left there, and these were given as having belonged to your mother, Anunda Bye, and your stepmother, Radha Bye. Look at them."

As he spoke he untied a bundle he held, and poured the contents at her feet; heavy gold and silver ornaments of some value, and a few rings.

Tara looked at them for a moment. The silver chain anklets, which were her mother's, were dabbled with blood, now dry on them; the gold pair had been made after those on her own feet for Radha's marriage, by her brother Moro. Enough—all were familiar objects. They swam before her eyes—the room seemed whirling round, and, weak as she was, she sank down again utterly unconscious, with Zyna crying over her.

"Let them remain," said Fazil, "she must see them when she recovers, else she will not believe. Show them to her one by one. I dare not stay;" and he left the room.

Tara had not however fainted, but she was gasping for breath, and Zyna called to Goolab to bring a fan, while she opened the casement of the window still more, to let in air. " He said—he said," sobbed Tara, trying to speak ; " lady, I cannot speak—I am choking—O ! why do I not die ? He said——"

" He said you were to look at them all, one by one," said Zyna, trying to check her own sobs and tears. " He is kind. Fazil, my brother, would not give you pain unless it were for good. Look ! here they are," and Zyna spread out the ornaments with her own hands, shuddering at the blood upon them.

Tara looked earnestly at Zyna ; the eyes were full of misery—so full that Zyna could not bear them— passed her hands over her own, pressing them tightly, then looked away. Tara turned the ornaments vacantly over and over, sighing, and, as it were, catching her breath convulsively. There was one, a ring with a sapphire set in it, with which she knew her mother never parted, for she believed that without it evil would happen to her, and that it had brought prosperity. It used sometimes to be put on the altar when they worshipped Lakshmee, the Goddess of Wealth—else it never left her mother's hand ; but it was there. Zyna did not know this then, but she saw Tara's hand tremble very much as she took it up and looked at it carefully. There was a dark stain inside, and Tara put down the ring, gasping, as it were, for breath, then took it up again.

Zyna watched wonderingly, the changing expres-

sions which passed over the beautiful features : first
despair; then, as it seemed to her, prayers were mur-
mured in a language she did not understand, and the
features appeared to relax, the upturned eyes glistened,
there was a look as if of hope or triumph upon the face.
She moved closer to Tara, still closer, as she thought
she saw tears gathering in the hot eyes. If Tara could
only weep it would be well. Zyna passed her left arm
round her, and gently drew the girl's head on her own
shoulder and bosom ; it fell softly there and rested ;
the hand which held the ring dropped on her lap, beating restlessly ; but the other grasped her so that it
almost caused pain. Kind nature did not suffer the
terrible struggle to continue longer, else Tara had died :
and with almost a shriek of pain, her tears burst forth
uncontrollably.

"Thank God for it," said Lurlee, who had entered,
and was standing over them, and who now passed her
hands over Tara, as Goolab had done ; " she will be
easier for this, and the worst is past : let her weep.
The blessing of Alla and the Prophet on thee, my
daughter," she said to Tara. " I salute thee with
peace ! Thou hast entered at a fortunate moment,
and there is joy following thy grief. Fear not ; thou
hast come to those who will be to thee what thou
hast lost."

" She will require much care, mother," said Zyna ;
" feel how she is trembling ; I will not leave her. Ah,
yes—that is the reason ; take away those things, Goolab ; wash them and put them by."

Goolab took them up, and with all her choicest epithets of "Poor little rose! my pretty dove! my lily! my own life!" she tried to soothe the girl; but Tara heeded no one.   Keeping the ring clutched in her own hand, she hid her face in Zyna's bosom, then suffered her gradually to lay her head down on her knee, and rock it softly.   She dared not speak, but tried to look up gratefully, sometimes, and then clung the closer to her gentle nurse.

"Hush," said Zyna, as fresh bursts of tears often occurred, "I know what has happened, and I will not leave thee, Tara; no, never now.   And he, my brother, says it too."   So they sat and lay—the two girls—long into the night; and gradually, unable to resist the kindness lavished on her, Tara spoke a little, and Zyna encouraged it, and heard wonderingly, Tara's simple tale of trial and sorrow.

That night, too, her future fate was the subject of earnest debate, often approaching the verge of passion, between Afzool Khan, his son, and the priest.   What could they do with a Bramhun orphan, a heathen unbeliever who was a captive, and a slave by the laws of war?   Long and earnestly did the priest plead that she should forthwith be sent to the royal harem.   So beautiful a slave would be cherished, loved, and have every luxury at her command; she might become the mother of princes, and the head of the state; and Afzool Khan supported this opinion, which was borne out by texts from the law, plausibly quoted by the Peer.

But Fazil opposed them both, gently yet firmly, and

at last almost fiercely. "She is my captive, if captive at all," he said; "my slave, taken in war, according to your own texts, Huzrut—and I can release her, or ransom her, or keep her, as I will. She has relatives at Wye, where we are going, and with your permission father, she can stay with us till then; we will be her safeguard, honourably and truly. After that," he added with some little confusion, "she can act for herself, and of her own free will; but to send her to the palace, to be decked out and noticed for a while, and then flung aside—no, father; better she died, or better still that we now turned her into the street, to shift for herself among her own people."

"That would be inhospitable son, if no more," returned his father; "well, boy, let her stay, and welcome. No matter," he thought to himself, "if he have his own way in this thing." The Khan was decidedly in good humour. The kichéri, kabobs, and some other dishes which were especial favourites, had been dressed to perfection by Lurlee, and were relished, as they can best be, with the zest insured by a long ride.

Lurlee had met him in good humour, and the stars were in propitious conjunction to welcome his arrival. The lady had nothing but good to say of Tara, whose beauty and sad history had at once deeply impressed her. "What if she be an infidel," she said, "she will make the better true believer. Let her stay with us, O Khan! she shall be a daughter to me," and the lady sighed. "There is nothing unlucky about the

period of her arrival, for the sun was in conjunction
with Jupiter, and she was born under Venus, she says ;
and as she is a Bramhun she knows all about her
horoscope and the planets ; besides, is not this Wednesday, and she arrived between five and six in the
evening, under Venus, so that she is born to us under
the same planet as she was born to her own parents ?
Is not that curious ? and by-and-by I shall call her
Fazila, according to the blessed scheme of nativity sent
by the prophets.   And listen further Khan," continued
the lady pausing, and examining her book.   " Her
name now begins with a T, and that stands for Air,
and is lucky, because——" and she was nearly saying
it aloud, only she checked herself in time, "because,"
she said to herself, " Fazil's name begins with an F,
and that means Fire, and fire and air always agree best,
because the one cannot exist apart from the other."

" I don't understand, Lurlee," said the Khan, " how
it is.   What about fire ? "

" Never mind," replied the lady knowingly, "you
will find out more by-and-by, Khan ; there is a good
deal to be done before then."

So Tara escaped another great peril which she knew
not of, and remained as an honoured and welcome
guest with her new protectors.   And in a few days,
when Afzool Khan had made the necessary arrangements, his army was ready to move on.   These need
no detail at our hands, except as concerns two characters in our history who did not accompany it.

The first was Kowas Khan, who, recalled by the

King to manage the affairs of his own troops, returned
from Sholapoor to the capital. The young man re-
gretted the necessity ; for to share a campaign in real
service with his friend Fazil, had ever been one of his
most cherished plans. The King's order was, however,
peremptory, and was obeyed. " When we return,"
said the old Khan to him as they parted, " the days of
mourning will be expired, and thou shalt have thy
desire."

With him was sent the Lalla, who, being naturally
of an unwarlike nature, rejoiced at the prospect of
escaping hardships of no ordinary kind. And was not
Kowas Khan the late Wuzeer's son, and nominal Wuzeer
himself ? He might become actually so, and what a
field for advancement was opened to him if this should
be ! " May your prosperity increase, may you be
victorious," he said to the father and son as he took
leave of them. " Inshalla ! your poor servant will
write you news of the city and court, after the true
imperial fashion, which is more his vocation than re-
cording battles ; only remember that your slave is
grateful."

Afzool Khan's army, now organised in all respects,
set forward on its march. A few miles only were
traversed daily, and it would require a month or more
ere they could reach Wye. Sometimes a house was
found for the ladies in a village or town near which
the forces encamped ; but more frequently they were
in the Khan's tents, which were infinitely pleasanter.
The two girls grew together, the more as the first

restraint passed away; and the lady Lurlee and Zyna were never tired of hearing from the lips of the beautiful heathen, the simple story of her life, her widowhood, and her strange rescue from dishonour.

Was Tara happy? Yes; when she thought of what her fate must have been had she not been rescued from Moro Trimmul, or even if Fazil had yielded to her first entreaties, and let her go without inquiry. She knew not then of the further escape from the royal harem which Fazil had secured; but as it was, gratitude to him had already become the main feeling of her life. Of her parents' death she had no doubt whatever now. The other members of the family would have claimed the property and cast her off. Widow and priestess combined, she would have been helpless against the insult and profligacy of men of her own faith, and now she was at least safe. She was grateful, therefore, and, for the most part, happy too.

But often, as she wept bitterly under the old memories of an innocent and happy home, the loving arms of her mother seemed clasped about her once more, and her caresses almost palpably felt, while the glistening eyes of the Goddess appeared to follow her, sleeping and waking, with a reproachful look of desertion. In these moments, Tara endured bitter grief; but ever at hand were the gentle remonstrances of her new mother and sister, and to them also were joined those of her deliverer which, in the constant association which grew out of a camp life, she felt becoming more and more powerful day by day.

CHAPTER III.

AMONG the events which passed at Sholapoor after the arrival of the Khan, was the disposition of the prisoner Moro Trimmul. Heavily ironed and closely guarded, he had been brought from Tooljapoor on horseback, his irons loosened from one leg, and, when they were again riveted, he was consigned to the custody of the Khan's own troop. When the fate of the Bramhun hung in the balance, and Fazil, fearing him, and knowing his indefatigable and successful attempts in propagating the political influence of the Mahrattas, had at first urged his execution, then his transmission to Beejapoor,—there was not a dissentient voice in the small council; but at Sholapoor the aspect of affairs had changed: the priest and his father had sent for Moro Trimmul, and examined him in private; and the sullenness of the man had apparently broken down before the threats of being despatched to Beejapoor, and submitted to his fate with the King.

The Khan and the priest were no believers in the honesty of Mahrattas; and at the second of these examinations, the Bramhun was plied with temptation

such as was difficult to resist, and to which he yielded
with apparent reluctance, but yielded nevertheless.
To assist them in speaking with the prisoner (for
though the priest spoke Mahratta perfectly well, yet,
as a language of infidels, rarely suffered it, as he said,
to defile his mouth ; and if he did, subjected that organ
to an excessive purification at the hour of prayer),—
a Bramhun, who belonged to the accountant's department of the state, by name Punto Gopinath, was employed by the Khan. Of this man he knew but little :
but he was a good Persian scholar, as well as an intelligent official servant of the kingdom, and the Khan had
no doubt of his fidelity.

Nor, indeed, Bulwunt Rao either ; who, a bad inter-
preter himself, had, on all occasions, been allowed to be
present, as a check upon the Bramhuns. Both had
joined in trying to persuade Moro Trimmul to disclose
the intentions of his master, and had always been met
with the same answer, that the Prince only desired
recognition of his rights, and that when he heard for
certain of the march of the force, he would be sure to
send ambassadors to explain what had occurred. So it
had come to this, that if ambassadors did arrive within
a few days, Moro Trimmul was to be confronted with
them ; otherwise, that he was to be sent back to Beejapoor, to be dealt with as a traitor.

To Bulwunt Rao, whose Mahratta mind was capable
of understanding and appreciating an indirect motive
of policy, the Khan's determination seemed perfectly
reasonable ; and if Moro Trimmul could by any means

be brought to consent to lead the force through the
defiles beyond Wye, some effect upon the Rajah's position might be obtained. If not, who was to do it?

To Fazil, however, the position taken up by his
father was so unintelligible, and so unlike his usual
straightforward mode of proceeding, that he feared
some extraneous agency was at work. It was not
so, however: it was simply the power which strong
minds exercise over weaker; and by the Bramhun's
cool contempt of death, his certainty that Sivaji
would beg for terms, and his willingness to assist if he
did,—the Khan's suspicions were overcome.

Nor was it strange, perhaps, that after a time the
Khan appeared to attach no particular culpability to
Moro Trimmul's attempt to carry off Tara. He had explained the act, by her father having tired of her presence
in the house as the jealous enemy of his sister, a new
and beautiful wife, and had requested him to take her
away to Wye, to devote her to one of the temples
there. Some little force was, no doubt, necessary; but
her father had authorised its being used, to prevent
interference by her mother. What did he care about
the girl?—as a widow she was impure, and her not
having performed the rites of widowhood, placed her
beyond the pale of respectability; yes, the Khan might
make a Mahomedan of her, send her to the King, or
do what he pleased with his slave, he had no concern
for her now.

The Khan thought this state of the case on the
whole more probable, in all its aspects, than Tara's own

story, heard through Lurlee and Zyna. It did not
affect her character, which Moro Trimmul spared no
words to commend.

So the Bramhun grew into favour ; and as he did so,
the flattery which he distributed to the Khan and the
priest had its effect, in procuring him liberty, first from
his irons, and then of speech with Gopinath and other
persons of his own sect, who came to converse with one
so well known by reputation. The position of all parties continued thus till a few days after the force had
left Sholapoor; when, one morning, as the Khan reached
the halting-place for the day, the arrival of envoys
from the Rajah Sivaji was announced in camp, and
without delay they were summoned to the Khan's
presence.

We need not follow the negotiations which ensued ;
we have only to do with those who took part in them.
Most of us know, too, what Eastern negotiations are,
when weakness is covered by temporising expedients
of falsehood or treachery. So it has been from the
first, so it will be to the end. Moro Trimmul had well
guessed what his master's policy would be when he
laid his fate upon the result ; and when he heard
from Bulwunt Rao that the envoys had proffered submission, and begged of Afzool Khan to advance and
partake of the Rajah's hospitality at Pertabgurh, where
the affairs pending in dispute could be amicably discussed, he was satisfied—he could understand what
was to come.

His own liberation soon followed. Of what use was

it confining an irresponsible agent, when real ambassadors had voluntarily met the Khan, and declared
their master's intention to throw himself on the royal
clemency? So Moro Trimmul was set free.

His first act was to seek Gunga. So long as he had
been kept within the fort at Sholapoor he had heard
nothing of her; but the day the force marched, he
had seen her, attended by two stout footmen with
sword and buckler, riding among the camp followers, as
the division of horsemen, under whose charge he was
placed, rapidly passed a crowd of them straggling onwards. She had not observed him, he thought, for she
made no sign of recognition. It had been otherwise,
however; and we must retrace a little this girl's proceedings, in order to comprehend her present position.

Under that strange fascination which often impels
women to endure more from men who ill-use them
than from those who caress them, she had been unable
to remain at Tooljapoor, and after a brief struggle she
had yielded to her destiny. When the Khan dis-
chafged her, and the temporary insensibility of Lukshmun had procured her the gold zone, which was valuable, the hard, mercenary nature which had grown out
of her vocation, rose as a wall between her and Moro
Trimmul, and yet but for a moment.

It said to her, "You have got all you can from this
man, his fate is evil; you have had many escapes from
him, and this is the last. Go! leave him, you could
not save his life if you would; the Mussulmans hate
him, and will destroy him, or imprison him for life.

Enough that you have escaped ; go, and be thankful."
This was what she thought, as she picked up the zone
when it rolled away, fastened it round her waist, and
walked out of the room.   Where was she to go ?   She
dared not visit the temple.   Dead. bodies were still
lying there, and there was blood about the streets. She
went to Anunda's house, and looked into all the courts.
She saw the dead negro lying among the flowers,
and, horrified at the sight, she started back; and just
as some men opened a door and tried to intercept her,
she fled away in terror.   She dared not trust herself in
the quiet parts of the town nor in the camp ; for there
were many who would have thought little of a stab
with a dagger, or open violence, to rid her of the zone
and the valuable ornaments she had about her.   The
bazar, however, was safe, and she might meet some
one she knew, and obtain protection.

There were many. Among them Janoo the Ramoosee,
now very tipsy, yet able to recognise her.   He knew
she was no friend of Anunda's or Tara's, and to her he
told the same story as he had done to Fazil.   "Dead,
all dead !" he cried, as he staggered away—"dishonoured
and murdered by the negroes ; and they are buried
in the hole beyond the well, without the gate. Go and
see—go and see."

She went up through the gate idly, and sat down
beside the great well. She dared not go beyond it. A
large peepul* tree hung over it, and a number of Hindu
soldiers were cooking under its shade. She asked for

* Ficus religiosa.

a few hot cakes, and they gave them, and she ate them
there. Then she wandered into the fields and gardens
beyond, and so round to the Pâp-nâs temple, and sat
down on the ledge of rock above the little stream,
which thence leapt plashing down the precipice, looking over the broad plain, over which the light shadows
of fleecy clouds were chasing each other.

Her eyes filled with tears, for there came back to
her, hard and depraved as she was, many tender memories of the man whom she had loved passionately ;—
feared, hated with bitter jealousy, and again loved with
that perversity which is part of the fiercest jealousy,
and distorts every semblance of truth to serve its own
purpose. The scene of Tara's inauguration came back
to her memory, and her beauty. " It was not his fault,
Mother," she cried out aloud ; " it was thine, to send
that lotos-faced girl to bewitch him, else he had been
true to me, and thou art rightly served for it. He
said thou wast a fiend, and feared thee not ; nor do I."

Yes, Tara was gone ; would the Mussulman boy, so
grand, so beautiful, ever give up so lovely a captive ?
Surely not. " Let him have her," she said : " she will
go away, far, far from me and him, and it is well.
Yes, it is well, and what have I to do but follow and
watch,—follow and watch ?"

Then she rose, remembering her store of money in
a pot under the fireplace, in a cloister of the temple,
where she had lived. Her clothes, her property, would
be gone ; what matter, if that were safe ?

So she rose up and ran lightly along the plain, back

to the gate, avoiding the new graves ; then passed
down the bazar and into the temple court. All the
dead had been removed. The scavengers were wash-
ing the court, which she crossed rapidly. As she
expected, her room had been plundered, all her clothes
were gone, but the fireplace had not been disturbed.
She closed the door carefully, then sat down for a
while with a beating heart, to see whether she were
followed or not ; no one came,—no one had cared to
stop her though she had been seen. With a small iron
bar which lay in a corner, she hastily dug up the clay
plastering of the hearth, and took out the brass vessel
she had hidden there, which contained her savings ;
there were upwards of a hundred rupees in it—wealth
to her.

Tying these coins carefully into her waistband, she
again went out into the court, and proceeded to the
temple. " Do not go there," cried a man sweeping ;
" it is not washed." But she went on.

It was not washed, and was ghastly with dried and
clotted blood. She looked into the shrine, to see what
had become of the image, venerated, feared, and yet
even detested. It lay there as it had fallen. No one
had yet dared to touch it, and the wicked eyes still
glistened and sparkled in the light of the lamp which
had been placed beside it. " Aha !" cried the girl exultingly ; " lie there, liar and murdering devil, as he called
thee. He did not fear thee, nor do I. Lie there, till
they pick thee up ; or why dost thou not rise thyself ?
Up, Mother, up ! shall I help thee ?" she cried mockingly,

as she seized the stone hand ; but she dropped it as instantly—it was wet and cold.

As she did so, she fancied the eyes turned spitefully
towards her, and a horrible superstitious terror came
into her heart when she looked at her hand and saw
it was covered with blood. Then she shrieked and
fled shuddering, out of the front entrance to the vestibule, across the court, up the steps, staying only for
a moment to wash hurriedly in the sacred cistern.
Thus she went into the bazar, and sought out a carrier
who she knew possessed a strong pony, who agreed
to take her to Sholapoor ; and, purchasing a heavy,
coarse cotton sheet, she wrapped herself in it, and,
mingling with the crowd of camp-followers, rode after
the force to Sholapoor.

For many days she could get no speech of Moro
Trimmul. She had seen him taken to rivulets and
wells to bathe, and he had also seen her ; but though
she daily tried, on one pretence or other, to get near
him, she was repulsed. It was enough, however, that
she knew where he was.

It was not long after his release ere he discovered
her. She did not importune him, and he could hardly
resist the devotion which had prompted her to abandon
what had been her home and follow his fortunes. He
trusted also to induce her gradually, again to further
his designs against Tara, which, now that her parents,
and, as he believed, also his own sister, were all dead,
appeared more probable of success than before.

If ever this selfish man had felt a pang of real grief

in his life, it was when he had heard of his sister's death. Poor Radha! whom he had settled at last so well, when any provision for her had become next to hopeless—Radha, who, with all her faults, was part of his own rugged nature, polished and set in a more beautiful frame. It was impossible not to grieve for her. This was the first impression ; afterwards there ensued an element of rejoicing in it, which daily grew stronger. That he was free—free to act : free from the keen perception and daring opposition of his sister, which, ever protecting Tara as with a shield, had only yielded to violence at the last.

Now Tara was within his reach, and, comparatively speaking, in a far greater measure than before. He knew her to be safe in the family with whom she had obtained protection. Their own high honour and strict respectability were guarantee for this. Knowing her helplessness, Moro Trimmul had but one source of alarm or apprehension : she might allow herself to be converted to the Mahomedan faith, or it might be done without her consent. Then, indeed, there would be no hope.

But, on the other hand, was she not a Bramhun—wonderfully learned for a woman, proud of this learning, and, above all, a self-professed devotee of the Goddess?

"No," he thought, "they may attempt conversion, probably will do so, but she will resist it : and yet she should not be too long exposed to a double temptation." Now, therefore, as before, he discussed plans with

Gunga as to what means could be employed to separate Tara from her new protectors, and carry her away into the wilds of his native province, where she could be effectually concealed ; and his pursuit of the girl grew once more into a fierce and morbid passion, absorbing and deadening all other feelings of his life.

CHAPTER IV.

"THE Gods be praised!" cried Jeyram Bhópey to Wamun Bhut, late in the day after the attack upon the temple. "He has opened his eyes once more. Speak, Vyas Shastree; you are safe amongst friends: the Gods be praised, and Toolja Mata, for this mercy, for we little expected to see you live."

"Who are you?" said the Shastree faintly. "I see very dimly, and it appears very dark.—Anunda! Tara!—"

"I, Wamun, speak to you," replied the elder of the two priests, "and this is Jeyram Bhópey. We carried you away, and you are safe in the house of Gunnésh Hurry, Putwari of Sindphul.—Look, friends," he continued, speaking to others without the door of the room, "the Shastree is alive, and hath spoken, and asked for his wife and daughter."

Vyas Shastree was sensible that the room darkened again, as a number of men crowded to the door; but, feeling sick and faint from the exertion of speaking even those few words, thought himself dying, and re-lapsed again into insensibility.

Very anxiously did all those friends watch around the wounded man; and it was long before he showed any appearance of rallying strength. Night passed, and they hardly expected he would see the day; but still he breathed, and as morning was breaking, a warm moisture took the place of the chill, clammy, death-like state in which he had remained previously, and then those attending him hoped that he would live.

He had received a fearful wound. Bareheaded as he was in the performance of the ceremonies so rudely interrupted, he had not thought of protecting himself; but, as the Abyssinians advanced, had caught a sword and shield offered him by a man in the crowd, who drew back and fled, and had passed to the front with some others, crying the shout of the Goddess, "Jey Kalee!" "Jey Toolja!" and catching blows on the shield rather than returning them. But when a gigantic negro before him was pressing upon the front rank of those who defended the entrance to the vestibule, so heavily that it seemed as if they must give way, the old soldier spirit within the Shastree was stirred, and he struck desperately at the man. Stung by the pain of the wound, the negro instantly returned the blow with a furious cut, which laid open the crown of the Shastree's head from back to front. Well for him that the shield had greatly broken the force of it, or he had died instantly; as it was, the Shastree fell stunned, and was trampled upon by the advancing crowd; and lay there, unconscious, until the early morning.

Then the two friends who had watched him fall, and

who, concealed in the recess behind the shrine, had
escaped slaughter, came forth and sought for him.
They found him under a pile of dead, still breathing,
but utterly insensible. It was impossible to take him
to his own house, for the gateway and bazar were
filled with Abyssinians, and they feared a renewal of
slaughter with the dawn; so they lifted the Shastree
from the ground, obtained a bedstead from one of
the closed archway rooms, put him upon it, and, being
joined by several of the Bhópey priests, had broken
open the postern by which Tara had been taken away,
and carried him at once, unobserved, to Sindphul.

Had Tara remained where she had been first
stopped, she must have seen her father borne past her,
and would have been saved; but Fazil Khan had
sent her palankeen to the trees by the back of the
rivulet, about a gunshot's distance from the path, out
of sight; and though those who carried the Shastree
were challenged by Shêre Khan's horsemen, there was
nothing suspicious in the fact of a dead body, for
so it seemed, being carried away, — and the little
procession had passed unnoticed.

Heera, the barber of Sindphul, was a skilful surgeon,
and on his arrival at the house of the Putwari or
accountant of the village, the Shastree's wound was
examined. The barber had seldom seen worse, and
during the time which had elapsed since he had received it, the Shastree had become weak from loss of
blood. So Heera shook his head. Still he did his
best: the wound was sewn up skilfully, and a com-

posing poultice of warm leaves and herbs applied to it, while the bruised body was fomented. All night had Heera watched anxiously with the friends about the Shastree, fearing the worst, for he was restless and feverish; but with the morning came refreshing sleep, and the warm moist skin for which the barber had so anxiously looked. Then he said, " If the Gods please, the Shastree will live. Let him be kept quiet, and the room darkened."

At first the women of his family were hardly missed. All those who could escape had fled into the fields and gardens around little Tooljapoor, and many into the deep ravine beyond the town, or to adjacent villages. Sindphul was crowded with them, and no one dare return till the Mahomedan force had passed.

The Bhóslay of Sindphul had searched again and again through his village and its hamlets for the Shastree's wives and for Tara, but in vain. He had sent men to look for them in their own house, but they were not there. The place showed the signs of violence we already know of; and the men in charge of it could only hope that Janoo Näik might account for them.

Janoo had been sought therefore, and found in the liquor-seller's shop drinking out his money ; and when asked for Anunda and Tara, said, with drunken solemnity, that he had buried them all. The idea had possessed him that this was the safest answer for all questioners, and he held to it the more pertinaciously as his drunkenness increased. It was impossible not to fear that the story might be true ; for all had seen Tara in

the throng of priests and priestesses, and knew also
that Anunda and Radha had been in the temple.

We left them crouching in a niche, as it were, of the
rock, overgrown by long pendant creepers and grass,
near the little spring, and there they passed the night.
At early dawn Janoo had come to them with his son,
and told them that their house had been attacked in the
night, and was no safe place for them. It was polluted,
moreover, and they could not return to it. That Tara
and the Shastree had escaped to Sindphul; that he
dare not take them past the force which was guarding
the town and pass, and that they must go to Afsinga,
where all was quiet. He knew they had friends in a
Bramhun's family which resided there, and thither
Anunda and Radha suffered themselves to be guided
by the boy, while Janoo, after seeing them safe across
the hill, returned to his post.

Weeping bitterly, hardly knowing whether to go on
with the lad or to return, at all risks, to Tooljapoor, the
two women had yielded to Janoo's well-intended but
mistaken direction. The path was stony and rough,
and their naked feet, unused to such places, were sorely
bruised and cut in descending the rugged track by
which, through the most intricate and gloomy ravines
of the hills, they were guided. It was hardly four
miles, perhaps, and yet, faint and wretched as they
were, the sun was high in the heavens ere they reached
their destination, and were kindly received.

They told their story; but what could be done?
Who could go to Tooljapoor? The Bramhun to whose

house they had betaken themselves was old and feeble,
but a student who lived with him, and who had been
absent since daylight to obtain information, returned
about noon. He had no news of the Shastree or of
Tara ; but he volunteered to go again to seek them,
and did so, returning at night with accounts of a fruitless search. Janoo, he said, knew nothing of them,
and he had found him telling the same story, that he
had buried Anunda and Radha out of sight,—and understood—what the faithful but drunken creature had
perhaps meant to convey to all inquirers—that they
were safely hidden away.

Perhaps Janoo would not have been absent so long
had he been sober; but the excitement and his pota-
tions together had been too much for him. When he
awoke, having lain down to sleep in the bazar, it was
evening, and they were lighting the lamps in the shops.
"It is too late now," thought he, "to go across the hills
for the Shastree's wives, and they are safer where they
are ;" so he betook himself to the house. His men
were there in charge. The dead negro had been taken
out and buried, and some of the blood washed away; but
the place was utterly defiled : the sacred fire had gone
out, and the whole premises must undergo purification
ere they could enter or inhabit it once more. Janoo
shrugged his shoulders—"They cannot live here," he
said ; "there is the hut in the garden at Sindphul, and
I will take them there and hide them in it."

So in the morning, before it was light, he set out
from Tooljapoor, and crossed the hills, with two of his

men leading two stout ponies for the women, and
reached Afsinga before the sun had risen. He brought
no tidings of the Shastree; but it was reported generally
in the town, he said, that he and Tara were at Sindphul; and, in any case, they must go there and live in
the garden till the house could be purified, and fit to
be again inhabited. This was scant comfort to Anunda
and Radha; but Janoo said that most families in the
town were in the same predicament, that he knew the
Shastree and Tara were not among the dead, and pro-
bability confirmed the report that they had fled in the
confusion, and were safe.

It was hardly four miles to Sindphul by the road at
the foot of the hills on the plain; and they set out,
after their hospitable hosts had insisted upon their
taking an early meal. Anunda would fain have gone
by Tooljapoor, but Janoo overruled it. There was no
one there; they would only sit down and cry at the
house door; and if the Shastree were at Sindphul, they
would be delayed going to him. Nobody had been
disturbed there; and the Bhóslay and the Putwari
would advise them for the best in any case.

All these arguments overruled Anunda, and they
set out with their guide. They met no one, except a
few men watching in their fields by the wayside, who
told them all was quiet. Janoo would not even take
them near the pass of Tooljapoor, but, striking across
the plain by the Gosai's Mutt, and through the great
mango grove, they reached Sindphul unobserved.

It is not a large village, and they were well known

there. Passing up the central street, they had greetings from many friends, both men and women. At
last they saw their own old gardener sitting weeping
at the door of the Putwari's house ; and Janoo, who
was leading Anunda's pony, took them thither. They
were both sick at heart as they dismounted and entered. The Putwari's wife and his married daughter
who lived in the house were kind people, and met
them in the outer court. " He is alive," said the dame;
" fear not. Heera has dressed the wound, and he has
spoken to my husband, and asked for you. We told
him we had sent for you, and that you were coming,
and, behold, the Gods have brought you." Then she
led Anunda, weeping, into the inner court, and Radha
followed. The men sitting about the door of the apartment got up, and, feeling they had no more to do, went
out, all but the old Putwari.

"Vyas Shastree," he said, as the women approached
the door, "be comforted ; they are safe, and have come
to you. Be gentle with him," he added to Anunda ;
" he is very weak, and Heera says if he is made anxious,
or disturbed, fever may come on ; therefore, be careful."

It was well meant to give them caution, but at such
moments, nature will have its course. The women had
existed—since the attack on the temple, and since they
had fled with Janoo—in a state of intense fear and
misery which cannot be described ; and yet one mercy
had accompanied this dread, that they had not fully
known what had happened in the temple, and so hope
had sustained them. Now, however, there was no

doubt; and in a paroxysm of mingled fear and thankfulness, they cast themselves beside the low bed, embracing their husband's feet, and weeping passionately. The Shastree was too weak to speak or move; he could only lift up his hand gently, as if to bless them and welcome them, while a faint but grateful smile spread itself over his pallid features.

For a little time, and as they sat silently beside him ministering to their wants—for Anunda was an unrivalled nurse, and had at once proceeded to arrange many things about him, as he liked—strange to say, they did not miss Tara; but Anunda's mind suddenly misgave her. Her husband, whom her arrival had aroused, had again fallen into a doze, and she went outside to ask for her. The whole court had been left to them, and the door of the outer one was closed. "Tara," she called gently, several times, but there was no reply. She might be asleep, she thought, in one of the rooms which opened into it, and she searched in each in succession. There was no one. Radha joined her. "Where is Tara?" she said. "She should have been with him." True, she should have been with her father, but she was not.

The women turned sick at heart and sat down. A nameless terror seized them, so absorbing, that they could say nothing, but that she was not. Anunda dare not ask. Of the two, Radha was most self-possessed. Looking through the door, she saw the old Putwari's wife sitting spinning outside it, and as if watching the place. She called her in, and the dame

saw at a glance what was needed. O the misery of
that mother's face! who, after trying to articulate
"Tara," which her lips formed, as though she spoke the
word, fell forward clasping the knees and feet of her
old friend, and groaning in her despair.

"The Gods have given thee one precious object,
sister, and taken the other," she said. "Be thankful
for what is spared thee."

Then Anunda thought Tara was dead, and so did
Radha; but the woman resumed—

"And yet, why should I say so, Anunda? We know
not; she has not been heard of. Let us wait. Hundreds of our friends fled from the temple and from the
town. Many we sheltered here all yesterday till the
force passed by; then they returned home. So Tara
may be at some village near, and we have men watching at your house and at the temple. The Bhópeys
will send intelligence if they get any."

"She is not in the garden?" asked Radha.

"No; we searched there long ago, and in all the
gardens. No, she is not here, and you must wait. She
was favoured of the Mother, sister, and will not be
deserted. At least we know she was not killed."

Anunda was comforted for the moment by this,
and the women went and resumed their watch by
their husband. It was a relief, perhaps, not to speak
—a relief, too, to find, in watching him and ministering to his wants, a diversion from the other care.
Sooner or later Tara might come in. Janoo had at
once gone in search of her; the Bhóslay had despatched

horsemen to every village around, and there would surely be news of her before nightfall.

But none came that night, nor the next day. The Shastree was not yet aware of Tara's absence; fever had begun—the fever of the wound—and he was unconscious of most things. Sometimes he recognised Anunda, and sometimes called Radha, Tara. It was a blessed thing then that he knew no more. Neither of the women relaxed for a moment in their work, and sat there by the bed, without sleep and without rest, looking for news of Tara; but none came. Messenger after messenger arrived, but with no tidings of her.

Late next day Janoo returned. He must see Anunda, he said; he had news of importance about Tara, and, so far as he knew, she was not dead.

Anunda went to the man outside; he might not enter because of his impure caste.

Janoo was a man of few words and scant ceremony, and he blurted out, " Moro Trimmul and Gunga took her away, lady. I was drinking last night with some of our people, who are strangers, and came from a distance, and who were dividing booty; and they said they had carried off a beautiful Moorlee as the disturbance broke out, and put her in a palankeen, and they were paid by Moro Trimmul, the reciter. They treated me and some of my people to liquor, and told us of this as a good piece of business. And I have not stolen them, lady; but the jewels you gave me are gone; they were given to Pahar Singh's hunchback, who came and asked for them in the Cucherri in my name:

but Pahar Singh will give them up; or if not, I will
burn a corn-stack of his every night till he does.".

All this was told rapidly and confusedly. The detail was hardly intelligible; but one great fact came
out beyond all others, and if it were true, better Tara
were dead—O far better!

"Wait," said Anunda, "and I will come to thee
again;" and she went in and whispered it all to
Radha. She saw the girl's face flush and her bosom
heave rapidly. "Gunga must have helped him," she
said, "else he had not dared it, and I will see to it myself." So they both went out to the Ramoosee, and
Radha at once declared she would go with him to the
town above, and make inquiries.

She was shrewd and active. Accompanied by Janoo
and two of the Bhóslay's retainers, she soon found the
man from whom Janoo had heard of Tara, and listened
to his story. They had known nothing of Moro Trimmul's purpose, he said, till that night of the recitation,
or how the girl they took was to be decoyed away,
or who she was; but as the disturbance began, she was
brought out by him in his arms, and then they took her.
Yes, he knew what had become of her. Moro Trimmul had been put in irons by the Mahomedan chief,
and Tara had been carried off to Sholapoor. He and
his companions had watched the palankeen from the
rocks in the ravine where they had hidden themselves,
because, if it had been left unguarded, they would have
gone to it.

It was clear enough now, therefore, that Tara was

gone, not dead. That would have been grief—bitter
grief; but here was more misery than death would
have caused. Who had taken their Tara? for what fate
was she reserved? They could only think of her beauty
as destined for some Mahomedan harem—reserved for
a fate worse than death.

It was piteous to see the mother and the sister-wife
prostrated under this misery and the state of their
husband; and it was with difficulty that Radha was
restrained from going at once to Sholapoor after the
camp, and endeavouring to trace and reclaim Tara. If
she had only done so—if this energetic girl, used to
rough ways and rapid journeys, had been allowed to
follow out her own plans, what misery might not have
been saved to all! Hard she pleaded, that she could
not be denied to her brother. She would force from
him, an account of Tara, and would bring her back.

But Anunda hesitated; and the Shastree, to whom
all was told, weak as he was in body, was more than
usually vacillating. The Mahomedan camp, full of
licentiousness, was no place for a Bramhun girl. "The
Shastree must be attended," Anunda said; and, in
Tara's absence, he seemed to cling the more fondly to
his young wife, and to miss her ministrations if even
she was temporarily absent. Finally, the matter was
left in the hands of their friends, the Bhóslay and the
old Putwari, and they decided that Radha must not
go; but a messenger should be sent, who, assisted by
friends and Bramhuns at Sholapoor, would do all that
was needful or possible.

In truth, all these friends thought that seeking for Tara at all was injudicious. They could not believe, considering her beauty and public vocation as a priestess, that she could have escaped observation, and they had come to the conclusion that her preservation from dishonour was impossible. Better she were dead ; or, if alive, reunion was henceforth impossible, for the hard rules of religious faith must exclude her from all assistance and sympathy. These were home truths which, sooner or later, Vyas Shastree himself would acknowledge ; and Radha's plan was overruled.

It was some day's before an answer came. Communications were necessarily slow when there were only foot messengers to carry them. The Shastree's fever had passed away, and his wound was progressing favourably. Mentally and bodily, he had passed a fearful crisis ; but natures like his bow to these calamities rather than break, and there was hope at least in the messenger who had gone, to which they all clung.

Little by little they heard enough to sustain this hope. The Bhóslay's correspondent, a banker in the town of Sholapoor, had spared no pains for the recovery of Vyas Shastree's child ; but beyond the fact that in the family of Azfool Khan there was a new Hindu slave, of great beauty, who was carefully secluded in the zenana, he could ascertain nothing ; and the inquiries, he wrote, must be continued in camp, for the force had marched, and was now some stages distant, going towards Wye.

Again, after an interval of weary expectation, and

the daily endurance of that heavy weight of uncertainty
which is so often worse than the bitterest agony of
reality, there came fresh news which they could not
doubt. A poor Bramhun of Sholapoor, incited by the
offer of reward held out by the Shastree's friends, had
proceeded to camp, and returned from it direct. They
never forgot that evening of his arrival. The Shastree
had, meanwhile, been removed to his own house, as
soon as it had undergone purification, and lay, weak
as yet, but convalescent, in the verandah of the inner
court, living, as he said, in sight of the objects most
loved by his lost child ; and it was almost an occupation to watch dreamily Tara's bright flowers glowing
in the sunlight. He was lying there, watching them,
as the evening sun declined, and the colour of its light
was growing richer as the shadows of the buildings
lengthened, and Anunda had just said he must retire
to his room ; but he was pleading to be allowed to stay,
when the man was announced without.

Weary and footsore, Radha and a servant poured
water over his feet, and led him in. "There was no
bad news," he said ; "none, Tara was well." Then they
all listened, with grateful hearts and tears of joy, to
the man's tale of having discovered her, though he
could not get speech of her or send a message to her ;
but in Afzool Khan's family there was a Bramhun girl
called Tara, who was an honoured guest; her people
had been killed, they said, and they were taking her to
Wye, to her relatives. He had watched several days
about the Khan's tents in hope of seeing her, but in

vain ; for the servants and soldiers, thinking him a spy, had beaten him and driven him off. Day by day the distance back to Tooljapoor grew greater, so he had returned. But there was no doubt ; the man described what he had heard distinctly, and they could now trace Tara from the temple to where she then was. She must believe they were all dead, and was going to their relatives at Wye : and she was at least safe from Moro Trimmul, whom the messenger reported to be in close confinement.

Now, for once, there was no indecision or vacillation in the Shastree's mind. He could bear easy travelling in a litter ; and Radha should have it by-and-by, when he grew stronger. He would not delay, and they could yet overtake the army at Wye, or soon afterwards. Very little of the household property had been lost, after all ; and Anunda's store of money was at last to prove useful. That night, as with thankful hearts they spoke of their lost child, they arranged plans for setting out to reclaim her ; and their friends, who crowded about them with congratulations next day, soon completed the necessary arrangements. The third day was a lucky one, according to the planets ; and they moved down the pass to Sindphul, followed by many friends, and the good wishes and prayers of all who had known Tara from childhood.

CHAPTER V.

A PLEASANT life was it to Tara. The daily stages of a large army encumbered with heavy materiel are necessarily slow at all times, and the country roads were not as yet dry from the recent rains, so that the force could not hurry on. The Khan himself was in no haste. On the arrival of the Mahratta ambassadors he had received them courteously, and insisted upon their being the guests of the royal camp. They had not much to say, beyond general protestations of attachment. Their master's demands were simple, they knew; but he would treat for them in person when he met the Khan. Meanwhile, supplies for the royal forces were abundant; the stages they arranged were shorter perhaps than the Khan, and especially Fazil, approved of; but they found grain and forage provided everywhere, and the camp bazar had always the appearance of a busy fair.

On his own part, Afzool Khan, yielding to the persuasions of Sivaji's agents, despatched an envoy of his own, the Bramhun Punto Gopináth, to Pertabgurh. Their master's mind, they said, would be relieved by it;

and as Sivaji had evinced confidence in sending his own
servants unsolicited, so a similar mark of courtesy could
hardly be refused. The Khan did not object to it.
The Envoy received his instructions, to act as circumstances might require, leaving all points of detail for
future arrangement; and Bulwunt Rao was placed in
command of the escort which accompanied him. In
this capacity he was safe against all local enemies; and
he went the more willingly, as he trusted, under this
opportunity, to interest the Rajah in his own affairs.

So there was no hurry, and it was a pleasant life.
Every day, or nearly so, there was a change ; the force
moved forward a few miles, or it halted ; tents were
pitched, thrown down, moved, and again pitched in
pleasant places; perhaps in some soft grassy plain
spangled with flowers, or in a stubble field with the
stacks of ripe grain standing around them. The
Khan's Durbar tent was open to all comers, where the
leaders of the various bodies of troops met every day
for business or ceremonial visits, as it might be : behind it the private tents enclosed by a canvass wall,
which afforded a large area. Before all, floated the
royal standard, and a place was cleared near it which
was appropriated for public prayer. Five times in each
day, if the force halted, did the musical chant of invitation to prayer resound from this spot ; and as often
did the devout among the soldiery assemble there, and
perform the stated devotions. Every afternoon the
priest and other divines preached to the people ; and it
was remarked that the sermons on the holy war, though

they were continued at intervals, were of quieter character than they used to be at first.

Perhaps the religious zeal of the Peer had relaxed
since the slaughter at Tooljapoor, and was satisfied
with the fact of the idol having been overthrown and
defiled. Perhaps the Khan supposed enough had been
done to terrify the Mahratta people, and that the rest
would follow upon negotiation.

There was very little change in the daily life : the
early march, the halt for the day, the household
occupations, and then the pleasant talk with Zyna
and Lurlee. Her tales of the old Hindu life, and
of her home pleasures and occupations, were told
again and again by Tara, often with bitter tears, and
yet told again and again, and heard by sympathising
friends.

Two different worlds, as it were, were thus brought
together. What did the simple Bramhun girl know of
the grandeur of Mahomedan nobles, of which only a
faint rumour had ever reached her ? To her unclean,
she would once have shuddered at nearer contact with
them, however rich or grand they might be. Now,
how different ! They had respected her honour, and
they also respected her faith ; and every day her little
cooking-place was arranged, with water brought by a
Bramhun for her bath and her drinking, which no one
interfered with. Sometimes, Zyna and Lurlee would
look on while the little maiden dressed her simple
meal, as she had often done at home,—amused, and
wondering at her dexterity ; and it was not long before

the Khan himself was a petitioner for some delicate specimen of her handiwork, which, it was remarked, he ate with infinite relish, and pronounced better even than Kurreema's efforts to the same end.

They procured the girl the books she loved, and eagerly, and with infinite animation, she would read and expound sacred texts, which even the priest admitted contained at least moral and virtuous doctrine. Occasionally, too, he was unable to control himself, and he answered the little preacher from his own books, hurling at her texts translated from the Koran into bad Mahratta; and half angry with, and half amused by, the seeming petulance with which she resisted conversion, allowed her greater liberties, perhaps, than he had ever been known to submit to before from "an infidel."

"See," she would cry, "Huzrut! here are God's holy words to us poor Hindus hundreds of thousands of years old, but yours are, after all, but a few hundreds. Surely the elder has precedence?" If she could translate the beautiful Bhugwat Geeta to him, that book so full of mystic religious doctrine, he could understand her better, she thought; but she had no words that he could comprehend, in which to convey the sense of the noble Sanscrit; and it must be confessed that her general attempts in argument were failures.

Kind Tara! gentle Tara! was any servant ill,—and the cold air and damp earth gave many fevers,—who so ready with knowledge of simples as the Bramhun girl? who so watchful, who so careful? In turn she

had tended Lurlee and Zyna, who suffered at first from
the change and exposure in camp. Then Fazil grew
ill too, and for several days could not ride. She could
ride : she had never travelled in a palankeen in her
life—her father could not afford one : so she gave up her
litter to him, and rode a stout ambling palfrey of the
Khan's which was gentle, and a relief on long marches
from his heavier war-horse ; and old Shêre Khan and
his men, her first escort from Tooljapoor, claimed
the privilege of guarding her as she rode, rapidly and
fearlessly, and managed the active horse with skill and
grace.

Once Moro Trimmul saw her riding with this escort
of heavily-armed men. She was wrapped in shawls,
and had twisted one round her head like a turban,
which covered her face all but her eyes. He concealed
his own face and person as she passed, but the fact
that she was riding with so noble a company to attend
on her, disquieted him. She is growing into favour,
he thought, and is in danger. It is necessary to act
before we reach Wye.

Whether Moro Trimmul was in camp or not, she
had not thought to inquire. Fazil had told her once,
with a very perceptible tone of disappointment, that he
had been released, and had gone away. He was never
seen in the camp, but, with Sivaji's envoys, put up in
villages near where the force might halt. They did
not vex her with his tale of her having been taken away
under her father's sanction, which Fazil, Lurlee, and
Zyna had never believed, and by common consent the

name of the Bramhun was never mentioned among
them.

Ah, yes, a pleasant time indeed! What more delicious to a young girl's heart than the consciousness of
awakening love? Could she help it? did she desire
it? Neither, perhaps; but it would come nevertheless:
and there would come too, with all the persuasive ad-
juncts of her own helplessness and dependence, the sense
of evident respect in which she was held by Fazil, and
his honourable reticence, even of speech with her. So a
new life, a new desire for life, was growing within her,
and increased day by day. Did she endeavour to
check it? Not then; it was too delicious.

Before it, the old home was fading away, the forms
of father and mother already becoming dim and
shadowy, as belonging to the past. The old temple
occupations, the preparation for daily duty, were being supplanted by other feelings, undecided as yet,
but ineffably tender. Did she regret that these were
growing into definite form in her own heart? Not
then. She had no certainty of what she thought,
and if any one, even Zyna, had asked her to define
what was passing within her, she could not have
done so.

O the wondrous stirring of that new life, shutting out
all the old! the gentle growing of an absorbing passion.
If Fazil spoke to her, she trembled; but not in fear.
She had no fear of him. No matter what he said, she
listened, and never replied. When he was ill, she took
to him the little soothing potions she had made, and,

as he lay tossing with fever, was conscious that they
would relieve thirst, and would not be forgotten. She
could speak to him then, a word only, perhaps, to tell
him to be patient, that he would be relieved if he
would be still. Even this was a fearful but an exqui-
site pleasure.

How often Zyna spoke of her brother! How precious
he was to her; how brave he was; how beautiful!
Had Tara ever seen any one like him? No; those
timid, loving eyes had never looked up to any one
before, far less to such a one as Fazil. What did she
know? She could only see that there was, in her eyes,
the godlike beauty the old poets wrote of Kāmdeo—
those soft, loving eyes which sometimes earnestly
looked into hers, before which she dare not open her
own. If he came into the tent accoutred, blazing
with cloth-of-gold and steel armour, she fled at once,
and from a distance watched Zyna embrace him, perhaps fasten an amulet upon his arm, or relieve him of
his heavy clothing and armour.

If Fazil were absent, Tara and Zyna would often sit
and talk of him. Poor little heart! how it fluttered
then. She could not tell his sister what rose to her
lips, but, as her heart swelled, she felt as if she could
do some great thing for him or for Zyna—defend them,
or avert evil from them—even if she died herself, it
would be welcome. Yes, the old story—the old story!
—the telling of which, in all its wondrous forms, will
never finish here, or finish, but to be renewed hereafter!

Did Fazil perceive this? Not yet. He had a true gentleman's best safeguard against presumption, an innate modesty in regard to women, which prevented it; and yet . . . how often he watched the lithe and graceful figure as it passed from his presence on some trifling errand, or the glowing intellectual face as it quivered under the excitement of explaining any portion of one of her old-world books which interested her,—or the quiet, demure expression which gathered over it, as she sometimes brought — for she would allow no one else to touch the vessels she cooked it in —her little daily contribution to his father's dinner, and waited apart with folded arms till he had told her, with a pleasant smile or joke, how much he liked it !

"Ah !" said Shêre Khan, after Fazil's first journey in the palankeen, and as he lay, languid and weakened by his fever, in the outer tent where his retainers could attend on him—"whom hast thou sent us, Meah ? They tell of Chandnee Begum of the Nizam Shahee's, but who, after all, was one of our royal race,—that she rode with her army of true believers, and fought with her enemies. By Alla ! this girl rides so that it is hard to follow her ; and we all say, there is that in her eyes which, had she a sword in her hand, nay, without it, would lead us, as only thou, or the Khan could lead us, Meah. Yes, she is a jewel of great price."

And Fazil liked to hear this ; he liked to hear old Goolab exhaust her vocabulary of endearment upon Tara, as she sat by him, rubbing his feet when the

fever oppressed him ; and when, in those feverish
dreams which are part of the disorder, strange fancies
beset him, the Bramhun girl often became a prominent actor in those unreal scenes of his imagination.

So it grew on. The habits of Eastern people do not
admit of those demonstrations and protestations of love
which form part of our social habits. But we have no
warrant for saying that their feelings are the less ardent or permanent. We think not ; and that there, as
elsewhere, they progress silently, and are afterwards
called into active exercise by occasion and opportunity,
and with possibly more energy and passion than among
ourselves.

When Lurlee had rallied the Bramhun girl sometimes upon her attachment to her old faith, now, she
said, hopeless,—and Zyna, throwing her arms round
her as they sat together in the twilight after evening
prayer, besought her to give it up—to come to them as
a sister, as a daughter,—and pleaded hard for this,—
Tara was sorely tried. Whom had she now to look to ?
whither was she going ? If there were some of her
mother's relatives at Wye,—and all she knew of them
was the surname,—what was she to do ? Even were
they there, what was she to do ? Against her, ever
rose up the hard cruel wall of Hindu widowhood ; the
servitude, the nearly inevitable dishonour among
strangers of her own faith, the hopeless weariness of
an unloved and uncared-for life ; and so, better death.
All this had passed through her mind before, at Tooljapoor, and then there was no alternative. Now ?

O how hard the new young life pleaded,—as these
thoughts passed through her mind—the certainty of
love on the one hand, even as a friend or dependant,
and of respect and protection from all evil, even though
to minister to the old Khan should be her only occupation. This, and to see Fazil daily—to see Zyna—to
be held to that rough old Lurlee's heart—to be the
child, for so they called her, of all the servants,—what
had the other life to compare with this? Even if
she found her people, what had they to offer her but
misery? for so it seemed.

And when, one day (Wye was now only a few stages
distant) Zyna told her what they wished—what they
all spoke of among themselves—what Fazil had proposed to his father,—and how the old Khan had at
first gently resisted it, desiring a high connection for
his son, and yet had conceded in the end;—when
Lurlee came and pleaded too, and told her, and proved
to her by the planets and the elements, that she would
be fortunate to the house and to Fazil—a loved and
honoured wife,—what could she say? The new life
now rose up within her vigorous and defiant against
all other thoughts; and its blessed shape—definite,
honourable, irresistible, and delicious to contemplate
—would not be repelled.

"Only give me time," she cried, hiding her burning
face in Zyna's bosom—"only give me time! It is so
sudden—so unlooked-for." Then she added, after a
pause, and looking up sadly, "I am his captive and
his slave; not of your people, lady, but a stranger, and

an infidel as the priest says; impure among my own
sect, and of no account but for shame and dishonour.
As such, I cannot come to a noble house. Ah, do
not mock me!"

"They say," returned Zyna, "that the Emperors of
Dehli sought brides from among the Rajpoots, and
esteemed them as honourable and as noble as themselves; and thou art a Bramhun, Tara, far purer and
nobler than they. But no matter : thou art our own
Tara, whom Alla hath sent to us, and whom we have
received thankfully, for him whose heart no one as yet
has touched. Let it be as we all will;" and Tara at
last said it should be so.

Was she grateful or happy, this desolate girl? O,
far beyond either ! All those dreamy imaginings which
at home, among her books and flowers, had taken no
definite shape, now assumed a palpable reality. In
her eyes glorious, in her heart Fazil was supremely
glorious also. She dared not look at him now, even
by stealth ; but there was ever a sweet assurance of
his presence—of his care—of his thought, which produced a kind of ecstasy, filling her mind with a sublime
devotion and innocent passion : often filling her eyes,
too, causing a strangely tight feeling at her heart as
if she could not breathe, and then a deep sigh as her
tears welled over ; and she hoped, with an almost deli-
rious joy, that she was to belong to him by-and-by :
no matter how far distant it might be,—only to
belong to him, and be for ever with him.

And so the time passed to them all. A pleasant

life which, day by day, grew to be more absorbing to
Tara, and caused indifference to outward occurrences.
But had her enemy been idle?

The force marched late one day. Moro Trimmul
had ascertained that the litters and followers generally, would not arrive in camp before nightfall. It
was dark, for there was no moon; and he laid his
plans accordingly. Day and night, he and Gunga,
in various disguises, had watched about the Khan's
tents, and had tried to get speech of the servants.
He dare not come openly, except to the Khan's
Durbar, where he heard nothing. He was nearly
hopeless of success, when he understood casually that
the evening march was determined upon. All the force
was not to move; but some only with the Khan, for
the sake of convenience of supplies and water. It was
a short stage—only four or five miles, and the Khan's
tents were to precede the force. He and his family
were to remain in a village for the night, and several
houses had been cleared for him. Thus much had
Gunga picked up, and for once, fortune seemed to
favour their designs.

Fazil had recovered, and again rode with his men.
Tara, therefore, once more occupied the litter, which
was closed, and carried with those of Lurlee and Zyna.
Had she continued to ride as she wished, nothing could
have happened. As it grew dark, Moro Trimmul—
with a small body of horsemen which he had detached
from the Envoy's and kept about his own person—followed Tara's litter at a distance, and yet so as not to

interfere with it. As it grew dark, and they neared
the place where they were to stop for the night, he
observed that Tara's palankeen was the last : he knew
it from the white devices sewn on the red cover; and he
dexterously, yet apparently unpremeditatedly, pushed
his horsemen between it and the others, in a narrow
lane, in which litters, horsemen, and soldiers were
much crowded together. Then he stopped his men,
pretending there was obstruction in front ; and so the
litters of Lurlee and Zyna, which were surrounded by
footguards and guides as usual, went on for some distance, never missing the one behind.

Moro Trimmul was exultant. At the next turn in
the road, his own servants, who had been instructed
beforehand, went to the bearers of Tara's litter, pretending to have been seeking them, and, abusing them
roundly for their carelessness in remaining behind,
bade them come on rapidly. The men followed blindly;
they knew they were to go to a village, and here was
one ; and, pressing forward, they presently reached a
house to which they were directed.

"Put down the palankeen. Gosha! Gosha! Murdana! Murdana!"* was cried by several voices ; and
a screen of cloth being stretched, as usual, from the
palankeen to the entrance of the court, and the door
of the litter opened, Tara emerged from it unsuspi-
ciously : then the door was instantly closed behind
her, a thick shawl was thrown round her head which

* Private! Private! The usual cry when Mahomedan ladies
enter or depart from a house.

almost stifled her, and she felt herself taken up by powerful arms, and carried rapidly onwards. She struggled violently, but a voice she knew but too well, hissed into her ear through the shawl, "Be quiet, else I will kill you;" and for a moment she lost consciousness.

CHAPTER VI.

TARA revived as the shawl was pushed roughly from her head, and the cool air reached her face; in another moment she was set down in a verandah, closed from the outer court by thick woollen curtains, in which a small lamp, placed in a niche, glimmered faintly. There could be no doubt now. Releasing her, Moro Trimmul drew himself up, panting with the exertion of carrying her, and looked at her from head to foot ere he spoke; while Gunga, advancing from a dark corner of the room, and bending lowly with a mock gesture of reverence, touched the ground near her feet, and then retreated a pace so as to see her better.

"Thou hast had powerful friends, Tara," said the Bramhun bitterly, and with a scornful sneer—"very powerful; even the enemy's general and his fair son; but the Gods are not with them, but with me. Once, in blood and terror, didst thou escape me; but not now, girl—never more. Now thou art mine, and there is nothing between thee and me; nor sister, nor father,

nor mother; only thee, and only me; and thou hast a
long account of misery to pay me."

"The holy Moorlee of the Goddess forgot her faith
and her vow among the cow-slaying infidels; and the
Mother hath sent me to bring her back from her dainty
lover, who rides in cloth-of-gold and bright armour,"
said Gunga, with another mock reverence. "Art thou
ready, O Moorlee of Toolja Mata? ready to be such
as I am, in her service? Come! there is thy master
and mine; be content that thou art saved the sin of
faithlessness to her. Didst thou think she — the
Mother," continued the girl, advancing a step at each
word till she was close to Tara, who shrank from her—
"the Mother would loose thee from thy vow to be the
petted toy of an unclean Toork? O Tara, didst thou
think it? Ah, yes! I know thou didst, faithless, when
the fair boy's arms were about thee."

"Silence!" cried Tara panting, as these bitter words
stung her to the quick. "Silence! thou art shameless,
Gunga. O what have I ever done to harm thee, that
thou hast such bitter enmity to me?"

"Thou art beautiful, and I hate thee for that. I
hated thee long ago, before thou wast a Moorlee," she
replied. "He loved me once, that Moro Trimmul
there; now he cries, 'Tara! Tara!' all day long, like a
sick child, and will not look on me. Thou wilt hate
me because I have taken thee from thy beautiful lover;
but, O Tara, more deeply do I hate thee for taking
mine from me. Look, he gave me this gold zone. It
is as heavy as thine—heavier. That is all I have left—

that is all. He will give thee another, by-and-by; not now, but when he has done with thee. Enough! Take her away, Moro Trimmul. I have done thy bidding, and earned the gold. Take her away—far away—ere I repent of this, the worst work of my life, and join her against thee. Go!"

"Gunga! Gunga! go not," cried Tara, seizing her dress. "There is pity in thy heart, let it come out to me. O leave me not to him, by your mother, by your——"

"Come," cried Moro Trimmul fiercely, casting his arm about her. "This is child's play, come. . . . Nay, Tara, gently, and it were better for thee—else I will strike thee," he said, under his breath, but with a terrible distinctness, as she struggled violently, shrieking as she did so. "Gunga! the shawl. Quick, girl —lest she be heard without. Quick! Bar the outer door."

It was too late. Several persons, among whom was an elderly Bramhun of sedate and respectable appearance, attended by armed retainers, came up the steps hurriedly and entered the room. Between the noise of Tara's shrieks and his own exertions, Moro Trimmul had not heard them, and with Gunga's aid had forced Tara to the ground, and was endeavouring to tie the shawl about her head, which she was resisting with all her might; but Gunga had succeeded in catching her hands, and Tara was much exhausted. Another instant, and she would have been helplessly in their power; but at this moment Gunga saw the curtain pushed aside, and one of the men enter with his sword drawn; and, loosing Tara, she upset the cruise burning in the niche, and fled into an inner portion of the dark apartment.

"Who art thou?" cried the man, darting forward and seizing Moro Trimmul's arm; "what murder is this thou art doing?"

He had had no time to escape, or even to rise from his kneeling posture to shake off the soldier's grip, and two others also caught him at the same moment; while the elderly man, calling earnestly for a light, raised up Tara, and disengaged her from the shawl which had been thrown about her. "Art thou wounded?" he said.

"By the Holy Mother," cried one of the men with whom Moro Trimmul was struggling violently, "be quiet, else I will drive my knife into thee. Bind him, brothers, he may be armed. Quick!"

At this moment a man bearing a lighted torch came into the court from the street, and ran rapidly up the steps into the room. As the light flashed upon the struggling group of men, the leader of the party recognised Moro Trimmul, and bid his retainers release him. As they did so, Tara, who had partly risen, sank again to the ground, clasping his knees, and crying piteously for protection.

The old Bramhun understood the situation at a glance. "There was another woman here,—seize her!" he exclaimed. She was not, however, to be found. "Peace," he said to Tara, "peace, my daughter; be comforted, no

one shall harm thee. Who art thou ? What has
happened ?"

"I am the unhappy daughter of Vyas Shastree of
Tooljapoor, who was murdered, and I am an orphan,"
she cried sobbing. "Oh, defend me from him; he
would have done me violence and dishonour."

"Moro Trimmul," said the old man sadly, "how
often hast thou been warned, and what new wicked-
ness is this ?—against a Bramhun girl too, and the
daughter of the man to whom thy sister was given!
Oh, shame !"

"She is a Moorlee," he replied sulkily, "and has
done dishonour to the Mother by living with Mahomedans in camp. It was from them I have rescued
her, and would have taken her to Wye, but she resisted.
I have done no evil, Pundit, nor intended any."

"Is this true, girl ?" asked the Bramhun.

"Quite true, Maharaj," answered Tara sobbing hys-
terically, and hardly knowing what she said : "only
take me hence, and I will tell thee all ; but I am not
impure,—I am not defiled,—I have nothing to be
ashamed of. Oh, put your hand on my head, and take
me to my people in Wye. Save me, else I shall die ;
or kill me, rather than let him or the woman come
near me. When I am alone with your family I will
tell them all."

"Come," said the man, who was Govind Narrayen,
the principal envoy of the Rajah Sivaji, and a Bramhun of wealth and high station in the country, best
known among the people under the familiar title of

Baba Sahib. "I am well known, and I knew and honoured your father, and grieve his death. Come with
me, and you shall go on with my people at once to
Wye. They leave the camp to avoid the confusion,
and will take care of you, and the bearers and palankeen are still in the street.

"As to you, Moro Trimmul," he continued, turning
to him, "I reserve my judgment till I have inquired from
this girl of what she complains. I bid you, however,
beware. The Maharaja is not what he used to be, and
will submit to no profligacy now. I take this girl as
my daughter, and she is safe against you. Beware!"
And so saying, and giving his arm for Tara to lean on,
while he partly supported her with the other, he led
her out, and once more placed her in the litter, which
was taken up and carried forward rapidly.

The Envoy and his escort had also moved with the
camp, and he had sent on his family to a stage some
miles distant. As he passed through the street of the
village where Tara had been set down, the bearers of
her litter, who had remained with it, hearing the stifled
scream from within the court, and alarmed by the sudden closing and fastening of the door, had stopped
Baba Sahib as he went by, and besought him to see
whether Tara was not in danger. He had dismounted,
some of his men had burst in the court door, and we
know the rest.

"Again baffled, O witch that thou art!" cried Moro
Pundit, flinging himself on the ground as Tara passed
out, and tearing up the clay of the floor in the agony

of his passion : " what sent that meddling fool to aid thee? If it had been only that proud boy she loves, ah ! I would have slain him and her together. Gunga ! Gunga ! where art thou? O girl, I burn—I choke ! She too is gone, devil that she is. If she had only helped me sooner I had stopped the screams, and no one could have heard them. Gunga ! dost thou hear? By ——," and he swore a frightful oath, " come hither, or I will come and stab thee : art thou too playing with me? Beware !"

The girl advanced from a dark corner trembling, yet without fear ; and as she did so, he raised himself on his arm, and she saw him grasp a knife at his waistband. " Kill me," she said, " if thou wilt ; twice I have aided thee, and twice the Mother hath saved her from us. I will have no more of it."

" No more !" cried the Bramhun, starting to his feet, and seizing her arm he shook her roughly—" no more ! This from thee ? I tell thee we have gone too far to recede. Will that old dotard be quiet? Will he spare my character? Not he. He has been my enemy from the first, supplanted me in my authority, crossed me in every design, and lastly in this—Why didst thou bungle with the shawl ? Coward ! witch ! devil !"—and he struck her violently on the face with his open hand at each word. " Why didst thou fail me ? Go !" and he flung her away from him, so that she tottered and fell heavily against the wall beyond. " Go ! may——"

Her fall and agony of mind prevented her hearing the frightful curses which followed. Once before, when

his sister had come to him, the paroxysm of passion
had been like this, but only once, and yet he had not
dared to strike her. She was not stunned, but O the
misery of her mind! She felt her lips were cut, and
her mouth was bleeding. The pain of this, the degra-
dation of having been struck, made the girl desperate.
If she had had a dagger she would have stabbed him
or herself. She could see him very dimly, for the
place was dark except the faint light which came in
from the drawn curtains. She saw that he was sitting, leaning against one of the wooden pillars of the
room, rocking himself to and fro. He had drawn his
knife, and a faint gleam of the naked blade was seen now
and again as he moved. Was she to die, or he? No
matter. In a frame of mind like hers death has no
terror. It is only the return to consciousness which
brings fear with it, and she lay crouching on the ground,
but watching him intently. If he moved towards her,
she knew she must die; but he did not move, and suddenly the rocking ceased, he seemed to fall heavily to
one side, and lay there motionless.

Was he feigning, in order to get her into his power?
No, it did not seem so, for he lay still, breathing
heavily. She had heard that thick heavy breathing
once before, and now recognised it again. Still she
was cautious. She rose gently, and stepping lightly
forward stood over him, yet near enough to the steps
to escape if he moved. The knife had fallen from his
hand, and lay beside him. She took it up, and placed
it in her own waistband. He was insensible; his tur-

ban had partly fallen off, and his face lay towards the
light, turned upwards. He could not harm her now,
—he was in her power. . . . The evil spirit within,
tugged hard at her heart, and she drew the knife.
Then the blood from her lip trickled into her mouth,
and the wound smarted and urged on her hand. If he
had risen and spoken a word to her, she would have
killed him; but as he lay so helpless, the girl's heart
once more softened. "It is my death, I know," she
said; "let him kill me; I cannot kill him, and this
faint will pass away. Now she is gone, he may love
me again." Poor fool, to think it!

Then she watched a few moments, and as she sat
down by him raised his head into her lap. The face
was cold and clammy; was this death? There was
no water, else she would sprinkle some on him, but
she fanned him with the end of her garment, and after
a while he opened his eyes gently. "Gunga!" he said,
stretching out his arms, "where art thou, girl? come to
me." It was the old tone of kindness, almost sad. Poor
fond fool, she did not resist it; and, wiping the blood
from her lips, kissed his forehead.

Meanwhile, Tara, sorely shaken in body and mind,
had been put into the litter. She heard the bearers
ask the old Bramhun whether they were to take her
to Afzool Khan's tents; and he had opened the door,
and said to her kindly that she had better come to
her own people, and that his wife and sister, who knew
them, would take charge of her, and be kind to her;

that they were at a village some miles further on, and he himself would escort her there.

She was helpless to object : in the first place, she dare not prefer the Mussulman noble's house, as strangers to her faith and to her own people ; nor dare she resist a Bramhun of the Envoy's powerful position in whatever he chose to do. She had no alternative, indeed, for he shut the door ere she could reply, the bearers took her forward at a rapid pace, and the night was somewhat advanced, ere she was again set down at the door of a respectable house in a village, and several women-servants, such as are menials in Bramhun families, kindly assisted her to alight, bringing what there was in the palankeen after her.

CHAPTER VII

It was a house something like their own at Toolja-poor. There was the master's seat, with its flowers and holy text painted on it; the verandah open to the court; the thick curtains between the pillars let down to exclude the night air, which was chill. The room was neat and scrupulously clean. She was once more in a Bramhun's house.

Before Tara sat two women, both elderly. One a stout and matronly figure, with a grave but kind countenance, and grey hair neatly braided, with heavy gold rings round her neck, wrists, and ankles, plainly but richly dressed, indicating rank and wealth; the other evidently a widow, clad in coarse white serge, her head clean shaved, and her wrists, ankles, and neck without any ornaments. She had strong coarse features, much wrinkled, small piercing eyes deep set in her head, and her skin was flaccid and shrivelled. She was the elder sister of the Envoy, and lived with him a life of austere penance and privation, and, as a Hindu widow, was a pattern of scrupulous attention to the rules of her faith. Neither rose to meet her.

Tara advanced and touched their feet in token of reverential submission and salutation. By the lady, whose evident rank had attracted Tara first, the action was received at least without repugnance, and perhaps with interest ; but by the other with marked aversion —she drew back her feet as though to prevent pollution, and shrank aside, evidently to avoid contact.

"Thou art welcome, daughter of Vyas Shastree," said the one ; " peace be with thee."

"And that gilded thing is called a widow and a Moorlee!" cried the other, with a scornful glance at Tara. "O sister, admit her not! Why has she any hair? Why is she more like a bride than a widow? —a harlot rather than a virtuous woman?"

"I am a widow and an orphan," returned Tara meekly, sinking down and trembling violently, as she addressed the first speaker. "I have been saved from dishonour, lady. O be kind to me! I have no one on earth to protect me now. They are all gone—all— and may God help me!"

"Your mother was one of the Durpeys of Wye, was she not?" asked the Envoy's wife, whose name was Amba Bye. "Do they know of thee?"

"I do not know, lady," returned Tara ; " they have never been to us, nor we to them ; but my mother was a Durpey, and used to speak of them."

"Her father lately married that wild sister of Moro

Trimmul's, and Sukya Bye is sure to know her," said
the widow.

"O not to her!—not to her!" cried Tara passionately—"do not give me to her? I beseech you by
your honour, by your children, lady, by all you love on
earth, not to give me to her. Do with me as ye will
yourselves, ye are matrons, but——"

"And why not, girl?" asked the widow, interrupting her.

"Peace! Pudma Bye," said her brother, now entering, and seeing that his sister's question had caused
pain, "the girl hath had a sore trial; listen to her, ere
thou art hard on her. Speak, daughter, let us know
from thine own lips how and why thou wast suffering
violence from Moro Trimmul."

"From Moro Trimmul!" exclaimed both ladies in a
breath.

"Yes, from him did I rescue her, sister, else she had
fared badly, I fear," returned the Envoy. "A violent
and wicked man,—who must be brought before the
council, to prevent further scandal. But speak, daughter,—thy name?"

"Tara."

"Tara: well, fear not. Amba Bye is strict, but
kind. Speak truly, we listen."

And Tara told her little story: how she had become a priestess when the Goddess called her; what
she knew of holy books; how she had been carried off
from the temple by Moro Trimmul, and how he had
persecuted her before. How she was taken by Fazil

Khan, and had been saved by him from the King's harem at Beejapoor. Finally, how they had treated her with honour and respect, and were taking her to her only refuge at Wye.

Ah, it was a sad story now: a glimpse of a heaven of delight now shut out from her for ever! She saw the stony eyes of the grim old widow wandering over her, from her glossy braided hair and the garland of jessamine flowers which Zyna had put into it just before they left camp, to the gold ornaments about her neck which Zyna would have her wear; and, above all, to the silken saree, and the gold anklets which Fazil liked, because the tiny bells to them clashed so musically as she walked. Over and over again, as she told her simple story, and was believed by the Baba Sahib and his wife, did his sister evince decided unbelief and scorn. But at the last her brother rebuked her.

"I rescued her myself from violence," he said, "and what she tells me confirms her whole story. Peace, Pudma! one so helpless and so beautiful should have thy pity, not thy scorn."

"Let her have her head shaved, and be such as I am; let her live with me, and bathe in cold water before dawn; let her say the name of God on her beads a thousand times an hour during the night; let her do menial service," cried the widow rapidly; "and then, if she can do these things, brother, she is a Bramhun widow, and true; else, cast her out to the Mussulmans with whom she has lived. Art thou ready to do all this, girl?" she continued, stretching out her long skinny flaccid arm, which was naked to the shoulder, and showed that the serge about her was her only garment.

Tara's spirit sank within her. Yes, such as the being before her were Hindu widows—such they would claim her to be. "It were better if I were dead," she groaned—" better if I were dead."

" Better if thou wast dead!" echoed the widow. "Ay, much better. Such as thou art, were better dead than live, in a harlot's guise, to be a disgrace to the faith!"

" Nay, peace, sister," said her brother—" I will have none of this. While she is with us, she is our guest and daughter, and shall be cared for tenderly. Take her away, Amba, and let her rest. I will see Afzool Khan at the Durbar to-morrow, and inquire if what she says be true; but my heart already tells me it is so."

Amba Bye rose and said a few soothing words to Tara as she stood over her and raised her up. " Come," she said, " I will not harm thee—come." And Tara rose and followed her to an inner room. The old lady had perhaps been afraid of her sister-in-law, or she was softened by Tara's beauty and grief, for, as she closed the door, she sat down and took her to her heart, laying her head on her bosom. " Thou art a gentle lamb," she said, stroking her head. " God help thee, child," and Tara clung to the kind heart, and felt, as it were, loving arms once more closed around her.

That night she slept with Amba Bye. Her sleep was at first broken, and full of fearful dreams; but wearied nature and youth in the end obtained their

mastery over her, and she sank into a deep slumber,—
so deep, that the sun was high in the morning ere she
awoke.

It had been a weary time to Zyna, Lurlee, and the
Khan's household, and even the Khan and the priest sat
up far into the night, speaking of Tara. No one had
slept. As to Fazil, he, with Shêre Khan, Lukshmun,
and a body of horse, rode round the country for miles,
all through the night, seeking Tara. No one dared speak
to him, and the men had never seen him so excited
before. He and Lukshmun, whose activity even sur-
passed his own, had stopped every palankeen ; every
cart or carriage which was covered ; every veiled
female they could see. Villages had been searched
also, but no trace of Tara was found—none ; and Fazil
returned home dejected and worn out, only, however, to
change his horse and the men, and to start once more
with Lukshmun, who would not leave him, on an errand
equally fruitless. That day (Fazil was still absent)
Baba Sahib sought Afzool Khan after the afternoon
Durbar, and told him what had happened : how he had
rescued Tara, how he had sent her on to Wye with
his wife and sister, and how she would be safe in his
hands ; and he heard in return how she was respected
and loved in the Khan's family.

" We cannot allow her, Khan," he said kindly, " to
remain with you, much as you have respected her faith.
It would be a scandal to Bramhuns, if the daughter of
Vyas Shastree were the guest even of Afzool Khan
and his household. It is not compatible with her

purity or her honour, which, now her father is dead,
her people must protect. We—that is, my wife and
myself—have charged ourselves with her for the present; and her people, the Durpeys of Wye, are rich
and devout,—they will receive and protect her."

Afzool Khan remonstrated as far as possible. Tara
had grown to be a familiar and beautiful object to him;
but he felt the Bramhun was right, and he must not
connect her name with his son's. He dare not mention
to Lurlee what had been done, but he told Fazil when
he returned, and so all knew of it.

"At least she is safe and in honourable keeping,"
said Fazil, when he had heard all, "and for the rest, as
God wills. But as for that Bramhun, father, he escaped
me once—it may not be again."

"Look!" cried Lurlee to Zyna, who was sitting
sobbing bitterly—"look! Had I only been careful,
this would never have happened. It was Sunday
night, and Saturn ruled from the second hour of the
first watch to the end. Could anything be worse? We
should not have moved at all. My pearl, my love, she
should not have left us! Hái! Hái! May the peace
of the Prophet be with her, and the protection of Alla
be upon her till we meet again!"

"Ameen! Ameen!" sighed Zyna, but she was not
comforted, nor was Fazil.

CHAPTER VIII.

MAGNIFICENT as is the scenery of the Western Ghauts of India throughout their range, it is nowhere, perhaps, more strikingly beautiful than in the neighbourhood of the great isolated plateau which—rising high above the mountain-ranges around it, and known under the name of Maha-bul-eshwur, from the temple at the source of the sacred river Krishna on its summit—is now the favourite summer retreat and sanatarium of the Bombay Presidency. Trim roads, laid out so as to exhibit the beauties of the scenery to the best advantage—pretty English-looking cottages, with brilliant gardens, and a considerable native town, are now the main features of the place; but at the period of our tale it was uninhabited, except by a few Bramhuns and devotees, who, attracted by the holiness of the spot, congregated around the ancient temple, and occupied the small village beside it. Otherwise the character of the wild scenery is unchanged. From points near the edges of the plateau, where mighty precipices of basalt descend sheer into forests of everlasting verdure and luxuriance, the eye ranges over a sea of rugged mountain - tops,—some,

scathed and shattered peaks of barren rock—others with
extensive flat summits, bounded by naked cliffs which,
falling into deep gloomy ravines covered with dense
forests, would seem inaccessible to man.

To some readers of our tale, this scenery will be
familiar ; but to others it is almost impossible to convey by description any adequate idea of its peculiar
character, or of the beauty of the ever-changing aërial
effects, that vary in aspect almost as the spectator
turns from one point to another.   Often in early
morning, as the sun rises over the lower mists, the
naked peaks and precipices, standing apart like islands,
glisten with rosy tints, while the mist itself, as yet
dense and undisturbed, lies wrapped around their
bases, filling every ravine and valley, and glittering
like a sea of molten silver.

Again, as the morning breeze rises in the valleys
below, this vapour breaks up slowly : circling round
the mountain summits, lingering in wreaths among
their glens and precipices, and clinging to the forests
until dissipated entirely by the fierce beams of the
sun.   Then, quivering under the fervid heat, long
ridges of rugged valleys are spread out below, and
range beyond range melts tenderly into a dim distance of sea and sky, scarcely separated in colour, yet
showing the occasional sparkle of a sail like a faint
cloud passing on the horizon.   Most glorious of all,
perhaps, in the evening, when, in the rich colours of
the fast-rising vapours, the mountains glow like fire ;
and peak and precipice, forest and glen, are bathed in

gold and crimson light; or, as the light grows dimmer, shrouded in deep purple shadow till they disappear in the gloom which quickly falls on all.

Westward from this great mountain plateau, and divided from it by a broad deep valley clothed with forests, the huge mountain of Pertabgurh rises with precipitous sides out of the woods and ravines below. The top, irregularly level, furnished space for dwelling-houses and magazines, while ample springs of pure water sufficed for the use of a large body of men, by which it could be easily defended. At various periods of time—by the early Mahratta chieftains of the country in remote ages, and afterwards by their Mahomedan conquerors—walls and towers had been added to the natural defences of the place, as well as strong gateways protected by bastions and loopholed traverses, on the only approach to the summit—a rugged pathway, which could hardly be called a road. Under very ordinary defence, the place was perfectly impregnable to all attacks by an enemy from without; and, at the period of our tale, it was held as his capital and choicest stronghold, among many such fastnesses in those mountains, by Sivaji Bhóslay, a man destined to play a conspicuous part in the history of his country and people in particular, and of India at large.

We have already informed the reader, in a somewhat desultory manner perhaps, for we are not writing his history, of the attempts made by Sivaji to establish an independent power; and, by taking advantage of

the weakness and distraction of the kingdom of Beejapoor, of which he was a vassal, — on the one
hand, and of the ambitious designs of the Emperor
Aurungzeeb on the other, to raise himself to a position in which he could secure the actual administration, and eventually the sovereignty, of his native
wilds.

Hindu history is in all cases unsatisfactory; and that
of the early Mahratta chiefs and principalities of the
Dekhan eminently so.   On the invasion of the Dekhan
by Alla-oo-deen, nephew of the then King of Dehli,
in A. D. 1294, the fort and city of Deogurh, now Dou-
latabad, was held by Rajah Ramdeo Jadow, who appeared then to have been prince of the whole country.
Whether he was so or not, whether the chiefs of the
wild tracts of the Ghauts and provinces lying on the
western sea-coast were his tributaries or vassals, or
whether they were actually independent of each other,
has never been ascertained; but, on the downfall of
the princely house of Jadow, no other ruler or chieftain seems to have made any resistance, and the
Mahomedans, gathering strength, and founding a
kingdom at Gulburgah, in the centre of the Dekhan,
gradually subdued the whole tract, establishing garrisons in the wildest parts, fortifying hills not already used as strongholds, and improving the defences
of others, in that noble, and picturesque style of
fortification which now excites our wonder and admiration.

One of the Mahratta families of ancient native nobility, though not of the highest grade, were the Bhóslays. The Jadows, though no longer possessing princely power, had descended into the rank of landed proprietors, or hereditary officers, under the ancient Hindu tenure, of the districts over which their ancestors had once held sway. Under ordinary circumstances, an alliance between the families would have been rejected by the Jadows; but one fell out nevertheless, and after a strange manner.

At the marriage of a mutual friend, Shahji Bhóslay, then a pretty boy, was present with his father, and the head of the family of the Jadows with his daughter, Jeejee, a child younger than the boy Shahji. The children began to play together, and the girl's father remarked jocosely what a pretty couple they would make. The remark was heard by the boy's father, who claimed it as a promise of betrothal, and, after some discussion, and objection as to disparity of rank, the children were eventually married. From these parents sprung Sivaji, who, with his mother, as remarkable a person in many respects as himself, became the originator and leader of the renewed independence of the Hindus of the Dekhan.

The women of India, particularly those of the higher classes and families, are invariably the treasuries of family events, and of deeds of departed or existent greatness. Jeejee Bye, an ambitious, perhaps unscrupulous woman, strove hard to excite her husband, Shahji Bhóslay, to exertion in the Hindu cause. She filled his mind with legends of the Jadows' power; she

sought out the histories of his own family ; she urged
him to assert his right to districts in sovereignty of
which he was only the official head ; and she actively
canvassed all the heads of the Mahratta families, with
a view to a combined resistance against the Mahomedan powers, then beginning to show symptoms of a
final decadence.

.And not without effect. Shahji, the servant and
vassal of the Emperor of Dehli as of the King of Beejapoor, rebelled in turn against both ; was restless and
unfaithful, lacking, while a bold, enterprising partisan
soldier, the higher qualities which could direct and
take advantage of such movements. He was frequently imprisoned, fined, and otherwise punished, but
nothing checked his wife's ambition. Left to herself
during his long absences and captivities with her
young son among their native wilds, surrounded
by rude retainers, she turned to him as soon as he
could comprehend her plans ; and by the mother
and son those designs were sketched out which, in
respect of utter hopelessness at first, and splendid success afterwards, have few comparisons in the world's
history.

As the boy grew up, his immediate retainers joined
him in wild enterprises against the Mahomedans,
which to the people savoured of madness, but which,
as they increased in boldness of design and execution,
were believed to be the deeds of one especially protected
by the Goddess Bhowani, the tutelar divinity of the
Jadow family. His mother, an ardent votary, pre-

tended to be occasionally visited by the Goddess in person, and, filled with her divine afflatus, spoke prophecy. Her son believed in her inspiration : and gradually his friends, Maloosray, Palkur, and others, with a superstitious faith, believed also. Undisciplined, often unarmed men of the Mawuls, or mountain valleys above the Ghauts, who were called Mawullees, and of those below the mountains towards the sea, called Hetkurees, joined the young leader: scaled mountain forts, or descended into the plains beyond the valleys, gathering arms and booty, occupying Mahomedan garrisons, putting their defenders to the sword, and never relinquishing what they had obtained.

So year after year passed, and the young Sivaji, as he grew stronger, became more daring and enterprising. Originally a few hundreds of half-naked, ill-armed mountain peasants, his forces of Mawullees and Hetkurees at last numbered many thousands of active, determined men. He had possession of some of the strongest mountain forts in the Western Ghauts ; he had built, and was building, defences to other isolated and naturally almost inaccessible mountains. He was arming them with cannon purchased by stealth from the Portuguese of Goa, or cast by his own skilful artificers ; and as he gained more perfect local strength, he was silently extending his intrigues to all the Mahratta families of ancient Maharastra by agents like Moro Trimmul, and awaiting the time patiently, till all could rise to overthrow the

Mahomedan governments which held them in sub-
jection.

Had those governments, after the spirit of the earlier
Mussulman invaders of the Dekhan, been intolerant of
Hindus, denied them privileges of worship, defiled their
temples, confiscated their ancestral rights, or otherwise harassed and oppressed them,—it is probable that
Shahji's first attempts towards throwing off the Mahomedan yoke would have met with better success. But,
on the contrary, there was now little or no oppression
or interference with them in any way; and many of the
Mahratta chieftains not only held estates in fief for
service, but joined the armies of the Mahomedan kings,
and fought with them bravely and faithfully. We have
ourselves a counterpart of this, in some respects, in the
Norman occupation of our own country; inasmuch as,
while some Saxon thanes then held themselves aloof,
and retired to the management of their own estates,
others were found who joined the invaders, or, gradually
imitating their manners, became incorporated with
them.

That Sivaji's prospects had assumed a more encour-
aging form than any of his father's, may easily be
imagined from the method in which they had been
maintained. The Dusséra, or festival of Bhowani,
throughout Maharastra, of 1657, the year of which
we write, was to show, by a private muster of the
people, what forces were available for a general rising;
and after that it would be determined how they were
to be employed.

We know what the object of Maloosray's mission to Beejapoor had been, and its result. Sivaji had heard already by express from the capital, of the death of the Wuzeer, the discovery of some of his own correspondence by the King, and the acceptance of the gage by Afzool Khan to undertake a campaign against him with a picked army. He had not heard since, nor had Maloosray arrived; but Sivaji knew that Afzool Khan was no laggard in war, and that he must prepare himself to meet the emergency.

A fascination for sacred plays which had possessed him from childhood, was a strange peculiarity of this man's character. As Sivaji grew up, no distance, no personal danger, deterred him from being present at any which could by any possibility be reached. Sometimes openly, and more frequently in a peasant's or common soldier's garb, the young prince, with a few chosen associates, would appear at places where his arrival was incomprehensible, and his disappearance equally abrupt and mysterious. In the latter days, these " Kuthas," as they are termed, became means of assembling his men without attracting suspicion; but his adherents well knew that the most exciting enterprises immediately followed them.

Soon after the arrival of the news from Beejapoor, notice of one to be held at Pertabgurh had been sent through the country, and from the earnestness and celerity with which the orders were circulated from village to village, the people at large were assured of the proximity of some notable event, and hoped, in their own expressive phrase, that, at last, the "fire would light the hills."

With this partial digression, and introduction to the Rajah's play, the day of which had arrived, our history will proceed

CHAPTER IX.

FROM a straggling, irregular village, which could hardly be called a town, nestling in a hollow under the mountain of Pertabgurh, a rude pathway, for it was little else, ascended to the fort above. Very rough, but very lovely, was this road. The forest, or jungle, had been partly cleared away from its sides, but noble trees still hung over it, affording grateful shade as it wound round ravines and shoulders of the mountain in gradual but easy ascent; and the huge broad leaf of the teak tree, the graceful and feathery bamboo, and other masses of luxuriant foliage, rich with great creepers now covered with flowers, which hung from tree to tree in graceful festoons, or clung in dense masses about their tops,—presented endless and beautiful combinations with the bold upper precipices of the mountain itself, and the distant ranges behind it. Farther up, as the air grew fresher in the ascent, and you looked down into deep gloomy dells, or abroad over the valley, or up to the rugged sides of the great mountain beyond,—a subtle blue atmosphere appeared to pervade everything; and this, the peculiar characteristic of

those high tropical regions, seemed to increase in depth
of colour,—and, without in reality obscuring the features of the scenery, to soften its rugged outlines, and
blend its almost savage elements into harmony.

It has been said of natives of India that they are
insensible to beauties of natural scenery. We admit
that Mahomedans to a great extent are so, but not
Hindus, still less Mahrattas, of these glorious mountains. Their sacred books, their ballads, and recited
plays, abound with beautiful pictures of natural objects;
and, living among combinations of the most glorious
forms in nature, peopling every remarkable rock,
deep dell, or giant tree with spiritual beings belonging peculiarly to each, who are worshipped with a rude
veneration,—insensibility to outward impressions and
their influence upon character would be impossible.

So now, at the time we speak of, a numerous company of men on foot were ascending by the pathway
already mentioned to the fort, and that light merriment
prevailed among them which ever accompanies the
enjoyment of fine scenery and pure mountain air, and
excites physical capability for the endurance of the
heaviest fatigue. Some ran or leaped, as occasional
level portions of road occurred; others climbed among
the crags and rocks by its side, or, knowing shorter
paths to the summit, struck out of the main road, and
breasted the steep mountain with a freedom and agility
only known to mountaineers.

Keen-eyed, lithe, spare, yet muscular men; low in
stature, yet of extraordinary power of endurance; often

heavily armed with long matchlock, and its accompaniment of powder-horns, bullet-bags, and other
accoutrements tied round the waist,—a long, straight,
heavy two-handled sword hanging over the left shoulder, or a smaller curved sabre fastened into the waistband, with a dagger or two, and a broad shield at the
back—such were Sivaji's Mawullees. Ordinarily unburdened with much clothing—a pair of drawers fitting
tight below the knee, a coarse handkerchief wound about
the head, and a black blanket thrown over all, or crossed
over the chest, leaving the arms free, sufficed for ordinary purposes ; on festival days, however, all were clad
in a clean suit of coarse cotton cloth, with a gay turban,
and scarf round the waist, and bunches of wild flowers
tucked fantastically into the folds of their head-dress.

This was a festival day—for their Rajah had ordered
a Kutha ; and all knew when this took place that it
was the prelude to some raid or foray—some distant
expedition in which honour and booty were to be
gained—and when the Mawullees would strike in,
hard and fierce, on the unsuspecting Moslems. The
" Dhunni," or master, as they called him, had been
unaccountably quiet for some time past ; but to a man
they knew he was not idle, and throughout that country, as in more remote provinces, the conviction prevailed that something unusual was to happen—some
manifestation of the will of the Goddess, whom all
feared and most worshipped. There was nothing apparent or tangible ; but expectation and excitement
prevailed nevertheless.

For several days previously, the usual messengers
had run from village to village among the Mawuls
or valleys of the ranges near Pertabgurh, giving news
of the Kutha. The players had come from Wye,
from Sattara, and other towns, and the Rajah's hill-
men had been clearing the usual place of celebration,
and were now decorating the royal seat, and stage for
the players, with green boughs and wild flowers. The
little town was already full of people, and others were
crowding up the mountain to make their salutation to
their beloved prince who, now seated in his hall of
audience, surrounded by a few friends, soldiers, and
priests, denied no one the privilege so dearly prized,
that of making a "salam" to their Rajah, and receiv-
ing one in return.

Up the mountain-side, through the grim gateways,
till they emerged upon the irregular plateau at the
top, the men poured in a continuous stream.   Some
singly or in small groups ; others in larger companies
headed by a pair of "gursees," or pipers, one playing a
drone, the other a reed flageolet, very strong and shrill
in tone, the combination of which, as well as the wild
melodies played, being curiously like bagpipes in effect.
Others had with them their village trumpeters ; and
shrill quivering blasts of their horns, accompanied by
the deep monotonous notes of large tambourine drums,
not unfrequently arose together or singly from different
parts of the ascent, and were answered by the Rajah's
horn-blowers stationed on the bastions above the
gates, and elsewhere in the towers above the precipices.

The fort was full of men, for several thousands were assembled in it: sitting in groups, rambling about the walls, or by the side of springs and wells, untying the bundles of cakes which each man had bound to his back, and making a noonday meal ; or proceeding to their chieftain's kitchen, received the daily allowance of meal bread, which was served out without stint to all comers on those occasions, and of which huge piles stood on the kitchen floor ready for distribution.

All the morning Sivaji had sat in his humble hall of audience, surrounded by some of his tried friends, and some Bramhun priests and scribes. No gorgeous palace was this, like that at Beejapoor, but a broad shed made by poles fastened together, and thatched with grass and teak-leaves, decorated gracefully and appropriately with leafy branches and wild flowers. At the upper end was the Rajah's seat, a low dais covered with coarse cotton carpets, on which the " guddee " or royal seat—a velvet pillow covered with gold embroidery, and a seat to match—had been placed temporarily. Below the dais, the leaders of large and small parties of men came—saluted—seated themselves by turns, and got up and departed with the usual salutation, but seldom without notice ; and while other men passed quickly by, the chief had a kind word of greeting or reminiscence or salute for every one. Many saw that his features were clouded with care ; but the news from the capital concerned no one, and the Kutha to come off that night would, they knew, prove the usual prelude of active service.

Seated as he was amidst a crowd of friends and attendants, the Mahratta Rajah seemed, in the distance, almost contemptible, from his small stature and plain, insignificant appearance. Dressed in ordinary white muslin, the only ornament he wore was the "jika," or jewel for the turban, which sparkled with valuable diamonds. A light red shawl drawn over his shoulders protected him from the somewhat chill wind, and before him lay his terrible sword Bhowani, and the large black shield of rhinoceros hide which he usually wore. A nearer view, however, gave a different impression. Somewhat dark in complexion, with a prominent nose, broad in the nostril; large, soft eyes, small determined mouth and chin; a thin mustache curled up at the ends, and bushy black whiskers shaved on a line with his ear,—formed a countenance at once handsome and intelligent: while his slight figure, apparently more active than strong, evinced, by its lithe movement even while sitting, a power of endurance which was confirmed by the expression of his face.

No one who had once seen the Maharaja ever forgot him. Though now mild in expression, if not sad, most about him had seen and remembered the face in other and wilder moods of excitement: in war, or in the actual hand-to-hand combats, in which he delighted, and from which he could with difficulty be restrained; while the impression that he was an incarnation of divinity, mingled awe with the respect and love which all bore him.

CHAPTER X.

THE morning ceremony was at length over, and, some-what wearied by it, and by sitting inactive so long, Sivaji rose and passed into his private apartments, to which the shed or pavilion was a temporary addition. The rough mountain fortress afforded no royal palaces. A few terraced houses, divided by courts, with some thatched out-offices and stables, stood on an elevated spot near the walls; and the Rajah's favourite retreat was a small vaulted apartment, which joined the fort-wall —indeed, formed portion of it—and from which a small projecting window, placed immediately above one of the deepest precipices, looked out over the valley and moun-tains, and commanded a view of part of the ascent.

It was a habit of Sivaji's to go to no ceremony, nor return from any, without saluting his mother. Did he ever leave the house or return to it, he touched her feet reverently, while she gave him her blessing. The son's faith in his mother was only equalled by her faith and love for him ; and as a pattern of filial piety and devotion, his example is still inculcated upon the Mahratta youth by many a village schoolmaster.

She met him at the threshold of the door, and, as was her wont, passed her hands over his face and neck, kissing the tips of her fingers ; while, bowing low, he touched both her feet, then his own eyes and forehead.

"Is Tannajee arrived, son," she asked, "that thou hast broken up the reception so early?"

"No, mother," he said ; "but come with me, for my spirit is heavy, and there is a shadow of gloom over me which thou only canst dispel. No, there is no news, and that vexes me."

She followed him into the apartment we have mentioned. A plain cushion had been placed near the window upon a soft mattress, and he flung, rather than seated himself, upon it, and buried his face in his hands, turning away from her.

She sat down by him, and again passed her hand over his face and neck, and kissed her fingers without speaking.

A mother's loving hand! O ye who know it, who possess it as the rude waves of life come breaking one by one against you, be thankful that it is there in its old place, soothing and sustaining like nought else of earthly comfort! Ye who have lost it, never forget how lovingly it used to do its blessed work. In times of anxious trial, perplexity, and sickness most of all,—ye shall feel it still, in the faith which leads ye where it is gone before, and awaits your coming. So, forget it not!—forget it not!

For a while both were silent. The mother knew the

feelings which filled her son's mind too well to interfere with their course. Still she sat by him, and
patted him occasionally as she used to do when she
soothed him to rest as a child. "If he could sleep,"
she thought, "this gloom would pass away; but it
will do so nevertheless."

He lay still, sometimes looking out into the blue air,
watching the swallows as they passed and repassed the
window in rapid flight to and from their nests, which
hung to the ledges of the precipices,—or the groups of
people ascending and descending the pathway to the
gates. Again, burying his face in the cushion, he lay
still, and his mother watched, and gently waved the
corner of her garment over his head, lest any insect
should light on him and disturb him. There was no
sound save the dull buzzing of flies in the room, and
sometimes the loud monotonous note of a great wood-
pecker from the depths of the ravine below.

He turned at length, and she knew the crisis was
past. "Mother," he said, "hast thou been with the
Goddess to-day? To me she is dim and mournful; I
ask my heart of her designs, but there comes no answer. Is her favour gone from us?"

"Who can tell her purposes, my life?" she replied,
"we are only her instruments. O fail not in heart!
If there be troubles, should we not meet them? If
she bid us suffer, shall we not suffer? But, O, fail
not—doubt not! Remember thy father doubted and
failed, and what came of it but weary imprisonment,
fine, pain, shame, and failure? O not so, my son: better

thou wast dead, and I with thee, than to doubt and
fail."

"The trial will be heavy, mother," he returned.
"Here we are safe, and I fear not for thee; but for the
rest, the cause is hopeless, and that is what vexes me.
Years of stratagem and arrangement are gone with that
man's death, and all we have planned is known."

"And if it be known, son, dost thou fear?" she exclaimed.   "What has been gained by these communications with a traitor?   O son, he who is not faithful
to the salt he eats, is untrue to all besides.   I—a
woman only—and the priests will tell thee not to trust
a woman's thoughts or designs—I tell thee I am glad:
I rejoice that a trial has come to thee.   One hour such
as thou hast passed now, with thine own heart to speak
to thee, is worth more to the cause than a thousand
priests or a lakh of swordsmen.   I tell thee I am
glad: for such things only can teach thee to trust thyself, and not to look to others."

"And thee, mother?" he said smiling.

"No, no—not to me," she replied quickly, "except
the Goddess speaks by my mouth.   No, not to me.   I
am but a woman else, fearful of thee, my son—fearful
of the bullet, the sword, the lance, the wild fray of
battle—fearful of——"

"Nay, mother," he cried, sitting up and interrupting
her, "not of the sword or the battle; there I am safe,
—there I fear not.   Were I but there now, this heavi-
ness at my heart would pass away.   'Hur, Hur, Mahadeo!' the cry—the shout rings in my ears and

urges me on; then there is no time for thought, as now in this silence."

"And it shall ring again, my son," she replied. "Fear not—doubt not, only act : that is all. Wilt thou be like thy father, drifted here and there by every current of rumour like a straw upon the sea? 'Such a one will not join, what can I do? Such a thing threatens, what can I do? This man says this, shall I follow it? That man says the other, shall I follow it?' So he followed as others led; so he acted as others advised. What came of all? only shame, my son. Had he said to all, Do this, they would have done it. O Mother, O Holy Mother," she cried, standing up and lifting her joined hands towards the deep blue sky, "come from thence—come from the air into thy daughter's heart; teach me what to say, how to direct him, or direct him thyself! O Mother, we do all for thy name and honour, and for the faith so long degraded : let us not fail or be shamed!

"Not thus, son," she continued after a pause—"not thus will the spirit come upon me, but in the temple must I watch alone and pray and fast, ere she will disclose herself to me; and I will do so from to-night. Yes, she will be entreated at last. Perhaps," she continued simply, but reverently, "the Mother is in sorrow herself, and needs comfort. No matter, I will entreat her."

"Surely she hath heard already," replied her son after another pause, "for my soul is better for thy words—stronger, mother. Yes, I see how it will be;

nor Moro Trimmul, nor Tannajee, nor Palkur, nor any
one but myself. I had thought to lay all these matters
before the people at the Kutha to-night, but I will not.
I will only say we must work for ourselves—against
the Emperor, against the King, and most against
Afzool Khan. If they will only trust in me—yes,
mother, if they will only trust in me—we shall have
victory, and I will not disappoint them or you."

" Now, a thousand blessings on thee, Sivaji Bhóslay,
for those words," cried his mother, passing her hands
over his head. " I have no fear now—none. Go to the
Kutha—tell them all that their time is come ; and when
you cry ' Hur, Hur, Mahadeo ! ' each shout of theirs in
reply will echo the death-cry of a thousand infidels.
Now, let me depart, my son ; it is well for me to go
to the Mother, and sit before her ; haply she may come
to me. Better to be there, than that a woman should
be near thee, when the woman's spirit has passed out
of thee."

" Bless me, then, my mother, and go ; nor will I stay
here long," he replied. " The shadows are even now
lengthening in the valleys, and I should have the people
collected ere it is dark."

She placed her hands upon his head solemnly :
"Thus do I bless thee, my son—more fervently, more
resignedly than ever. Go, as she will lead thee in her
own time. To all thy people thou wilt not alter, but,
to the Moslems, be stone and steel. Trust no one—ask
of no one what is to be done, not even of me. Do
what is needful, and what thy heart tells thee. Show

no mercy, but cut out thine own path with the sword.
If thou wilt be great, do these things ; if not——: but
no, thou wilt be great, my son. She hath told me so ;
and thou wilt reckon the true beginning of it from
that silent watch there, by the window. I go now, but
stay not thou here. See, there are none ascending,
and even those descending the hill are fewer. Go to
them."

He watched her intently as she left him and disappeared behind a curtain, which fell before a door of
the apartment leading to the small household temple.
An expression of triumph lit up his large dark eyes
and expressive features. "She said I must act for
myself," he cried aloud. "Yes, mother, I will act for
thee first, and then for the people ; and there shall be
no idle words again—only 'Hur, Hur, Mahadeo!'
when the fire is on the hills."

CHAPTER XI

THE servants and attendants of the lady awaited her without, and preceded her to the temple, which was situated in a court by itself,—a small unpretending building, which her son had built at her request. The usual priests sat by the shrine, feeding the lamps with oil, and offering flowers and incense for those who needed their services. This, too, had been a busy day for them, for the Rajah's temple had been opened to those who came to the fort; and many a humble offering and donation of copper coins to the priests, from the soldiery, had been the result. The court had now been cleared of all visitors, and the doors shut. As the lady advanced and sat down before the shrine, the priests made the customary libations and offerings, and stood apart, not daring to speak, for her visions of the Goddess were well known, and much feared, and this might be the occasion of one of them. So, as she sat down, the priests and her attendants shrank back behind the entrance to the sanctum, and awaited the issue in silence.

Very different from Tara, as she had sunk down in

her strange delirium before the shrine at Tooljapoor,
the Maha* Ranee, as she was called, but more simply
and lovingly the "Lady Mother," was perfectly calm
and self-possessed.   A small, grey-headed, slightly-
formed woman, of graceful carriage and shape, which
had altered little, if at all, from the best period of her
youth : nor, except in her hair, had age apparently
told much upon her ; for the arms were still as round,
the skin of her cheek as soft and downy as ever, and
the firm springy tread of the small naked foot showed
no decline of vigour.   Her son often told her she was
yet the most beautiful woman in Maharastra ; nor indeed, in the clear golden olive of her skin, in the delicate mould and sweet expressive character of her
features, above all, in the soft lustre of her eyes, had
she many rivals.

She had seated herself directly before the shrine, on
which was a small gold image of the Goddess upon a
golden pedestal ; and the water-vessels, lamps, and other
articles of service were also of gold.   The full light of
the lamps within shone out on her, and glistened on
the white silk garment she wore, with its broad crimson
and gold border—upon the jewelled bracelets on her
arms—and the large pearls about her neck.   The end
of her saree, heavy with gold thread, had fallen a little
aside as she seated herself, and her soft throat, and a
little of the crimson silk boddice below, could be seen—
enough to show that if the face were calm, the bosom
was heaving rapidly, and under the influence of no

* *Maha*—great.

common emotion. No one dared to speak to her, or
interrupt her thoughts or prayers, whatever they might
be ; and when she seated herself before the shrine in
this manner, the priests and attendants knew she expected a " revelation," and had to wait, even though it
might be for many hours, for the issue.

When it came, it was with various effect. At times
calm, with glistening eyes and throbbing bosom, her
hands clenched convulsively, she would speak strange
words, which were heard with a mysterious reverence,
and recorded by an attendant priest ; at others, the
result was wild delirium, when they were obliged to
hold her, and when the excitement was followed by
exhaustion, which remained for days.* Now, however,
she sat calmly, her eyes cast down, but raised occasionally with an imploring look to the image, seldom
altering her position, and seemingly unconscious of the
time which passed.

Long she sat there ; the shadows of the mountains
lengthened, till only their peaks shone like fire, and
then suddenly died out. The moon rose, and the
little court was white under her silver beams, and
still the lady sat and moved not. The chill night
breeze at that elevation had caused an involuntary
shiver to pass over her, which her favourite attendant
thought was the precursor of the usual affection, but
nothing followed ; and seeing it was caused by cold,

* A series of very curious and most interesting papers on this subject, by the late Xavier Murphy, Esq., were published some years
ago in the ' Dublin University Magazine.'—M. T.

had, apparently unobserved, cast over her a large red
shawl, which fell in soft folds around her person. It
was far in the night when she arose from that strange
vigil; and, dreamily passing her hands over her face
and neck as if to arouse herself, sighed, and advancing
to the threshold of the shrine, joined her hands together, and bowing reverently before the image,
saluted it, and silently turned away.

"Not to-night, Bheemee," she said to a woman who
approached her bearing her sandals, and laid them
down at the entrance to the temple,—"not to-night.
The Mother bids me go; she is sad, and will come
another time. Hark! what is that?" and she paused
to listen.

A hoarse roar, a cry as though of a wail of thousands
of voices, came from all sides at once, floating up
the precipices, echoed from the rocks, and reverberating from mountain to mountain. It seemed to those
present, who were already filled with superstitious
expectation, as if spirits cried out, being invisible, and
that some unearthly commotion was in progress around
them. In the pure mountain air, still as it was, these
sounds seemed to float about them mysteriously, now
dying away, and now returning more faintly than
before, till they ceased, or only a confused perception
of them remained. The fierce shout or wail, however,
occurred but once; what followed was more diffuse
and undecided.

"Something has moved the people more than ordinarily, lady," said a priest who advanced from the outer

court. "The assembly can be seen from the bastion yonder, and I have been watching it while you were within; if you would look, follow me."

She drew the shawl more closely around her, and went with him through the court to the bastion, which, situated on the edge of an angle of the precipice, commanded a view of the town and valley below. The moon shone clear and bright, else she had looked into a black void; but the air was soft and white, of a tint like opal, as the moon's rays caught the thin vapours now rising. Some thousands of feet below, was a bright spot in a dell, filled with torches, which sent up a dull smoke, while they diffused a bright light on all around. There were many thousands of people there, mostly men, and there was a glitter as of weapons among them, as the masses still heaved and swayed under the influence of some strange excitement. She could make out no particular forms, but she knew that her son sat in the pavilion at the end, and about that there was no movement. As she looked, the shout they had first heard arose more clearly than before—"Hur, Hur, Mahadeo, Dônguras-lavilé Déva!"*

"O Mother," she cried, stretching out her arms to the sky, and then to the dell below, "enough! thou hast heard the prayer of thy daughter: thou wast there with him, not with me. Now I understand, and it is enough. Come, Bheemee, it is cold," she said, after a pause,

* "O Mahadeo! the fire has lit the hills!"—the Mahratta invocation to battle; which is used also as the heading to all threatening notices.

and in her usual cheerful voice, "thou shouldst have been yonder in the Kutha, girl, and all of you. Well, the next, to-morrow night, will be a better one, and you shall all go, for I will go myself with the Maharaja ; come now, they will not return till daylight ;" and descending the steps of the bastion, she followed her servants, who preceded her, to the private apartments.

Below, Sivaji had been busy since before sunset. He had descended the mountain on foot, attended by his body-guard, and a large company of the garrison of the fort—a gay procession, as, accompanied by the pipers and horn-blowers of the fortress, it had wound down the rugged pathway in the full glare of the evening sun; and, amidst the shouts of thousands, and a confused and hideous clangour, caused by the independent performances of all the pipers and drummers of the clans assembled—the screaming, quivering notes of the long village horns, the clash of cymbals, and the deep tones of some of the large brass trumpets belonging to the temple, which had been brought down from the fort,—Sivaji passed on round the village to the spot which had been cleared for the Kutha.

It was a glen from which all wood had long been cleared away, and short crisp grass had grown up in its place, which, moistened by the perpetual drainage of the mountain, was always close and verdant. Near enough to the village to serve as a grazing ground for its cattle, the herbage was kept short by them; and the passage round and round its sides of beasts of all kinds, goats and sheep, cows, bullocks, and buffaloes, had worn

them into paths which formed, as it were, a series of
steps, rising gradually to the edge of the forest above.

In the midst was a bright green sward, soft and
close, and of some extent, and at all times of the year
the resort of the village youth for athletic exercises—
wrestling, leaping, archery, shooting with the matchlock, or, most favoured of all perhaps, the sword-play-
ing, for which the Mahratta soldiery were most celebrated. A projecting mound, which might have been
artificial, and was possibly the partly completed em-
bankment of some intended reservoir, stretched nearly
across its mouth, and while its grassy surface afforded
seats to many of the spectators, it shut out the valley
beyond, from all observers.

At the upper end of the dell, which in shape was a
long oval, and slightly raised above the level sward,
was the Rajah's seat, a platform of sods and earth,
covered with dry grass, and then with carpets from the
fort, upon which the Guddee, or seat of state, was placed.
Directly the Rajah had retired from the morning ceremony, the cushions had been taken down the mountain
and placed on this dais, which afforded room also for
many personal friends and priests who attended the
ceremony with him.

In the centre of the sward, but near the upper end,
was the place for the players. The smoothest portion
of turf had been selected, and around it wattled screens
were built, made of leafy branches, for entrance and
exit, and also to allow of changes of dress, rest during
intervals of performance, and the like. The stage, if

it might be called one, was bounded by wild plantain trees cut off at the root, and set in the ground so that the broad leaves continued fresh and green, and above these were twined branches of teak with their large rough foliage, bamboos, and other slender trees readily felled and transported ; while long masses of flowery creepers had been cut from the forest, and hung from poles at each side above the players' heads in graceful festoons. Inside all this foliage, were huge cressets of iron filled with cotton-seed soaked in oil, and all round the area below, and especially round the Rajah's seat, similar torches had been arranged, which would be lighted as the ceremony began, and illuminate the whole.

Before the stage, there was a small altar of earth, on which brightly polished brass vessels for pouring libations were set out, and above them, upon a silver pedestal, a small silver image of the Goddess had been placed for worship.

Early in the afternoon, people had begun to assemble there, and after the Rajah's arrival in the town, a new procession was formed to accompany him to the place. Thousands had rushed on before it ; along the valley, over the shoulders of the mountain, and as best they could, so as to secure good places for the sight; and by the time the head of the procession crossed the little brook which bubbled out beneath the mound, and ran leaping and tinkling down the valley, and had entered the glen,—the whole of its sides and the mound had grown into a dense mass of human beings closely packed together. There were comparatively few women ;

those who sat there were for the most part the Rajah's Mawullees and Hetkurees, armed as if for battle, ready, if needed, to march thence on any enterprise, however distant or desperate.

A clear space had been left for the advancing procession. In front the Rajah's pipers, playing some of the wild mountain melodies, which echoed among the woods and crags above, broken now and then by blasts of horns and trumpets, and the deep monotonous beat of many large tambourine drums, the bearers of which were marshalled by the chief drummer of the fort, who, with his instrument decked with flowers and silken streamers, strutted or leaped in front of all, beating a wild march. Then followed Bramhuns, bareheaded and naked to the waist, carrying bright copper vessels of sacred water, flowers and incense, with holy fire from the temple on the mountain, chanting hymns at intervals. After them, the players and reciters, male and female, in fantastic dresses, wearing gilt tiaras to resemble the costumes seen in carvings of ancient temples, among whom were the jesters or clowns, who bandied bold and free remarks with the crowd, and provoked many a hearty laugh and sharp retort. After these the Rajah's own guard, some with sword and buckler only, others bearing matchlocks with long bright barrels, who marched in rows with somewhat of military organisation ; then the servants ; and last of all Sivaji himself. Slowly the procession passed up the centre ; then the leading portions of it dividing on each hand, the Rajah, advancing, mounted the small platform. Ere he seated himself he saluted the assembly, turning to each side of it with his hand raised to his head, and all rose to welcome him with clapping of hands and shouts which made the wooded glen and the precipices above, ring with the joyous sound. Then all subsided into their seats, and the preliminary sacrifices and offerings began.

CHAPTER XII.

WE need not describe them. After the sacrifice of several sheep before the altar, to propitiate the Goddess in the form of worship peculiar to lower castes, the Bramhuns continued the rest of the ceremonies. Here were the same recitations of religious books, the Shastras and Poorans; the same processions sweeping round the altar with offerings, and hymns chanted by the Bramhuns at stated periods; the same invocations of the deity to be present, as we have already seen in the temple at Tooljapoor; and as they proceeded, shadows lengthened, the sun disappeared behind the mountains, and gloom fell rapidly on the glen and its people.

Very soon, however, it was lighted up; men bearing huge copper vessels of oil on their shoulders, went round the area pouring cans full upon the cotton-seed in the iron cressets, and then lighting them, and a blaze arose from each which illuminated a large space around. Gradually the whole were lit; and the effect was as strange as beautiful.

Tier upon tier of closely-wedged human beings, whose white dresses and gay turbans and scarfs ap-

peared even brighter by night than by day, arose on
all sides, those nearest the light being clearly seen,
while the others, rising gradually to the top, were less
and less distinct, till they seemed to blend with the
fringe of wood above, and disappear in the gloom.
Below, about the place of performance, and around the
Rajah's seat, the illumination was brightest; and the
thick smoke of incense rising from the altar hung over
all like a canopy, diffusing its fragrance to the farthest
edges of the assembly. Above, the grim mountain
precipices hung threateningly over all, fringed at the
top by walls and towers, hardly perceptible in the
distance, except where they projected against the sky;
and on which, and on the woods, as the night advanced,
the bright light of the moon fell with a silvery lustre
which our northern climate does not know.

To act a Hindu play is by no means so simple a
matter as to act an English one. It frequently lasts
several days. On this present occasion it would occupy
three nights. There was the introduction, the middle,
and the catastrophe. There would be pleasant witty
interludes of broad farce between the scenes, acted by
the clowns in various characters; satires upon Bramhuns, and priests generally, being a favourite subject:
upon landlords and tenants: upon servants and masters: upon lovers—merchants—in short, upon all social
topics. There would be political satires also; and the
Rajah would see himself represented according to the
popular belief, whatever it might be, flatteringly or the
contrary, and would take the joke good-humouredly.

So the entertainment proceeded. We, who sit for an hour or two with a languid indifference, or real approbation, as it may be, of theatrical representation here, can hardly appreciate the intense absorption of a Mahratta audience at one of their religious plays, where gods and demigods, represented by clever players and singers, engage in earthly struggles of love or war, and evince human sympathies and passions. So hour after hour passed, and Rajah and people alike sat and listened and watched; now to a grand scene from the Mahabarut or Ramayun; now to a merry farce, or description by the " chorus" of what was to come next; now to a plaintive mountain ballad introduced into the general performance.

It was near midnight, perhaps, when a single horseman suddenly turned the corner of the mound, and, entering the area unperceived, where it was not crowded, rode slowly up the centre. His noble horse seemed jaded and weary, for it moved languidly, yet, when it saw the lights and people, raised its head and gave a shrill and prolonged neigh. Its flanks were smoking, and its coat a mass of foam, proving that it had been ridden hard and fast.

The rider's face was tied up, as is customary with Mahratta horsemen ; but as he advanced he unwound the scarf about it, and the stern features and flashing eyes of Tannajee Maloosray appeared to all. For an instant he was not recognised, and his advance, indeed, had hardly been noticed at the upper end of the assembly; but some one who saw him cried " Tannajee !"

and the name spread from mouth to mouth, rising into
a roar of welcome among the people, as the rider
struggled on through the crowd which now pressed
about him.   Dismounting near the altar, Tannajee
gave his horse to a servant; and as Sivaji and all
about him rose to meet him, he ascended to the royal
seat, and was embraced by his prince in a loving greeting.   He had been long absent, and was expected;
but his sudden arrival alone, and at that time of night,
boded strange tidings; and while his arms were yet
around his friend, Sivaji anxiously asked what news
he had brought.

"Of sorrow, yet of joy, my prince," replied Maloosray, disengaging himself.   "I heard the news at Jutt,
and I made a vow which only that altar can clear me
of, that I would not sit or rest till I had told it to you
and to the people.—Rise, all of ye !" he shouted to the
assembly in that voice which, clear and sonorous, they
had often heard above the wildest din of battle, "and
listen to my words !"

They rose to a man instantly, and with a rustling
sound : after which, there was perfect silence.   Every
face of those thousands was turned towards the speaker.
Every form, from the highest tiers to the lowest, bent
forward in eager expectation of what should follow.

"Listen," he continued, "O beloved prince and
people : we have fallen upon evil days, for the Goddess,
our Mother, has been insulted, and her temple at Tooljapoor desecrated.   Yes," he continued, lifting up his
hand to stay the cry which was about to break out,

" Afzool Khan has cast down the image of Toolja
Mata, plundered the temple of its wealth, slain the
Bramhuns, and sprinkled the blood of sacred cows over
the shrine ; and now the altar there, and the Mother,
are my witness that I have told this grief to ye
truly ! "

Then burst forth that strange wild cry which the
lady mother had heard above in the fort.   Some wept,
others shrieked and beat their mouths, or cast their
turbans on the ground.   Individual cries, no matter
whether of grief or revenge, were blended into one
common roar from those thousands, which ascended to
the sky, and, reverberating from side to side of the
glen, went out through the woods,—up the mountain-
sides and precipices of the fort,—softened by distance,—yet uniting to produce that unearthly yell or
wail which had arrested her as she left the shrine, and
caused the watching priests to shudder.

Apparently, the people waited to hear from their
prince a confirmation of the news, or intimation of
what was to be done ; for, at a motion of his hand
they were once more silent, and listening with rapt
attention.

"I thought the Holy Mother was in sorrow," he
said, " for she has hidden her face from me these many
days, and my mother too sought her, but in vain.   And
now we know the reason.   O friends ! O people !
shall it be so ?   Shall the Mother's temples be desolate ?   Not while Sivaji Bhóslay lives, and ye live !
Better we died in honour than lived to be pointed at

as cowards, while she is unrevenged! Listen," he continued, using the same gestures as Tannajee to keep the people quiet, as he took up the sword lying at his feet. " This, ye all know, is named after the Mother; see!" and he drew it slowly from the scabbard, "she hath a bright and lovely face, but it must be dimmed in Moslem blood: let her drink it freely! So I swear, and so ye will answer to my cry—Hur, Hur, Mahadeo!"

As he spoke he flung the scabbard passionately on the ground, and waved the glittering blade high in the air. Already was men's blood fiercely stirred by his words, and the Rajah's action rendered them almost uncontrollable. Not one of all that assembly who wore a sword was there, that did not draw and wave it as his chieftain had done; and the light flashing from polished weapons, and the frantic shouts of the old war-cry, as men swayed to and fro, still more excited the rude soldiery—" Hur, Hur, Mahadeo! Dôn-guras-lavilé Déva!"

No wonder that the sound had gone up the lofty mountain, and was the more clearly heard as the Ranee, looking from the tower above, saw far below the heaving masses in the glen, and caught the bright glitter of their weapons.

But there was silence at last. It seemed as if the men expected to be led there and then against their hereditary foes. That, however, was not to be yet. During the clamour, Maloosray had told his chieftain that Afzool Khan's army was on its march, and that means must be taken to oppose it. So the Rajah once again spoke out in those clear ringing tones which were heard by all.

"Not now, my people," he cried—"not now. If we have sworn to revenge the Mother, she will wait her time, and herself deliver this arrogant Moslem into our hands. Then, O my friends, shall she drink infidel blood and be satisfied to the full. So fear not : if this news is terrible, it is yet good ; so let us rejoice that we have the more cause to be united in avenging it. And now sit down once more ; and play on, O players ! Who shall say that Sivaji Bhóslay and his people were scared from their Kutha by Afzool Khan ?"

"That means, my friends," cried Pundree, one of the clowns, after turning a preliminary somersault in the air, then resting his hands on his knees, and wagging his head with mock gravity, "that the master intends to kill the old Khan himself, and that the Mother will eat him. Now, as I am going to eat the sheep that have been killed there, just to save her the trouble, she will be very hungry—very hungry indeed ; and if her belly is not filled by Afzool Khan, ye are to kill all his people and satisfy it. Else beware !—No one likes to be hungry, good folks ; and I for one, am always ill-tempered and beat my wife when there is no dinner, or it is badly cooked. I dare say the Mother is much the same, and if she be so, nothing goes right in the world ; so see that ye strike hard, my sons, and get plenty of food for her when the master bids ye. Do ye hear ? Do ye understand ? As for the cooking of it, ye may leave that to the devil; and remember that I, Pundrinath, the son of Boodhenâth, have told ye all this, and will bear witness against ye and Tannajee Maloosray if ye do it not; and so—beware, beware!"

And then, amidst the laughter caused by the quaint speech and actions of the privileged jester, the play proceeded, while Sivaji heard from his friend Maloosray the tale of the Wuzeer's death, the Kótwal's execution, and the sack of Tooljapoor.

It was more than ever evident to Sivaji, that to attempt to oppose Afzool Khan in the field with the men about him, would be madness; but he might be drawn on, by specious promises of submission, into wilds where his cavalry and artillery would be useless, and in those jungles the men then present would be ample against ten thousand Mahomedan infantry.

Then it was determined to send those agents to Afzool Khan's camp with whose arrival there we are already acquainted.

CHAPTER XIII.

But the arrival of an Envoy from the Mahomedan General was an event of no small importance to the Rajah Sivaji. In order to further the plan he had conceived, and partly executed, in the despatch of envoys to the Mahomedan camp—it was his object to disarm all suspicion; and while assuming an appearance of insignificance and weakness which should impress upon the mind of a new-comer his insufficiency to make any resistance, the Rajah was making arrangements which, as Maloosray and other friends knew, boded action of no ordinary kind. When the time came, he would act, he said, as the Goddess directed. His mother had been silent for many days, and almost constantly sat in the temple before the altar; and it was certain there would be some special revelation. She had spread the end of her garment* before the Mother, and she had never done so, they said, in vain; but she was silent, and so they waited.

Afzool Khan's envoy had been received with the

---

* *Pulloo fusarné*—the most earnest and humble supplication that a Mahratta woman can make.

utmost distinction. When within a few miles of the fort he had been met by a deputation of Bramhuns and inferior military officers, and delayed only long enough to have the necessary astrological calculations made as to a propitious moment for entrance into the town. There, a house was assigned to him : servants of the Rajah appointed to attend on him : and his escort was supplied with forage and food in abundance. Nothing was wanting to give assurance of simple but earnest hospitality.

The day after, an audience of the Rajah was fixed upon. The Envoy was desired to choose his own time ; and the astrologer in his suite, with that of the Rajah, having ascertained a lucky conjunction of planets, the Envoy was carried up the mountain-side in a palankeen to the fort-gate, where sheep were sacrificed before him, cannon fired from the ramparts, and the fort pipers, drummers, and horn-blowers, performed a rude and very noisy welcome. Then the men on guard at the gate, with others of the garrison of the fort, formed a street, which reached as far as the Rajah's pavilion ; and the palankeen being carried along this, amidst the firing of matchlocks and shouting of the title of the King of Beejapoor by the royal bard and herald in his suite, the Envoy was set down before the same rude pavilion which we have before described, where the Rajah Sivaji awaited him.

To all appearance an insignificant little man, dark, youthful in appearance, with only one ornament in his turban, dressed in the plainest clothes, and without even

the gold embroidered cushion on which he had been
seated on the day of the Kutha.   Punto Gopinath
wondered much when he remembered the exaggerated
accounts of the Prince which were sung in ballads, told
by bards and reciters, and were believed by the people.
Was this the saviour who was to come ?   Was this the
man who was to rescue the Hindu faith from obloquy, if
not from destruction :—protect Bramhuns, foster learning, endow and enrich temples ?   Above all, was this
the man who was to defy the forces of Beejapoor, the
fierce Abyssinians, the fiery Dekhanies ? the noble park
of artillery ?   There were no troops, no means of offence
visible.   True, the fort itself was strong, but the garrison was small, and unworthy of consideration in com-
parison with the thousands who were even now nigh
at hand.

These thoughts hurried rapidly through the Envoy's
mind as he passed up the street of men, and the Rajah's
authorities and higher order of servants, who stood on
each side of this approach to the hall itself.   Puntojee
Gopinath was a big man in every sense of the word.
His body was large and corpulent, and he stooped
much.   His head was wrapped in a white cashmere
shawl, which increased its naturally disproportionate
size.   His features were massive but flaccid, and his
cheeks shook, while his head wagged from side to side
as he walked.   His eyes were large, but red and watery;
and the protruding under-lip, full, and set in deep lines
at the corners, gave him an air of pompous self-sufficiency.

With all this, the Bramhun was a shrewd, astute

person. He was vain, and usually confident. Now, however, as he saluted the Rajah, he felt the eyes which scanned him from head to foot had already taken a measure of him, which might be favourable or otherwise. Perhaps it was flattering, perhaps mortifying; he could not say which. They were in any case different eyes to those of his own rulers and officers, who were Mahomedans. Their eyes took things for granted, and he was accustomed to placid acquiescence, or perhaps to occasional fierce bursts of passion, which never affected him. These eyes, on the contrary, were restless and inquisitive, leaving an impression that they had seen and understood hidden thoughts, and would bring them out, lurk where they might.

Perhaps, for the first time in his public life, the Bramhun was disconcerted; but it was no time to show this; and recovering himself, he offered the prescribed salutation, and sinking into the seat pointed out to him, which was beside, but rather in front of the Rajah, with a loud exclamation of Ram-chunder! which was his habit—he settled himself on his heels after the most approved courtly fashion, placed his hands gravely upon his knees, twisted up his mustaches, and felt his habitual confidence return.

We need not, perhaps, follow the conference. The Envoy, as instructed, at first took a high tone as to outrages and treason on the part of the Rajah, and of the clemency and wisdom of the sovereign he represented. There should have been no attempts at insurrection, because the cause was hopeless by force, and the royal

ear was ever open to suppliants for justice, if timely
submission were made.

The Rajah did not reply personally, but this pitiless
scrutiny of the Envoy continued without interruption,
and the address was answered by Krishnajee Bhaskur,
one of his own Bramhun officers, eloquently and yet
respectfully:—What had been done ? No redress had
been given for injury, for extortion, and local oppression. In despair, some retaliation had been made. It
was the mountain custom, even by village against village; and did not affect higher relations, which would
only become the more firmly consolidated when the
cause of quarrel was past. " But," he added, in conclusion, " the details are private matters, and will be discussed better in privacy, and through Afzool Khan
alone, does the Rajah wish to have them arranged.
What have we here to oppose him ? We have no
concealments, no means of defence against such a
force as his ? "

" Indeed, no," said Sivaji smiling. " An army of
elephants has been sent to crush ants' nests, as the
proverb hath it ; and if the noble Khan will remain,
and take charge of the country now under me, I will
resign it to him cheerfully, and become his servant.
Wilt thou say this to him ? "

" Indeed, my prince," returned the Bramhun, putting
up his joined hands, " we who were in Beejapoor well
know how much Afzool Khan helped your father, when
he was confined, in the old Sultan's time; and how much
the rigour of his imprisonment was softened by the

Khan's kindness. Ah! he is a humane and generous man, and has no personal enmity against you, my lord."

"We will at least put it to the proof," returned the Rajah good-humouredly. "You are witness that you have seen no preparations for defence or resistance, and the sooner he comes the better. We cannot hurry him and the force, but we will at least make preparations for a peaceful entertainment; and if the Khan will accept of our rude mountain hospitality instead of the Jehâd we hear he has been preaching against us, it will be a happy thing for all."

"A happy thing indeed!" said Bulwunt Rao, who, in the suite of the Envoy, had as yet sat silently, and had not been recognised; "and when public affairs are settled, private justice may be done to suppliants like me, who, only for state quarrels, dare not have entered this fort."

"Who art thou, friend?" asked Sivaji; "a suitor to me, and from Beejapoor?—a Mahratta among Moslems? Who art thou?"

"I may not mention my name here, my lord," said Bulwunt Rao, rising, and again saluting the Rajah reverently; "but I can tell it in private. One whom injustice and evil fate have led where he is, and who, only for them, would have been serving you."

"How can I serve thee?" asked the Rajah sharply; "I am not usually hard of access; therefore come to me when thou wilt, and I will hear thee."

"I will come," returned Bulwunt Rao, looking round to all, "and put thee, Sivaji Bhóslay, to the proof. Men

vaunt the Rajah's justice," he continued—" he will find
much to do for me ;" and he sat down again.

An awkward pause ensued in the assembly, which
no one seemed inclined to break : and the person who
officiated as master of the ceremonies, having observed
a signal from the Rajah, brought in flowers, with pân
leaves, and distributed them in order of precedence to
the Envoy and all his suite. Bulwunt Rao, however,
would take nothing.

" If justice is done me," he said, rising again, " my
share of flowers will come with it, and will be hung
about my neck in honour ; if not, they will hang here,"
—and he touched his sword-hilt—" better."

"This savours of a threat, sir," said Sivaji, with
flashing eyes.

" The meanest will turn against oppression," returned
Bulwunt ; "and Sivaji Bhóslay has just pleaded this
in extenuation of his own acts. I, too, make the same
reply, my prince ; and when you know my history, you
will confess I am no traitor to Mahrattas."

" All are dismissed," said the Rajah rising ; " see
that these gentlemen are safely escorted below ;" and
amidst the confusion which occurred in many persons
rising, and as the Durbar broke up, he whispered to
the Bramhun who had been spokesman, and who was
one of his most confidential servants, " See that the
Khan's Envoy be separately accommodated. I must
visit him privately to-night, and thou must be with me,
Krishnajee ; I will come to thee at the first watch."

CHAPTER XIV

THE Rajah passed into the inner chamber, and found his mother sitting at the window alone, looking over the road which ascended to the fort-gate. He prostrated himself before her, as was his wont, and, sitting down opposite to her in silence, fell apparently into deep thought. She did not interrupt him ; but as the trumpet sounded, and a salute of cannon was fired from the ramparts, and the Envoy's procession passed out, and wound down the pass—she saw him following the palankeen with his eyes, while his lips moved gently, as though he spoke to himself. As it disappeared behind a shoulder of the mountain, he turned to her and smiled.

"Mother," he said, "you saw the Khan's Envoy. I expected some stupid, wrong-headed, supercilious Mussulman, but behold he has sent a Bramhun, and with him a Mahratta, whom we should know, but no one recognises him. I think the Mother will give both to me, yet you said one only."

"My vision was but of one," she replied, "and it will be enough. Who is the Mahratta ?"

"They said his name was Bulwunt Rao, mother, but he did not mention his surname, and no one knew it," returned the Rajah.

"It must be Bulwunt Rao Bhóslay, Tannajee's cousin," replied the lady. "I know of no other Mahratta of good family in Beejapoor. He is a relative of our own.

"Ah!" exclaimed her son, "yes, it must be he; and I have promised him justice, mother; but what of Tannajee?"

"It cannot be, son," she said; "that is a blood feud, and blood only will quench it. Tannajee did but revenge a murder, and you cannot quarrel with him. Let it be; no good will come of it."

"Nevertheless I will try, mother; and if the Bramhun——"

"Fear not," she returned. "If he be a true Bramhun, the Goddess hath given him to thee. I will go to her. It is my hour for watching, and I will pray her to guide thee."

Sivaji sat as before, looking out over the rugged mountain-side and the pass, now glowing in the rich tints of an afternoon sun. If he could only get Afzool Khan into his power, and hold him sure as a hostage, he might make his own terms. Would the Bramhun aid him in this? A word from him and the matter was secure. If he could only be persuaded to write, a swift messenger might be sent to the camp, with one of his own officers to guide on the army. Once the troops entered the defiles they were at his mercy. There was no escape

—the whole must surrender or be slain; but he well knew the old Afghan would not agree to dishonour, and to separate him from his force, was therefore his chief anxiety. As yet the temptation within him had assumed no more definite form; and in respect to the final result, his mother, strange to say, was altogether silent; but she had again taken up the position she had assumed before the shrine for many days past, and his belief in her inspiration was not to be shaken.

Late that night, muffled in a coarse blanket, and accompanied only by the Bramhun before mentioned, and a few attendants, the Rajah descended from the fort by a steep and rugged pathway, which led from a postern directly to the town, and, leaving the men at the gate, they passed rapidly on to the house where the Envoy had been located. It belonged to the Josee or astrologer of the town, in whose science the Rajah had much faith; and, as was usual with him on all occasions of great enterprise, the aspects of the planets had been consulted, and declared to be favourable at the hour at which they had purposely timed their arrival. The Josee met them at the door. "The Pundit is sitting within," he said, "reading, and there is no one with him. I have prepared the writing materials, too, as directed, and they will be brought if you call."

"Wait, then, in the outer court, friends," said the Rajah to his attendants. "This must be done between us alone. Not even thou, Krishnajee, must know what passes between us."

Punto Gopinath was sitting in the inner verandah of

the second court of the house, as the Josee had said, reading. He looked up as the old man entered and said, "There is one here from the Rajah, who would speak with you."

"Admit him," was the reply; and Sivaji could see as he entered, that the Bramhun drew towards him a short, heavy dagger-sword, and placed it so that the hilt lay close to his right hand. "Be seated friend," said the Envoy, "and tell thy business. What doth Sivaji Bhóslay desire of me?"

The Rajah's face was tied up with a handkerchief, which partly concealed his mouth and changed the tone of his voice, and he had passed his hand, covered with white wood-ashes, across his nose, eyes, and forehead, as he entered, which altered the expression of his eyes very considerably. It was evident that he was not recognised.

"Sivaji Bhóslay desires the prosperity and advancement of Bramhuns," replied the Rajah, "and to enrich them is his sole care. He worships them; and would fain have them as powerful as in the days of the ancients, and in this desire thou canst assist."

"I assist! How, friend? I, a Bramhun, am a receiver, not a giver,—and am only a servant to the unclean," he added with a sigh.

"It need not be so, Pundit. The fame of thy learning hath preceded thee, and the Maharaj desires thy friendship and welfare. I am sent to tell thee this."

"What can I do?" said the Envoy restlessly. "What

would he have me do ? and who art thou to speak thus
to me ? "

" No matter who I am—I am authorised to speak,"
replied Sivaji. " Look, here is his ring as my authority.
'Is he a Bramhun,' the Rajah said, 'and come with
Moslem followers to sit in my Durbar ? Alas, alas !
that such should be, that the pure and holy should
serve the unclean. This is indeed the age of iron, and
of debasement.' "

The Bramhun writhed in his seat. " There are many
besides me," he said, " who serve the people of Islam."

" Who serve the destroyers of Toolja Mata, the
defilers of her temple, the slayers of Bramhuns, and of
sacred kine everywhere ! O shame—shame ! " cried the
Rajah eagerly.

" I was not at the shrine when the affray took place,"
said the Bramhun apologetically. " I could not help
it."

" Has then a Bramhun's holiness become so debased
that he says only, I could not help it ? " returned the
Rajah. " Is it pleasing to the Mother, think you, that
her people should fawn on those whose hands are red
in the blood of her votaries ? "

" I would fling my service at the feet of Afzool Khan,
and even of the Sultan himself, could I but serve with
Hindus as I desire to serve," exclaimed the Bramhun.

" The opportunity might be found, friend," answered
the Rajah, " if it were truly desired; but proof of
fidelity would be required,—would it be given ? What
is the Maharaj's desire ? Dost thou know it ? "

"I guess it," said the Bramhun; "for I am not easily deceived by appearances, and I understood his looks to-day, if I mistake not. Could I only speak with him? Canst thou take me to him?"

"I can tell thy message to him," replied the Rajah, "and will deliver it faithfully. He chose me, else I had not dared to come."

The Envoy appeared to hesitate for a moment. "Impossible," he said—"impossible that I could tell another, what Sivaji himself should alone hear; it could not be."

"Dost thou know me, friend?" returned the Rajah, as he untied the handkerchief which concealed his face, and with it wiped the white ashes from his eyes and forehead—"dost thou know me? It is thus that I salute a holy Bramhun;" and he rose and made a lowly reverence, touching the feet of the Envoy respectfully.

The man strove to return it, but was prevented. "It cannot be," continued Sivaji; "here thou art a Bramhun, and I a Sudra.* Let it be as I wish. It is for thee to receive the honour, not I."

"What would you have me do, Maharaj?" replied the Envoy, now trembling much. "I have done evil in helping the unclean, and would now expiate it if possible."

"I have had many things in my mind, Pundit," replied the Rajah, "and the Mother sends perplexing thoughts; but one thing is clear to me—she must be avenged."

* The lowest of the four divisions of Hindus.

The man echoed the words—" She must be avenged."

" Yes," continued the Rajah, "day and night, by old and young, rich and poor, man or woman, there is but one cry going up from Maharastra—'Avenge the Mother!' and yet before that force we are powerless."

" Where are the Mawullees? where are the Hetkurees we have heard of, and the gallant Tannajee?" cried the Bramhun excitedly. "What art thou doing, Sivaji Bhóslay? Men say of thee that thy mother holds thee back, else ' the fire should be on the hills.'"

" Good!" returned Sivaji smiling; " it is as I thought, and there is yet a Bramhun who is true. What dost thou advise?"

" Hark!" said Gopinath, "come nearer. If I bring Afzool Khan and his men within the defiles, will it content thee? If I do this, what wilt thou do for me?"

" I have prepared for that already,—a Jahgeer,* a high office, secular or among the priesthood, as thou wilt,—double thy present pay whatever it be,—an ensign of rank, and—my friendship. Look, Pundit," cried the Rajah, springing closer to him, and drawing a small bright knife from his breast, " it were easy to slay thee,— for my knee is on thy weapon,—and so prevent my proposal being known : but it is not needed. Fear not," he added, for the drops of sweat were standing on the Bramhun's brow under the terror he felt—"fear not! only be true, and Sivaji Bhóslay will not fail thee. When he has a kingdom thou shalt share its honour."

" Give me time to write," said the man, trembling

* Estate of landed property.

under conviction of his own treachery and the excess
of temptation to which he was exposed ; "I will give
the letter to-morrow."

"Impossible, Pundit," replied the Rajah : " the messengers are ready without, and they will bear what
must be written to the Khan."

"Who will take the letter ? "

"The Bramhun who spoke for me this morning; he
and some horsemen are now ready."

"But to the Khan himself there must be no harm
done," said the Pundit. "To him and his son I owe
many kindnesses ; for the rest, as thou wilt. Keep the
family as hostages."

"As guests yonder," replied the Rajah ; "he will
be safe, he and his. Shall I send for writing materials ? Krishnajee! Sit there," he continued, as his
attendant entered ; "see that what is written is
plain."

And the Envoy wrote in the Persian character, in
which he was a proficient, and which the other secretary
understood :—

"I have seen the Rajah, his fort, and his people, and
there is nothing to apprehend. They are all beneath
notice ; but in order to settle everything perfectly, and
to inspire terror, my lord should advance with all the
force, according to the plan devised here, which the
bearer, one of the Rajah's secretaries, will explain personally, and which would be tedious to write. In a
strictly private interview, which will be arranged, the
Rajah Sivaji will throw himself at the feet of the Envoy

of the king of kings, and receive the pardon which he
desires. More would be beyond respect."

"It is enough," said Sivaji, when this writing was
explained to him—"it will have the desired effect.
Take this letter, Krishnajee, and set out for camp at
once."

"Stay," added the Envoy, "let him accompany my
messenger,—the Mahratta officer who spoke so boldly
to-day. It were better he went, and he will not refuse
duty. Enter that room and close the door, my lord,
while I send for him;" and he called to an attendant
to summon Bulwunt Rao.

It was not long ere he came in, flushed somewhat,
as it seemed, with drink. "Who is this?" he said.

"The Maharaja's Secretary, who will accompany thee
to camp. Go at once, if thou art fit, Bulwunt Rao; it
is needful that Afzool Khan receive this as soon as may
be."

"I am ready, Maharaj, to ride up Pertabgurh," he
replied; "and he?"

"I attend you," said the Secretary; "come, we must
leave this when the moon rises;" and they went out
together.

"Enough," said the Rajah, emerging from his concealment. "Generations hereafter will record how
Punto Gopináth served his prince. Fear not—it will
be well with thee and thine hereafter."

CHAPTER XV.

THE letter despatched by the Rajah Sivaji, as we have recorded, was received in a few days by the Khan, and its tenor was not doubted. There was nothing in it which could in any degree disturb the Khan's complacency, or awaken suspicion. If he chafed at the idea of a bloodless campaign, and his friend the Peer, in the ardour of his bigotry, sighed at what now promised to be a tame conclusion to an exciting commencement,—Fazil, on the other hand, and with him the commander of the Mahratta contingent in camp, and others who had more sympathy with the people of the country than their elders, rejoiced that it was to be so ; and that a valuable ally and confederate was to be secured to the dynasty which they served, by means which appeared at once just, merciful, and binding upon both.

The new Envoy who brought the letter, pleased the Khan and the Peer extremely. In the first place, he spoke the Dekhan court language fluently, and was a fair Persian scholar. He was known to the Khan as having served in a subordinate department when he himself held the administration of Wye, and he gratefully acknowledged—as he reminded the Khan of—former benefits. The first envoys could not communicate with the Khan except through interpreters. True, his son was usually present, or occasionally the holy priest himself, who might be induced to assist; but the Khan would have better liked to manage these Mahratta envoys himself, and now there was the desired opportunity. Day after day, as the army advanced without check, by easy but continuous stages, the new agent was in close attendance, and very frequently, with the others, was summoned to private conferences. Fazil, too, had his share in them, and to every outward appearance no room existed for suspicion of any kind.

They had now entered the Rajah's own jurisdiction, and were treated more as honoured guests than as an invading army. Supplies were provided at every stage, forage was abundant, difficult places in the roads were found cleared for the artillery, and the people met them with goodwill and courtesy, which was as pleasant as unexpected. Any idea of resistance was out of the question. The usual village guards, or here and there a few horsemen in attendance on a local functionary, were all that was seen of the Rajah's forces; and the Khan was amused and gratified with the Envoy's descriptions of how—to attract attention to his affairs—his master had caused the belief to gain ground that he was possessed of an army of vast power.

In short, all the obstructions and dangers which had

appeared so great at a distance had passed away ; and
as the Khan led his troops more and more deeply into the
mountainous district, he could not but feel that if they
had been opposed in those rugged defiles, the struggle
would have been difficult as well as desperate.   The
enemy would have had a stronger country to retreat
upon, and one more easily defended, while, in proportion, the advance to him would have been beset with
peril which could hardly be estimated.

Very frequently Fazil asked particulars of the fort
of Pertabgurh from Bulwunt Rao, who described it
clearly enough,—an ordinary hill fort, with a garrison
strong for local purposes, but, after all, only such as
Mahratta chiefs and gentry kept about them ; strong
in their own position, but helpless for offence. Where,
then, were the armies which Sivaji was said to possess?
Bulwunt Rao, in reply, pointed to the village people,
all soldiers, he said, from their youth, and accustomed
to arms : but among them there was no symptom of
excitement, nor could Bulwunt Rao, suspecting nothing himself, discover any cause for alarm : and so
they proceeded.

Meanwhile, the programme of a meeting had been
arranged by the agents between the Khan and
Sivaji. Both parties had mooted points of etiquette,
which could hardly be overcome. The Rajah, as a
prince, could not visit the Khan first, nor could Afzool
Khan, as the representative of royalty, visit the Rajah ;
but they could both meet, and the barrier of ceremony
once broken, it mattered little what followed. No troops

were to be present. Attended each by a single armed
follower, the place of meeting was fixed on a level spot
at some little distance up the mountain of Pertabgurh,
where the Rajah, the Envoy said, had already prepared
a pavilion, which would be fitted up for the occasion.
If the Khan pleased, he might bring a thousand of his
best horse—more, if convenient—to witness the ceremony from below; but only one attendant besides
the palankeen-bearers could advance to the conference.
Nothing was to be written, and the agent already at
the fort would attend the Khan on the one hand, while
another of the Rajah's, if possible or needful, would
accompany him from above. No objection appeared,
and none was made, to these arrangements.

So the army reached its final stage near the village
of Jowly, a few miles distant from the fort; and
the last preparations were made that night by both
parties. The morning would see the Khan set out
early accompanied by fifteen hundred chosen horse—
some Abyssinian, some Dekhani, others his own retainers,—all picked men; while the remainder of the
army should rest from its labour and exertion, which,
on account of the rough mountain roads, had been
exceedingly great for the last three days.

At Jowly, too, the camp was more than ordinarily
pleasant. A plain of some extent, and which for the
most part was under cultivation, afforded ample room
for all the force. The grassy slopes of the mountains,
by which the plain was surrounded, furnished abundant supplies of forage; a brawling stream ran under

the hills on one side, and the Rajah's usual supplies of
food of all kinds were abundant at moderate prices in
a bazar which, consisting of rough sheds and small
tents, was located near the village on the other.

Let us see how the night was passed by both parties.

The Khan's tents had been pitched on an even sward
which bordered the rivulet, and several fine trees were
included in the area enclosed by the canvas walls.
Under the shade of these, Zyna and Fazil had sat most
part of the day. A few carpets and pillows had been
spread there, and the cool fresh mountain air, the
brawling murmur of the brook, and the grand and
beautiful scenery by which they were surrounded, so
different to the bare monotonous undulations of the
Dekhan, were in themselves more exciting than it was
possible for them to have imagined from any previous
description. But the loss of Tara's society was pressing heavily upon both. All they heard daily was, that
she was well and among her people, who were taking
care of her. She would remain with them at Wye ;
and as the army returned, she should see Lurlee
Khanum and Zyna once more, and take leave of them,
for she could not be permitted to sojourn with Mahomedans. This the Envoy had told the Khan and
Fazil the day before.

It was a dreary prospect for Fazil, and apparently
a hopeless one. Should he ever see that sweet face
more? ever hear the music of the gentle voice, at
once so timid and yet so reliant ? There was no hope
that the Bramhuns among whom she had fallen would

now give her up voluntarily. It was impossible to think it. Did they know what he had asked and she had half-promised ?—would her life be safe even if they did ? Hardly so, indeed ; or, if safe, would be spared at the price of the disfigurement which awaited her, according to the strict rules of her faith. What they had arranged among themselves, therefore, could not be openly prosecuted ; and, in defiance of his father's cautions, and the apparently smooth progress of public affairs, no effort to demand her, or to recover her by force, could be made as yet.

"Let us settle everything with this Mahratta first, and as we return by Wye, we will have the girl, or know why," the stout old Khan used to say; for he had grown to love Tara very dearly, and missed her presence, though in a different manner, as much as any of them. "Fear not, Fazil, the Kafirs shall not possess her."

So Zyna and Fazil had sat most part of the day, revolving over and over again how best Tara might be assisted or rescued, while blaming themselves a thousand times for that neglect of special precautions for her safety which had resulted in her abduction.

" If only Moro Trimmul could be found, and brought once more to account," Fazil said, grinding his teeth, " it would go hard with him ; " but he was not to be heard of. The Envoys in camp declared he had at once proceeded to Pertabgurh to clear himself to the Rajah Sivaji and the lady mother, of whom, in particular, he was an especial favourite ; but he was not now even

there : he had been sent to a distance ; where or why
it was not known ; and it was impossible to trace him.
Bulwunt Rao, Lukshmun, and the lad Ashruf, had all
been employed in turn as spies, but had failed to discover him—he was not to be heard of.

It was now late, and the lady Lurlee came and
joined them before the evening prayer. She had been
busy after her own fashion, and as the priest and some
others were to dine with the Khan, had prepared several of her most scientific dishes. She had no doubt as
to the issue of the morrow's interview. In the first
place, who could resist her husband ? and were not the
planets unusually favourable ? She and the priest
had compared notes from behind the screen in the
tent ; and though he laughed at the curious jargon she
had collected on the subject, yet, a steadfast believer in
astrology himself, had explained to her how peculiarly
fortunate the conjunction was to be at the hour cast
for the meeting, and she had fully believed it. If
Tara had been there, all would have been perfectly
happy ; but, as Lurlee said, the planets told her it
was only, after all, a matter of a few days' delay ;
and, indeed perhaps, after to-morrow she might be
demanded.

Fazil, however, in spite of these assurances, was
not easy ; and after he left the tents for the evening
prayer, had taken counsel with Lukshmun who, in
regard to Tara, had taken the place of Bulwunt Rao,
to whom Fazil dare not intrust his secret. The day
she had disappeared, and Fazil's misery was apparent,

the hunchback had divined the cause; and a few inquiries in his capacity of spy had confirmed his
suspicions.

"I know but of one thing to do, master," he said, as
the young man confided to him his dread of violence
to the girl—"send me back to Wye, where she is ;
give me but ever so small a note, and I will deliver it
into her own hand ; and if I can bring her away, trust
to me to do so. I can traverse these forests and mountains by night ; I can hide her away or disguise her ;
and if she be true to thee, she will come. Give me the
boy Ashruf, and a little money, and let us go, even now.
He is without ; call him."

"Ashruf," cried the young Khan to the lad, who
was standing near the tent door, and who entered at
once ; " wilt thou go with Lukshmun ? "

" My lord," replied the lad, " he and I have arranged
this already. They do not know us here, and he
has been teaching me a Mahratta ballad which she
knows, and we can sing it in Wye to-morrow. If he
had not spoken I should have told you of our plan.
My lord, we will bring her away silently, and no one
shall be the wiser. Yes, I will go into the fire for my
lord, if he will but prove me."

" And Bulwunt Rao ? " said Fazil.

" He is in the clouds," replied Lukshmun, " in the
hope of getting back the family estate ; wind has got
into his head, and he is beside himself. To my mind,
the Rajah would be far better pleased to have him put
out of the way than to favour his pretensions ; but

Bulwunt says he has been promised 'justice;' and so,"
added Lukshmun, with a hideous grimace, "he will
have his own way, and what is to be is to be ; only
write the note, master, quick, and let us go ; he won't
help us."

"Alas!" replied Fazil, "I can only write Persian ;
but she knows my signature, for she used to see me
write it. Stay, however," he continued, unfastening a
thin gold ring from his wrist, "she will remember this
better, and understand it ; take it with ye, and may
God speed ye. Go at once! Bring her, if possible,
or mark where she is, and we will go, Inshalla! and
fetch her."

The priest was chanting the Azân, and Fazil passed
out into the usual place of prayer, which was nume-
rously attended. After its close, the Peer, his father,
and all who were to stay to dinner, assembled for the
repast, which was served immediately. There was no
forward movement of tents that night ; and the guests
sat till a late hour discussing the probable events of
the morrow, and the possibility of an early counter-
march, at least as far as Wye, where the open country
was preferable to their present confined situation among
the mountains.

CHAPTER XVI.

WAS there equal confidence in the fort? We must now go there, and listen to the midnight consultation, which may be prolonged till daylight; and yet men on the eve of some desperate enterprise for which they have prepared themselves, need more rest, and often sleep more calmly, than at any other period of their existence.

It was the same chamber that we have formerly seen; but the window of the oriel is shut, for the night wind at that height is cold and bleak, and thick, quilted curtains, which have been let fall before it and the doorway, exclude all air. Sivaji, Maloosray, and Palkur are sitting together, but are silent, for the Rajah's mind is troubled.

"If I only knew what she would have me do," he said at length, looking up. "Hast thou prepared all, Tannajee?"

"Master," he replied, "everything is ready. By midnight, or a little later, Moro Trimmul and the rest of the veterans will be in the woods near Jowly, around the camp. Every position has been marked out, and

will be silently taken up. Nothing can escape out of
that plain, and they will await the signal of the five
guns from hence. The Bramhun swears," he continued, after a pause, "that he will take the pretty sister
of the young Khan, in revenge for his seduction of the
Tooljapoor Moorlee.

"He dare not," said Sivaji quickly. "I have heard
that girl was an honoured guest in Afzool Khan's
family; the Bramhuns say she was. No, he dare not
touch her; and I have warned him not to do so."

Maloosray shrugged his shoulders. "Perhaps," he
said; "God knows! but Moro says otherwise. Let it
pass; it is not our business; but he will be none the
less active to get the whole family into his power."

"And you, Nettajee?" said the Rajah, turning to him.

"There are five thousand of my best Mawullees
sleeping in the thickets east of the fort-gate. They
will close in behind the Beejapoor people as they pass,
and when we hear the horn, I think, master, few will
escape—yes," he continued, fixing his large black eyes
on the Rajah, and slightly twisting his mustaches,
"few will escape."

"O the blind confidence of these Beejapoor swine!"
cried the Rajah laughing, as he lifted up his hands.
"They have neither eyes nor ears, else they had guessed
we are not as we seem. But the Goddess Mother has
blinded and deafened them, and it is as my mother said
it would be."

"Where is she?" asked Maloosray; "she should
bless us ere we go forth."

"She is in the temple, and uneasy. As the time comes on, they think she will have a visitation," he replied. "Ah! here is some one to tell us. What news, Bheemee?"

"The lady mother is uneasy, Maharaj, and rocking herself to and fro. It is coming on her, and ye should be near to listen."

"Come, friends, let us go," said the Rajah; "on this revelation depends my course to-morrow."

It was but a few steps, and the place is already familiar to us. The low porch and dark vestibule, the small shrine within, from whence a strong light is shining into the gloom, resting sharply upon the figure of the Ranee as she sat before it, not quietly now, as when we saw her once before, but with her shoulders and bosom heaving rapidly, her eyes shut, or if opened for a moment flashing with excitement, her lips trembling and already speckled with foam; and that peculiar sharp, rocking motion of her body, which always preceded the final attack.

The men stood by reverently. No one dared to speak. The attendant Bramhun offered flowers from time to time, and kept up a low chant or incantation, while occasionally he threw grains of coloured rice upon the altar.

Suddenly the lady stretched forth her arms and shrieked wildly. Maloosray would have rushed forward, but Sivaji held him back. "Wait," he said in a low tone, "no one dares to interrupt her; wouldst thou go to death between her and the Mother? She will come—listen."

There was first a low muttering in which nothing
could be distinguished ; but words at last followed, to
them terrible and awful, as, believing in the dread presence of the Goddess, the lady poured them forth with
gasps.

" O, I thirst !   My children were slain—and no one
has avenged them.   Blood ! blood !   I thirst.   I will
drink it !   The blood of the cruel—of the cow-slayers!
All, all—the old and the young ; the old woman and
the maiden ; the nurse and the child at her breast ;
all — all — all !" she continued, her voice rising to a
scream.   "They who love me, kill for me ; for I thirst,—
for I thirst now, as I did for the blood of the demons,"
and the voice again sank to a low whisper which was
not audible.

These words had come from her by spasms, as it were ;
painfully, and with much apparent suffering.   She
shrieked repeatedly as she uttered them, and clutched
at the air with a strange convulsive movement of both
hands : sometimes as if apparently drawing to her, or
again fiercely repelling an object before her.   At last
she stretched forth her hands and her body, as if following what she saw, and, looking vacantly into the space
before her with a terrified expression of countenance, the
hands fell listlessly on her lap, and her features relaxed
into a weary expression, as of one who had endured
acute pain.   Then she sighed deeply, opened her eyes,
looked around, and spoke.   "Bheemee, I thirst," she
said gently,—" bring me water."

Sivaji alone had remained with his mother and the

Bramhun of the temple, who, as she spoke them, recorded the disconnected sentences. The Rajah's companions, fearless before an enemy, were cowards before the dread presence in which they believed.

"Ah, thou art here son," she said, turning to him. "Did I speak? Surely the Mother was with me," and she sighed deeply, again drawing her hand wearily across her eyes.

"Come and rest, mother," he replied, raising her up and supporting her tenderly. "Come, thou art weary."

"Weary indeed, my son," she said,—"there is no rest for me till all is finished. Come, and I will tell thee everything;" and he followed her into her own apartments, where she lay down. The attendant brought water, and she drank a deep draught.

"What did I say, son?" she continued. "But no matter. It is all blood before me—carnage and victory! Blood!" she cried excitedly, grasping his arm and looking intently into his face. "Art thou ready? ready for victory!—ready to cry 'Jey Kalee! Jey Toolja Mata!'"

"Ready, mother — yes. There is no failing anywhere. The men are at their posts, and the signals have been decided upon. No one will escape us now."

"No one will escape," she echoed,—"no one must escape—no—not one—not even he."

"Ah, mother," cried Sivaji, "not so; surely with pledged honour, soldier to a soldier, and a solemn invitation, it could not be."

"It must be, son," she said gloomily, "else the

sacrifice is incomplete and of no avail. Wilt thou risk
that for thine own sake—for my sake—for the sake of
our faith ?   I see it all," cried the lady excitedly,
"passing before me—a triumph of glory over those
defilers of the temples of the Gods ; thy rapid rise to
power ; the legions of the hateful Mahomedans trampled
in the dust by greater legions of thine own.   'Jey
Sivaji Rajah !' shall be cried from Dehli to Raméshwur.* Wilt thou now turn back ? wilt thou be forsworn to her—to the Mother who is our life ? Wilt
thou be as vacillating as thy father ?   Beware ! thou
art more committed to her than he—and does she spare
backsliders ? "

"He is but one to be spared, mother, and that because
of my promise," he pleaded.

"I tell thee it cannot be, my son. She will have
him—the slayer of the priests—the murderer of hundreds of the people about her shrine. And that priest
of his who, as all say, led the slaughter, cast down her
image, and trampled on it ! O son, canst thou hesitate ?
art thou—so firm and true always—now grown weak ?
have I borne one in travail who is degenerate ? Choose
then, now—victory and future blessing, or the result
which thou knowest, and we all know, if we fail her—
the death which must ensue. Both are before thee ;
choose, boy ! I can say no more !" and she turned away
her face to the wall.

But she had conquered, for there was no defying
her will,—always the mainspring of the Rajah's actions

* The celebrated Hindu temple in the southern point of India.

—and, backed by those seemingly divine revelations in which he devoutly believed, he did not resist her.

"Mother," he said, rising and prostrating himself before her, "I know—I feel that the Goddess is speaking from thy mouth still. I hear and obey. Bless me, O my mother, and my hand will be strong; put thy hands on my head, and the Mother will guide the blow surely."

"I do bless thee, Sivaji Bhóslay," she returned, placing her hands on his head, "in the name of her who directs us, and with her power I endue thee. Go, and fear not, but do her bidding—thou shalt not fail."

He rose. "I will but speak with Maloosray and dismiss them," he said, "and return. Make up a bed for me here, for I would sleep near thee mother, to-night."

"Get thee to thy post, Nettajee," he said to Palkur, as he met them without; "there is no fear now; victory is with us—she hath said it. Let the men sleep and be ready."

"And what will you do with him—the Khan?" asked Maloosray.

"You will see to-morrow," said Sivaji excitedly. "You will be with me, and will share the danger. This was reserved for you, O well-tried friend!"

"Enough," said Maloosray to Palkur; "let us go, for the master needs rest;" and, saluting him, they departed.

Sivaji returned to his mother. A low bed had been prepared in the room, and she was sitting by it. He

took off his upper garment and turban, and, having
performed his ablutions, lay down, and she patted him
gently, as she used to do when he was a child.   He
would have spoken, but she would not listen, and he
urged her to sleep herself, but she would not leave him ;
and when the dim light of day broke gently into the
chamber, he awoke, and found she had not stirred from
his side.   " Arise," she said, " it is time.   Food is prepared for thee.   Eat, and go forth to victory !"

He obeyed her ; bathed, worshipped earnestly in the
temple, and ate heartily.   Then he returned to her,
and, in the simple words of the old Mahratta Chronicle, " laid his head at his mother's feet, and besought
" a blessing.   He then arose, put on a steel cap,
" and chain armour, which was concealed under a
" thickly-quilted cotton gown ; and, taking a crooked
" dagger which he hid under his sleeve, and the
" ' tiger's claws ' * in his right hand, he girded his
" loins, and went out."

* A treacherous and deadly weapon, in the shape of tiger's claws,
which, fitted on the fingers, shuts into the hand.

CHAPTER XVII.

THE morning broke, calm and beautiful. Long before
the highest peaks of the mountains blushed under the
rosy light which preceded the sunrise, the Khan and
Fazil, with Zyna, had risen and performed their morning prayer. The deep booming sound of the kettle-
drums woke the echoes around, and reverberated from
side to side of the valley, retiring to recesses among
the glens, and murmuring softly as it died away
among the distant peaks and precipices. As yet, the
valley was partially filled with mists, which clung to
its wooded sides ; but as the sun rose, a slight wind
sprang up with it, which, breaking through these
mists, drove them up the mountain, and displayed
the scenery in all its fresh morning beauty, as though
a curtain had been suddenly drawn from before it.

Behind them were the stupendous mountains of the
Mahabuleshwur range ; before, at a short distance,
and divided from them by a chain of smaller hills,
rose up the precipices of Pertabgurh, glittering in the
morning light, and crowned by the walls and bastions
of the fortress.

Long before daylight the lady Lurlee had risen, and, careful for her husband, had, in conjunction with Kur-reema, cooked his favourite dish of kichéri and kabobs. " It was a light breakfast," she said, " and would agree with them better than a heavier repast, and dinner would be ready when they returned." So Afzool Khan, his son, and the priest, ate their early meal, not only in joyful anticipation of a speedy return, but of accomplishing what would result in honour to all concerned.

They remembered afterwards, that as an attendant brought before the Khan the usual mail shirt he wore, and the mail-cap, with its bright steel chains, over which his turban was usually tied when fully accou-tred, he laughingly declined both. " They will be very hot and uncomfortable," he said, " and we are not going to fight. No, give me a muslin dress," which he put on. A few words about ordinary household mat-ters to Lurlee, a few cheering sentences to Zyna, as he passed from the inner and private enclosure of the tent, and he went out among the men.

Fazil followed, fully armed and accoutred for riding. There had been a good-humoured strife between Fazil and the priest the night before, as to who should be the one armed follower to accompany his father, and he had chosen the priest. " Fazil was too young yet," he said, " to enter into grave political discussions with wily Mahrattas, and would be better with the escort." So the soldier-priest, like the Khan, discarding the steel cap, gauntlets, and quilted armour in which he usually accoutred himself—appeared, like Afzool Khan, in the plain muslin dress of his order ; and having tied up his waist with a shawl, and thrown another over his shoulders, stuck a light court sword into his waistband, which he pressed down on his hips with a jaunty air, and called merrily to Fazil, to see how peacefully he was attired.

The escort awaited them in camp, and the spirited horses of fifteen hundred gallant cavaliers were neighing and tossing their heads as Afzool Khan, Fazil, and the priest rode up. "Forward!" cried the Khan cheerily ; and as the kettle-drums beat a march, the several officers saluted their commander, and, wheeling up their men, led them by the road pointed out by the Bramhuns and guides in the direction of Pertabgurh.

At that time, single men, who looked like shepherds tending sheep, and who were standing on crests of the hills, or crouching so as not to be seen, passed a signal that the Khan and his party had set out. It was still early, and the time when, of all others perhaps, armies such as the Khan's, were most defenceless. Many, roused for a while by the assembly and departure of the escort, had gone to sleep again ; others, sitting over embers of fires, were smoking, preparing to cook their morning repast, or were attending to their horses, or in the bazar purchasing the materials for their day's meal. The camp was watched from the woods around by thousands of armed men, who, silently and utterly unobserved, crept over the

crests of the hills, and lay down in the thick brushwood which fringed the plain.

As the Khan's retinue neared the fort, parties of
armed men, apparently stationed by the roadside to
salute him as he passed, closed up in rear of the escort;
and others, moving parallel to them in the thickets,
joined with them unseen. Quickly, too, men with axes
felled large trees, which were thrown down so as to
cross the road, and interlaced their branches so as to be
utterly impassable for horsemen ; and all these preparations went on in both places silently, methodically,
and with a grim surety of success, imparting a confidence which all who remembered it afterwards attri-
buted to the direction of the Goddess whom they worshipped. As it was said then, as it is still said, and
sung in many a ballad, "not a man's hand failed, not
a foot stumbled."

At the gate of the fort the Khan dismounted from
his horse, and entered his palankeen. Before he did
so however, he embraced his son, and bid him be careful of the men, and that no one entered the town or
gave offence. He could see, looking up, the thatched
pavilion on the little level shoulder of the mountain,
and pointed to it cheerfully. "It is not far to go,
Huzrut," he said to the Peer, "I may as well walk
with these good friends," and he pointed to the Bramhuns who attended him. But Fazil would not allow
it, nor the Peer either. "You must go in state," they
said, "as the representative of the King ought to do,"
and he then took his seat in the litter.

" Khoda Hafiz—may God protect you, father!" said
Fazil, as he bent his head into the palankeen, when the
bearers took it up ; " come back happily, and do not
delay ! "

" Inshalla !" said the Khan smilingly, " fear not, I
will not delay, and thou canst watch me up yonder."
So he went on, the priest's hand leaning upon the edge
of the litter as he walked by its side.

On through the town, from the terraced houses of
which, crowds of women looked down on the little procession, and men, mostly unarmed, or unremarkable
in any case, saluted them, or regarded them with
clownish curiosity. No one could see that the court of
every house behind, was filled with armed men thirst-
ing for blood, and awaiting the signal to attack.

The Khan's agent, Puntojee Gopinath, being a fat
man, had left word at the gate which defended the
entrance of the road to the fort, that he had preceded
the Khan, and would await him at the pavilion. He
had seen no one since the night before, and he knew
only that the Khan would come to meet the Rajah.
That was all he had stipulated for, and his part was
performed. He believed that Sivaji would seize Afzool
Khan, and hold him a hostage for the fulfilment of all
his demands; and the line of argument in his own
mind was, that if the Khan resisted, and was hurt in
the fray which might ensue, it was no concern of his.
But he did not know the Rajah's intention, nor did the
Rajah's two Bramhuns who had ascended with him ;
and they all three now sat down together upon the

knoll, waiting the coming of Afzool Khan from below,
and the Rajah from above.

As the agreement had specified, except one each,
there were to be no armed men : no other people were
present but one, who seemed to be a labourer, who was
tying up a rough mat to the side of the pavilion to
keep out the wind and sun. Gopinath looked from time
to time up the mountain-road, and again down to the
town, speculating upon the cause of delay in the Rajah's
coming ; and the others told him he would not leave
the fort till the Khan had arrived below, and showed
him a figure standing upon the edge of the large bastion
which overhung the precipice above, relieved sharply
against the clear sky, which was fronting towards the
quarter by which the Khan's retinue should come, and
apparently giving signals to others behind him.

"Your master is coming," said the Secretary, "they
see him from above ;" and, almost as he spoke, the
bright glinting of steel caps and lanceheads, with a
confused mass of horsemen, appeared on the road to the
fort, among the trees, and they sat and watched them
come on. Then the force halted in the open space before the outer gate, where the Khan's little procession
formed, and entered the town. After that, the houses
and the trees of the mountain-side concealed them.
How beautiful was the scene !

The wind had died away, and the sun shone with a
blaze of heat unknown elsewhere, striking down among
those moist narrow valleys with a power which would
have been painful, but for the cool refreshing air by

which it was tempered. The distant mountains glowed
under the effect of the trembling exhalations, which,
rising now unseen, tempered the colours of the distance to that tender blue and grey which melts into
the tint of the sky. The rugged precipices above were
softened in effect; and the heavy masses of foliage, festoons of creepers, and the dense woods, rich in colour,
combined to enhance the wonderful beauty of the spot.
There was perfect silence, except the occasional monotonous drumming notes of woodpeckers in the glens,
and the shrill chirrup of tree-crickets which occasionally broke out and was again silent.

In a few minutes, the shouts of the Khan's palankeen-bearers were heard below, and the litter suddenly
emerged from a turn in the road, being pushed on by
the combined efforts of the men. The Bramhun's heart
bounded when he saw the figure of the priest beside
the litter, holding to it, and pressing up the ascent
vigorously. "Will he escape?" he said mentally;
"the Mother forbid it,—let her take him!" A few
more steps, and the palankeen was at the knoll; it
was set down, and the Khan's shoes being placed for
him by a bearer, he put his feet into them and got
out, speaking to the priest, who was panting with his
exertion.

"Is he not here, Puntojee?" cried the Khan to the
Bramhun, who saluted him respectfully.

"No, my lord, not yet. Ah! look," he continued,
as he turned towards the pass, "there are two men on
the path, and that one, the smallest, is he."

The men coming down appeared to hesitate, and waved their hands, as if warning off some one.

"It is the bearers," said one of Sivaji's Secretaries. "The Rajah is timid, and fears the crowd he sees."

The Khan laughed. "Good," he said to the men. "Go away; sit down yonder in the shade. You will be called when I want you;" and as they got up and retired, the two men advanced slowly and cautiously down the pathway.

Afzool Khan went forward a few paces as Sivaji and Maloosray came up. "You are welcome, Rajah Sahib. Embrace me," he said to Sivaji. "Let there be no doubt between us;" and he stretched forth his arms in the usual manner.

Sivaji stooped to the embrace; and as the Khan's arms were laid upon his shoulders, and he was thus unprotected, struck the sharp deadly tiger's-claw dagger deeply into his bowels, seconding the blow with one from the other dagger which he had concealed in his left hand.

Afzool Khan reeled and staggered under the deadly wounds. "Dog of a Kafir!" he cried, pressing one hand to the wound, while he drew the sword he wore with the other, and endeavoured to attack the Rajah. Alas! what use now were those feeble blows against concealed armour? Faint and sick, the Khan reeled hither and thither, striking vainly against the Rajah, who, with the terrible sword now in his hand, and crying the national shout of "Hur, Hur, Mahadeo!" rained blow upon blow on his defenceless enemy. It was an

unequal strife, soon finished. Falling heavily, Afzool
Khan died almost as he reached the earth.

Meanwhile, Maloosray had attacked the priest with
all his force and skill, but the Peer was a good swords-
man, and for a short time held his ground. Neither
spoke, except in muttered curses, as blows were struck ;
but Tannajee Maloosray had no equal in his weapon,
and as he cried to the Rajah, who was advancing to his
aid, to keep back—the priest, distracted by the assault
of another enemy, received his death-blow, and sank to
the ground.

"Jey Kalee !" shouted both.   "Now blow loud and
shrill Gunnoo, for thy life," continued the Rajah, "and
thou shalt have a collar of gold."

The man who had appeared to be a labourer, seized
his horn, which had been concealed in the grass, and
blew a long note, with a shrill quivering flourish at the
close, which resounded through the air, and echoed
among the mountains ; and thrice repeated the signal.

Then a great puff of smoke, followed by a report
which thundered through the valley, burst from the
bastion above. Those who were looking from the fort,
and the Rajah himself who ran to the edge of the
knoll, saw the wreaths of fire which burst from the
thickets about the plain where the Mahomedan cavalry
stood, and a sharp irregular crash of matchlock shots
came up from below, and continued. Hundreds died
at every volley, and there were writhing, struggling
masses of horses and men on the plain—loose horses
careering about ; and some men still mounted, strove

to pierce the barriers which had been made on every side, crowded on each other, and, falling fast, became inextricable. Soon, too, the Mawullees, under Netta-jee Palkur, emerged sword in hand from their ambush, and attacked those who survived. Some escaped ; but of the fifteen hundred men who had ridden there in their pride that morning, few lived to tell the tale.

.   .   .   .   .   .

Moro Trimmul had taken up his position over night on a hill overlooking the main camp of Afzool Khan's army. A few boughs placed together formed a cover and screen on a high knoll, which commanded a view of the camp beneath, and of the summit of the fort whence his signal was to come. He sat there watching, and observed the force below, careless, without a guard, without weapons—the men sitting idly, wandering about, or cooking, as it might be. Every moment seemed interminable ; and the eyes of those who looked with him were strained towards the fort.

" One," he cried at last, as the first puff of bright smoke burst from the bastion—" two—three—four— five ! Enough. It is complete, my friends. Now, cry ' Hur, Hur, Mahadeo !' and upon them. Spare no one ! Come, friends, let us sack the Khan's tents first, where I have some work of my own to do."

" Beware," said an elderly officer, who stood near him—" beware, Moro Punt, of the master, if thou disobey him in this. He will suffer no insult to the women."

"Tooh !" cried Moro Trimmul, spitting contemptu-
ously, "I am a Bramhun, and he dare not interfere
with me. Come !"

Ten thousand throats were crying the battle-cry of
the Hetkurees, as they burst from the thickets upon
the bewildered army. Why follow them? In a few
hours there was a smell of blood ascending to the sky,
and vultures—scenting it from their resting-places on
the precipices of the mountains, and from their soaring
stations in the clouds—were fast descending upon the
plain in hideous flocks.

Shortly after the Khan had left—he could scarcely
have reached the fort—two figures, a man and a boy,
ran rapidly across the camp at their utmost speed
towards the Khan's tents—they were the hunchback
and Ashruf. When Fazil had dismissed them, the
night before, they had taken the road to Wye; and
immediately beyond the confines of the camp, where
the road ascended a rocky pass, had been seized by
the Mahratta pickets posted there. In vain they
urged they were but Dekhan ballad-singers; they
were not released. "Ye shall sing for us to-morrow," they said, "when we have made the sacrifice,
the ballads of the Goddess at Tooljapoor;" and,
bound together, they lay by the tree where the
party of men was stationed. There they heard all,
but were helpless.

"Ah, masters," said Lukshmun, as daylight broke,
"unbind us; we are stiff with the cold; we will not
run away; and I will sing you the morning hymn of

the Goddess, as the Bramhuns sing it at Tooljapoor.
See, my arms are swelled, and the boy's too."

"Loose him, brother," said one of the men, "we
shall soon now have the signal. Wait you here," he
added, as Lukshmun finished the chant, "and we will
fill your pouches with Beejapoor rupees when we come
back."

"Alas!" said the hunchback, with a rueful face,
"this little brother came from Wye last night, to
say my elder brother, Rama, was dead. Good sirs,
let me go and bury him," and he began to sob
bitterly.

"Let them go, Nowla," said another of the men ;
"they will be only in our way ; we can't stop to guard
them."

"My blessings on ye, gentlemen! Only let us go
now, and we will come to you and sing congratulations when you have won the victory," said Lukshmun
humbly.

"Go," said the men, "but do not return to camp,
else we will slay you if we see you there."

"They will die, or worse," said the hunchback,
whispering to Ashruf, "for Moro Trimmul is the leader
here. Come, let us save the Khan's wife and the lady
Zyna," and they turned into the jungle in the direction
of the camp.

The boy was bold and quick-witted. As they ran
on, "I can get into the zenana," he said, "under the
tent wall, and perhaps we can make them change
clothes, and fly—but if they stay ?"

"I will get the ponies ready," replied the other, and they ran the faster over the plain unperceived.

They reached the tents, and the boy entered as he said. Who would believe them? Zyna heard the tale with sickening dread, and Lurlee, assured by the others, at first disbelieved him, and threatened him with stripes. The women-servants crowded round, and some began to shriek, and were with difficulty pacified; others mocked him and turned away. Still the boy urged: and the hunchback, desperate, and dreading the delay, now found his way into the enclosure, and prostrated himself before them.

"I know the country," he said: "fly! take what jewels you can carry, and come. God be with them, lady!" he continued, as Zyna and Lurlee cried aloud for their husband and brother—"God be with them! they are mounted and will escape, and we may yet meet; but stay not here, else ye will die, or be dishonoured, and the Khan will kill me."

Then another voice was heard without, shouting. It was Shêre Khan, who had been left in charge of the private camp. "Go!" he cried, "I see men moving in the woods, and there is confusion and treachery." And others said the same. Then, too, they heard the five guns of the fort, and there broke from the mountains around a hoarse roar of voices, "Hur, Hur, Mahadeo!"

This decided them. A hurried change of clothes, some coarse garments thrown over them, and the ponies being led within the enclosure, the ladies were lifted

on them and carried out. O to see the stupid misery
of those women! Hitherto secluded, they could understand nothing; they had no power to resist; and
why they should be taken out among men, when
the shouts and screams of the camp were growing
wilder every moment, they could not understand. So
they wrung their hands in speechless terror.

"Come with the ladies, Shêre Khan," cried Lukshmun; "come, save thyself, old man!"

"No," he replied sadly; "my time is come, and the
sherbet of death will be sweet. Go thou, and all of
ye who can," he added to those who had gathered with
the women. "Quick! quick! else it will be too late."

The shouts of "Hur, Hur, Mahadeo!" were already
mingling on the confines of the camp with the battle-
cries of the Mahomedans, who had rallied in small
parties, and the flood of attack was there stayed
for a little: this saved the fugitives. Close by the
enclosure of tent walls ran the rivulet, and its banks
were high and covered with brushwood on the sides,
which concealed the party. Lukshmun, with a true
freebooter's instinct, led Zyna's pony down the bank,
accompanied by some of the terrified women-servants,
and Lurlee followed. So they proceeded at a rapid
pace down the stream, meeting no one, and concealed
from view.

They heard the hideous din of shouts, screams, and
shots increase behind them, but it gradually softened
with distance, and in a little time Lukshmun turned
up the sandy bed of a tributary brook, on the sides of

which the jungle was thicker, while the bed was narrower and more tortuous ; and, bidding every one tread only in the shallow stream which flowed in the midst, in order to afford no traces of footsteps, he hurried on, still leading Zyna's pony by the bridle. " Fear not, lady," he said confidently,—" the worst is past, and God will be merciful ; fear not."

In the camp there was but a short resistance. On the one hand, the desperate valour of the mountain sol- diery, the certainty of plunder, revenge for Tooljapoor, and the example of Moro Trimmul and other leaders ; and on the other, the helpless, disorganised, bewildered mass before them, rendered the assault irresistible. The first attacking bodies were succeeded by mass upon mass of fresh assailants from all quarters, and these successive tides of men surged resistlessly across the camp, overwhelming all.

When Moro Trimmul and his party reached the Khan's tents, they found no one. The tracks of the ponies, where they had descended the bank, were, however, visible, and were taken up by his followers, who dashed forward like bloodhounds on a scent. " Away after them, Kakrey!" cried the Bramhun to a subordinate officer. " Thou art a better tracker than I. Bring them to me,—then," he added to himself, " Fazil Khan, we will see who wins the game,—you or I."

CHAPTER XVIII.

THE ambassador's family, with whom Tara had received protection, had arrived at Pertabgurh the day before the events related in the last chapter. At Wye some traces of her mother's family, the Durpeys, had been found, but they were now residing at or near Poona: it would require several days to communicate with them; and a much longer period for them, or any one of them, to come for Tara and take her away. Meanwhile, therefore, there was no resource but to stay where she was, and to endure, what was daily becoming more and more insupportable.

Personally, Govind Rao, the Envoy, was kind to her, and continually renewed his offers of assistance and protection; but from his sister, the widow Pudma Bye, Tara had to endure insult and ill-usage, from which the Envoy's wife was unable to save her. Few, indeed in the house, chose to risk the bitterness of Pudma's tongue, or the virulence of her spite. Her brother even, feared her, and avoided her as much as possible.

So she employed herself in ascetic penances and religious exercises, fasted long and often, and mortified herself in various ingenious ways, with a view to establishing a character for sanctity which should make her famous. As might be supposed, she, the general distributor of the family alms, had many friends among the priestly Bramhuns, who attended the house and partook of her brother's charity ; and it was an object with many, by flattering her vanity, to make those alms as large as possible, and to induce her to undertake ceremonies which could not be performed without priestly aid, and, necessarily, money.

The chief of these priests was one Wittul Shastree, an elderly man of grave aspect, but with a hard expression of countenance, which might proceed from austerity or avarice, or both combined. He was the agent or commissary of the prince superior of the Bramhuns of the province, and held authority sufficient for the disposal of cases of heretical error, misconduct as to caste affairs, and other matters of religious discipline. On grave occasions of ceremony he directed these proceedings, and, in virtue of his office, was in proportion feared by all who might by any possibility come under his influence or power.

Tara's presence in the family could not be kept a secret. The fact of a widow existing there who wore silken garments and jewels, and who had not her head shaved, was an infringement of caste discipline which required prompt investigation ; and as the Envoy arrived at the fort, the Shastree betook himself to Pudma Bye, as well to receive the donations which were his due since she had been absent, as to make inquiry.

The Envoy himself was absent at the Rajah's Cucherri. Amba Bye was busy arranging her house after her long absence, and Tara was assisting her with an alacrity and intelligence which at once surprised and gratified her. On her own part, the worthy, good-natured dame was not slow in evincing warm affection : which had arisen out of the helpless condition of Tara on the one hand, and the loving confidence which she had displayed on the first evening of their companionship.

Ah! it was a cruel struggle for the poor girl. Perhaps we, who belong to another creed and faith, can hardly estimate it. And yet the springs and motives of human action have parallels so close everywhere, that we can at least follow the events which had to be endured, alike without aid, and without sympathy.

Poor Tara ! could she deny herself the secret contemplation of the noble youth who, she knew, was her lover ? Could she forget the sweet companionship of Zyna, the rough but loving caresses of the Khan's wife, and the hearty greeting of the Khan himself ? Alas, no ! it was impossible, and yet all these were in direct antagonism with her own creed, with the people of her own faith. What had she been taught to believe, but that Bramhuns were the gods of the earth—divine emanations, incapable of sin, and only resting here for a while in expiation of the errors of former births, till they were absorbed again into divinity, as a drop of rain-water in the sea, or as the sparks falling back into the fire !

She herself was a Bramhun of the highest rank and

caste : the very idea of a Mahomedan should have been
abhorrent and repellant to her. Was it so ? Alas, no !
She, an orphan as she believed herself, had felt her
sorrow soothed, and her honour powerfully protected :
she had been received into loving communion with a
noble family : she could not help contrasting their
soft polished manners with the rude homely speech and
rough demeanour of those with whom she now was—far
ruder among those mountains, than even among the
people of her own town.

Again, and far above all, that bit of the old old story
which she had heard and believed, when she knew herself to be beloved, would not be forgotten.   It lay at
her heart, rankling sometimes and chafing, because so
impossible—and again was remembered in a sweet
confidence which, though more impossible, was yet
inexpressibly soothing.   "He will remember me—he
now thinks of me," she would say to herself in the
lonely night, when oft-times a bitter cry was wrung
from her, which no one knew of ; " and he would take
me away if he could—ah yes ! he would have done it
—if he could."

From the first moment antipathy was conceived
against Tara by Pudma Bye, that virtuous lady had continued to brood over it with increasing dislike to her.
She had tried to excite in her brother abhorrence for
Tara's condition ; and, failing that, in Amba Bye, with
whom she had as little success.   Both believed Tara to
be a priestess of the Goddess whom they feared.   The
Envoy had tested her knowledge of sacred books, which

was nearly equal to his own, for he did not pretend, he
said, to be a scholar ; and in several disputations with
other Bramhuns who, attracted by the news of Tara's
learning, had come to hear her read and recite what
she knew, she had acquitted herself with favourable
impressions upon all.   But the woman's hatred of the
girl's beauty, and her ascetic austerity which would
have made Tara like herself, could not be controlled ;
and, under the influence of the Shastree, was likely to
have full scope.

But Wittul Shastree could not restrain himself; and,
unable to get speech of the master and mistress of the
house, Pudma Bye was resorted to—a willing communi-
cator of all that she herself thought, all that she had
said and argued, and all that she had heard of Tara's
sojourn with the impure Mahomedans. As for herself,
she did not, she said, believe Tara's story of Moro
Trimmul's outrage ; she, on the contrary, believed what
he said, that it was a meritorious attempt to withdraw
her from a scandalous position—scandalous alike to
herself and to the faith.

The Shastree's mind was at once made up as to his
course.   There had been several offensive stories
current in regard to young widows lately, and not
without reason : and they had escaped his punishment.
This at least was sure—the Envoy dare not deny, and
could not evade his power ; and if Tara appealed to
the Rajah himself, it would be on a point of caste discipline with which he—Rajah though he was—would
not dare to interfere.

" Let us hear her first," he said to the lady, as, having listened to Pudma Bye's account of Tara, he sat in the outer verandah of the house the morning after their arrival, while Tara was within ; " wilt thou call her, daughter ? we should not judge unheard."

Poor Tara's heart failed her sadly when Pudma called her. She clung to Amba Bye instinctively, trembling as she saw the priest sitting without, and protested against meeting him. " He is a stranger to me ; what have I to do with him ?" she said. " Let me go away. I am not his to be questioned, but the Mother's at Tooljapoor."

"Go," whispered Amba Bye to her; "he is all-powerful here,—over the Rajah, over my husband, over all. Go, tell him the truth. I will not leave thee. Go, Tara."

"Wilt thou now screen her, sister?" cried Pudma Bye in a shrill voice, and stretching out her bare skinny arms to Tara. " Is her shame to be our shame— we that have no spot or stain upon us ? If thou art bewitched, I, that perform the nine penances daily, should not be exposed to this ! Come, girl ! it is pollution to touch thee—nevertheless, come, else I will drag thee to him."

" Go !" cried Amba, frightened at the other's voice of threat and scorn combined, of which she had had long and sad experience in the house. " I dare not keep thee now,—she is terrible. Go, Tara, and answer what they ask thee. Say the truth and the Mother will hear thee. O that my lord were here !

O that he were here!" and she sat down sobbing and
wringing her hands helplessly.

"Come," cried Pudma, as, seizing Tara by the arm,
she pulled her forward. "Art thou a child, to be
ashamed,—thou that art a Moorlee?"

Tara's limbs trembled so that she could hardly move.

"Ah, Mother," she prayed silently, "I am not false
to thee yet; let me not be tried more than I can bear.
I will go, even to death, but not to shame. O Mother,
not to shame! Let me go, lady," she continued to
Pudma Bye, "I will follow thee."

She did so, and, bending down submissively before
the priest, stood up with her hands joined in an attitude of supplication. For a moment the stern man's
features relaxed into an expression almost of kindness,
certainly of extreme interest. The youth of the girl,
her gentle grace, the sad but beautiful expression of
her face—above all, its purity of expression—sent conviction to his heart that there was no room for
calumny, none even for suspicion.

Pudma saw the hesitation, and, herself resolute,
resumed rapidly and passionately—

"Is that a figure to be a widow and a priestess—that
thing with a golden zone, and necklaces and ear-rings,
and a silken garment like a harlot? Is that a widow
who daily combs her hair, braids it, puts sweet
flowers and oils into it, decking it for a lover? O
Shastree, is that what a virtuous widow should be?
Is that a condition of penance and austere privation
whereby to inherit life eternal?"

The Shastree's features changed rapidly. "It cannot be," he said; "such adornment and beauty is not of a virtuous woman. Now I believe thee, sister, and thy brother must be spoken to. He cannot keep a thing so offensive in his house, and be among us."

"Hear me, my lord," said Tara, appealing to him piteously. "I am pure—I have done no evil—I am an orphan and a Moorlee, but not as others; such as I am, the holy Bhartee Swami, whom I have served hitherto, hath made me. Write to him if you will——"

"What is this?" said Govind Rao, who entered at the moment, interrupting her; "what art thou asking of her, friend? Let her alone; she is my care."

"Look," returned the other rising, "if thou art satisfied to have one like that remaining in thy house, the Swami must know of it, and there will be a fine, and shame will come to thee among the council. If she be a widow, let her be treated as widows should be. If—— "

"If I am a Moorlee of the Goddess, as ye call me," said Tara interposing, "I am already shameless in your eyes, and no widow: let me go. No Moorlee is asked what she does, or what she wears. The Mother will not have those near her who are disfigured, and I cannot break the vow I have made to her; she would destroy me."

Panting and excited, flushed with the desperation of her speech, Tara stood erect, with her eyes flashing, her glowing beauty exciting the involuntary admiration of the men, and the virulent hatred of the woman who sat with them.

"See, brother!" cried Pudma Bye, "look at the witch—look at her glowing eyes. It was by these shameless eyes that she won men's hearts at Tooljapoor. Beware! beware of yourselves, lest ye too fall! Ah!" she continued with a scream, "put her away—kill her; but let her not go—Bramhun as she is—to the cow-slayers!"

,   "Peace," said her brother; "why this spite, Pudma? what hath she done to thee? Peace, and begone to the inner rooms. Begone!" he cried in a louder tone, and stamping his foot, "begone! Dost thou not hear?"

"I hear," she replied doggedly; "but I will not go, unless the Shastree bid me. Choose now between us: send me out of thy house to thy shame, and keep her, to thy worse shame; or send her away. There can be no compromise between good and evil, shame and dishonour."

"She speaks truly, friend," said the Shastree mildly. "It must be done. How do we know she is a priestess?"

Tara had not entirely lost the presence of mind which she naturally possessed, though she found it failing rapidly. "Put me to the proof," she said quickly,—"the proof. If there be a temple of the Mother's here, let me sit in it before her a night and a day—haply she may come to her child, as she did at Tooljapoor. Ye can watch me too, there. If she come not—then she hath abandoned me, and ye can kill me if ye please, sirs; better ye did so, for I am indeed friendless."

"Not so," cried the widow; "thou hast friends, Tara, many and powerful—myself the greatest of all; but—not as thou art. Choose!"

"I have chosen, lady," said the girl sadly. "Take me to the temple now—even now,—and leave me there. A vessel of water is enough, and a woman to watch me at night, if ye will not watch yourselves. I have already eaten, and want no food. I would go to the Mother."

"It is some device, brother," said Pudma suspiciously; "some device to fly, to escape, or——"

He smiled and shook his head. "It requires a braver heart than a girl's to face the mountain-paths alone at night among the bears and the panthers, sister, and nought but a bird could escape down the precipices. Why these unjust suspicions? Art thou ready, Tara? If so, follow me, and thou too, Shastree; we will settle this matter at once. There is no one now in the Rajah's temple. He has already paid his devotions, and is preparing to meet the Khan. Come, the ordinary priests are there, and there is no fear of her. Come, Tara, fear not. If thou art true, the Mother will defend thee. Dost thou trust her, girl?"

"Take me to her," she replied. "I have no refuge but with her. I am ready." Then she turned to embrace Amba Bye, who now entered sobbing, and fell upon her neck.

" I will come to thee by-and-by," she whispered.
" It is but a step, and I will watch with thee at night.
I have a vow to pay to the Mother. Go with my
husband."

We know the place already. It was where Sivaji's
mother had sat. A few words to the attendant priest
by Govind Rao and the Shastree, explained the ordeal
to which Tara had voluntarily subjected herself, and
she was permitted to approach the shrine and make
her obeisance and offerings. They watched her, and
saw that she did her office as one used to the duty ;
and when it was finished, she went before the shrine,
sat down, and began to chant the morning hymn of
the Goddess in low and sweet tones, rocking herself to
and fro.

" There can be no doubt of this, Shastree," said
Govind Rao,—" she is what she tells us."

" She may be," he replied, " but till the Goddess
comes into her and speaks by her mouth, she may not
be fully believed. Let us leave her," and they went.

Tara grew absorbed in her devotion : she noticed no
one. By-and-by a gun was fired from a tower near
her, and four others followed. Then a pause ensued,
and the priest fed the lamps with fresh oil, tinkled the
bell on the shrine, and poured libations to the image,
renewing these ceremonies with much earnestness.
Tara scarcely noticed them, for though it was broad
noonday without, it was dusk within the closed vestibule. By-and-by a girl, bearing a tray of lighted
lamps, and garlands of flowers, entered, but so that

her face could not be seen, and, delivering some to the priest, began a ceremony herself, which was strangely familiar ; and as Tara turned her head for an instant, she saw that it was Gunga, and that she herself was recognised.

Gunga clapped her hands with joy. " At last," she cried excitedly, " at last ! See, I am worshipping for the victory which he has gained by this time. Hush ! thou wilt see Zyna here presently. Moro will bring her captive ; then there will be three with him—I, and thou, and she. Ha, ha, ha ! a merry three, girl. Dost thou hear, O Tara ? " But some strange chill had struck at Tara's heart, and, sinking down on the floor, for a time she was insensible.

CHAPTER XIX.

GUNGA'S appearance is easily explained. On his arrival at Pertabgurh, Moro Trimmul had been sent to bring up some of the Rajah's Hetkurees from the Concan, the tract below the mountains next the sea, and he had besought the post of honour in the ensuing attack upon the Mahomedan camp, which had been granted to him.

In this he had two motives : the one, personal distinction, and the desire of retaliation for Tooljapoor, which was shared commonly with all Bramhuns ; and, secondly, and probably most urgent, the desire of revenge upon Fazil Khan, and, if possible, the capture of his sister and family. That either Afzool Khan or his son would survive the fight, he did not think possible, or if they escaped death, and were captured, that they would be spared.

Of the Rajah's intentions in regard to the Khan, he had no idea ; and when Maloosray and Palkur were with their prince on the night preceding the Khan's visit to the fort, Moro Trimmul was in company with his own men, placing them in positions in the woods, ready to obey the signal which had been communicated to him. Gunga, therefore, had been sent on to the fort under charge of his servants, and directed not only to have the house swept and prepared, but, as the guns were fired from the fort, to offer sacrifice for him in the temple, and await his coming.

"Dost thou know her?" asked the Bramhun priest of Gunga, when he heard her speak to Tara, and observed the effect of her address.

"Know her?—Yes, Maharaj," returned Gunga, "she is a Moorlee of the temple at Tooljapoor, and I am another,—that's why I know her."

"It is curious," said the man musing. "There, raise her up till my wife comes; we have had charge of her given to us, and she is to watch here to see if the Mother comes to her to prove herself what she says she is. Did she ever prophesy?"

"The Mother came to her once," replied Gunga, "when she was made a Moorlee; but I never saw her come afterwards. If she would be a true priestess, she perhaps would come; but she is only half a one at heart, and that's why trouble follows her."

"What trouble?" asked the priest.

"Oh, her father and mother are dead, killed in the fight at Tooljapoor, and she is here, among strangers, with no one to help her; is not that trouble enough, Maharaj?" replied the girl. "And she is so beautiful, too; they say she is a witch, and steals men's hearts and throws them away; but I don't know that she is —she is only beautiful—look at her."

"Ah! that's the worst I have heard yet," said the man musing.

"Yes, but she is pure, quite pure, sir," returned Gunga earnestly, "not like me and the rest of us; and we envied her, and I hated her; but I don't hate her now, and when she wakes I will tell her so. Tara, Tara! wake! She is not dead, sir, is she?" continued the girl dreamily, pushing away Tara's hair from her face, and looking into her eyes: "she does not answer me. O speak to her!"

"No, she is alive," replied the Bramhun, feeling her hand and forehead. "Wait, I will bring some water."

"Would she were dead—dead ere he came," Gunga muttered to herself. "He will not spare her now— ah me! not now: and in the heat and confusion of victory, who will care for her? All those she loved last, too, are dead—all gone—and that fair boy with the rest! Ah me, better she died! Tara, drink! here is water!"

A woman came with a brass vessel full, and helped Gunga to raise her up, while she poured some into her mouth, and sprinkled her face gently. They saw Tara heave a great sigh; and presently, as the woman fanned her with the end of her garment, she awoke and looked drearily around her—first to the woman, then to Gunga, against whom she was re-clining. Her first impulse was to rise, but in the attempt she sank down again, and buried her face in her hands.

"Why art thou here?" she cried piteously. "O

Gunga, go ! leave me." She did not yet comprehend
what had been said of victory, for she made no allusion
to it.

"No, Tara, not now," said the girl—"not now. I
will tell thee why. Go," she continued to the woman. "You are kind. Go now. I have that to say
to my sister which no one must hear. Go ! We are
priestesses, and will serve the Mother in our own
fashion. But if I need shelter for her, wilt thou give
it ?"

"Ah," replied the dame, "we are poor people, and
can do little ; but the Maha Ranee is kind and just—I
will speak to her."

"True," replied Gunga absently; "if needs be, I
will come to thee again—now, go. Tara !" she continued, stretching out her hands to her imploringly
when the woman had gone out—"O Tara, look up ! look
up, and see if I be like what I was ;—cast me not away
now, for we are both in the like misery! O Mother!"
she cried to the image on the altar, "bid her speak to
me, ere it be too late ;—bid her trust to me, and save
herself! Tara, behold I kiss your feet ; trust me now,
as I swear on them not to fail you. No, no, never,
never more—never more, except in death. See what
I do!"

She arose, went to the shrine, and prostrated herself
before it on her face, so that her hands embraced the
feet of the image. "O kill me, Mother—O kill me,
Mother !" Tara heard her cry, in a passionate burst
of weeping ; "kill me, if thou wilt, for touching thee,

who am not worthy ; but hear me, and help me to save
Tara. She is thy child. O let me save her for thee.
I will,—I will, if thou wilt bid her trust me, for I am
not lying now. I am true to thee and to her!"

The words were almost inarticulate, and gasped or
sobbed, rather than spoken. They fell strangely on
Tara's ears as Gunga still moaned rather than spoke.
"Mother—O Mother, I am true, I am not lying ; bid
her trust me ! bid her trust me ! "

It was impossible to resist them. Tara rose and
went across the vestibule to her. " Gunga," she said,
" get up, I am here : what wouldst thou of me ? "

The girl arose, put away the dishevelled hair from
her face, and again bowed before Tara, embracing her
knees. She was not repulsed this time. The priest
had watched the scene wonderingly—he could not
understand it. Tara was standing beside the door
of the shrine, the light from within streaming out
upon her. Her slight figure was drawn up to its full
height, and her beautiful features were calm—almost
sublime in their expression. Lying at her feet, and
clasping them, was the other girl, still moaning in
apparent agony.

"She hath done some terrible crime," thought the
Bramhun, " and the other will intercede for her."

" O Tara—O Tara," cried Gunga piteously, " I dare
not look up to thee now ; all my shame is rushing back
into my heart ; my words and my touch are alike pollution to thee ! O Tara, I dare not ask forgiveness—
I who have wronged thee so foully. Speak, for time

passes quickly, and they will be here—wilt thou trust me now ? O Mother, Mother ! what can I do ? what can I say to make her trust me—to make her forgive me ?"

"Look up, Gunga," said Tara, sitting down, and gently parting the hair on the girl's forehead, "what hast thou done ? It was he, not thou ; see, I forgive thee freely."

"O yes, it was he, not I," she cried,—"I resisted, and he used to beat me. Yes, he beat me cruelly only yesterday, when he left me, and then it came into my heart to save thee ! Yes, the Mother told me—I know it now—to come here, and I have found thee. Listen !" she continued rising, and looking hurriedly about her. "There is no one near—all are gone. Come ! come ! we are not seen ;—come at once,—do not delay : we can escape during the confusion. Hark ! they are fighting below—come ! I tell thee the tigers and the bears on the mountain, are better for me and thee than they. Dost thou not hear ?"

"It is the men firing for the Khan's arrival," said Tara gently ; "there is no fighting. Who should fight ?"

"Ah no," cried Gunga, "they are attacked,—the Khan is already killed. I heard it as I came in—they are all dead or dying. O Tara, I tell thee that no one will escape,—no, not one. Hark ! the din increases, and thou art here : alas ! alas ! O Mother ! tell it to her," she exclaimed, with passionate gesticulation, to the senseless image before them—"tell it to her—she will not believe me—Tara, dost thou not hear ? "

Just then, an eddy, perhaps, of the mountain-wind, brought up to them from the deep valley below, a hoarse, confused din of shouts, shots, and conflict. It could not be mistaken. Tara had heard it once at Tooljapoor, but this was far more tremendous.

" Come ! " again shrieked Gunga, seizing her arm, and dragging her away — " come ! It is our last chance for life—do not throw it away. We can get out and hide among the bushes; and I will never leave thee Tara, never."

But she spoke to one now wellnigh bereft of sense. The Khan killed, the rest attacked, and the fierce turmoil of the fight coming up stronger and stronger, till the fretted roof of the temple seemed filled with the sound, overpowered Tara; for at last, the hideous truth seemed to flash upon her, as she sat down and buried her face in her lap in an attitude of mute despair; but Gunga would not let her rest.

" Ah, I am believed now," she cried wildly: " listen ! Moro Trimmul, with thousands upon thousands, has attacked the camp, and he swore to me to bring the Khan's wife and daughter hither. O Tara ! will he spare them? He swore he would not, and he beat me when I pleaded for them. Look ! here are bruises on me. I tell thee he will not spare them or you. Come ! "

" I will die here,—I will not go from the Mother, Gunga," replied Tara. " I am her child now—only

hers : let her do with me as she wills, I will not go.
Save thyself, care not for me," and she arose and prostrated herself before the shrine. "O Mother," she
cried piteously, " I will not leave thee again. Death
or life, what matters it to me? let it be as thou
wilt. I have promised not to leave thee, and I am
here waiting." Then rising, she seated herself as she
was used to do before the shrine, and spoke no more.

"I can at least die with thee, Tara; I will not leave
thee," said Gunga. " Whatever comes, let it come to us
both; I am as ready to die as thou art—I will not go."

They sat there long. The sun declined, and the
evening was drawing in. Once only Gunga had gone
out to see whether she could gain any intelligence, and
had returned saying the doors of the temple enclosure
were shut. The Bramhun priest had disappeared like
the rest, but there were shouts as if of victory which
rung through the building in bursts, evidently growing
nearer. Tara seemed not to hear them. It might be
that utter despair possessed her, or, as Gunga hoped,
that some manifestation of the Goddess was about to
take place. She scarcely moved now, but when the
shouts grew louder she shuddered, and drew the end of
her garment more closely around her as if she were cold.

It was thus that the Maha Ranee, Sivaji's mother,
found her and Gunga as she entered with her attendants for the evening prayer and worship, and to give
thanks for the victory.

As the lady had approached the temple, the attendant priest told her of Tara, and why she had been left

there by the Shastree and Govind Rao, and the tale
had excited her curiosity if not her compassion.

"She is sitting there before the Mother," he said,
"and does not speak. Perhaps she will answer you,
lady, but it seems as though a fit were coming on her.
I will tell her at least that you have come," and stepping forward he advanced to Tara and whispered in
her ear.

The Maha Ranee followed, and paused as she entered
the vestibule. The light shone full upon Tara, and
her expression of deep misery could not be mistaken.
Long afterwards, the first sight of that pale, wan, despairing face recurred to the lady with pain, and she
never forgot the look of hopeless grief which Tara had
first turned upon her.

"There is no inspiration in that face," said the lady
to the priest,—"none. It seems to me the Mother
hath forsaken her. Of what is she accused?"

"She was taken from the Mahomedan chief, we
hear," said the Bramhun, "and was to have become a
Mussulmani. They say, too, she is a sorceress, and
does evil with her eyes; but Govind Rao placed her
here, and knows about her."

"I fear her not," cried the Ranee, with flashing eyes.
"Who is she, that she dare sit in my presence? Put
her out! Away with thee, wench!" she continued to
Tara, "get thee hence! If thou art forsworn, begone!
The Mother hath drunk blood to-day and will not
spare thee! Take her away, Bheemee—she is an
offence to us."

"Get up, girl," said Bheemee roughly, as she advanced, followed by several other women—"get up;
dost thou not hear? else we will cast thee out."

Gunga came forward boldly. "Do not touch or hurt
her," she said: "I fear she is not now in her right
mind. If I may take her, I will look after her. Get
up, Tara," she whispered in her ear: "come, we will go
and hide ourselves. Come, for thy life come!" and
she tried to lift her up and drag her away.

But Tara could not rise; her limbs seemed paralysed
by grief or terror, and she did not evidently understand what had occurred. Not noticing the Maha
Ranee, she disengaged herself from Gunga, and once
more stretched out her arms to the shrine before her,
and cried in piteous tones which affected many around
her to tears, "O Mother, I will not leave thee: do with
me as thou wilt, even to death!" and so lay moaning.

"Send for Govind Rao and Wittul Shastree, lady,"
said the old Bramhun priest, who was sobbing and
wiping his eyes: "they know of her, and you will hear
about her from them."

"Good," replied the Ranee, already softened, "let
them be brought instantly,—they are without. We
will await their coming."

Some little time elapsed, and others assembled.
No one knew what was going to happen. After a
while Tara seemed to regain sense and to remember why she was there, for she sat up, and they saw
her lips moving as if in prayer. As the trumpets
sounded the setting of the first watch at sunset, and

the great kettledrums and pipes played the evening
music in the Nobut Khana* above the gate, the
Bramhun priests entered with the usual offerings, and
began to chant one of the evening hymns of praise, as
they moved round the shrine in time with the faint
clash of the silver cymbals, which one of them carried.
Then, timidly and faintly at first, but increasing in
power as she sang, Tara joined the chant.   It was
an emotion which she could not restrain, and which
not even the sense of desolation and dull misery
which had overwhelmed her, could repress.   She was
unconscious of the effect it produced upon those who
listened to her, as her full rich voice rose above the
hoarse and unmusical chant of the priests ; but as it
gradually ceased, and the sound died away in the recesses of the temple, it affected many of those who
heard it to tears, and was never forgotten.

"No wonder," said the Ranee, who had listened to
the hymn with emotion which she hardly chose to acknowledge,—"no wonder they say she is a sorceress.
See, she has no fear—no perception of what is to happen, or who are around her.   That is not natural; it
is magic, and may not be looked upon."

"Lady," said Wittul Shastree, who, with Govind
Rao and the other Bramhuns, now approached her,
"we attend you ; what are your commands?"

"We doubt the girl yonder, and they tell us she is

---

* The place for a band of music, allowed only to persons of rank
by royal permission, and which plays at stated periods during the
day.

dangerous, and a sorceress.; we would have her removed ere we render sacrifice for victory," she replied ;
" but the priests tell us she is there by your order. Is
it so ?"

" By her own will," said the Shastree ; " not our orders.
We would have made her over to the council for chas-
tisement and discipline, because, as a priestess of Kalee,
she hath been residing among the Mahomedans ; but
she claimed ordeal and sanctuary with the Goddess,
and we sent her here. Has any vision appeared to
her ?" he asked of the attendant priest.

" None," replied the man. " They have been talking
together, she and the girl beside her, who wanted her
to get up and go away ; but she has not stirred since
the five guns were fired, and she was told of the
victory."

" I will ask her again what she wishes, lady," said
Govind Rao, " but better than I, Moro Trimmul should
do it, who, we hear, has married his sister to her
father. He, too, is without with the Rajah ; they have
just come up into the fort."

" Let him be called," replied the lady, " and keep out
other strangers. Be ye all seated, sirs," she continued
to the Bramhuns who had accompanied the Shastree,
" while this inquiry lasts."

CHAPTER XX

THE inner part of the vestibule was not large,—a square room, supported upon massive stone pillars at the corners, with a slightly raised dais all round; and as the Bramhuns entered and took their seats, Tara could not avoid noticing them, and appeared more conscious of surrounding occurrences than before. Thinking she would rise, Gunga approached to assist her, but Tara motioned her away. "My time is not yet come," she said; "I will not go;" and again she drew her garment about her, and resumed her silent position.

But not for long. There was a sudden movement among those without, and a way was cleared for one who came in rapidly.

"Who wants me here?" cried a strong manly voice, apparently hoarse from shouting. "A girl! what girl? Let me pass."

As he strode in through the men who were sitting behind, Tara turned her head, and suddenly beheld her enemy.

She rose at once, excited and defiant, so noble in her

manner, so expressive in her abhorrence, that Moro
Trimmul shrank back a step, abashed.

"Begone!" she cried, stamping her foot. "There is
the Mother; not a second time shalt thou take me
from her. My fathers," she cried, appealing to all
around, "he would twice have dishonoured me, and I
have been saved. Now I am under your protection, O
give me not to him! Take me to the mother of the
Rajah; she will protect me."

"She is here," said the Shastree, stepping forward;
"and thy fate shall be decided before her. Fear not,
daughter."

"Friends," said Moro Trimmul, looking round, "have
care for my honour! Twice have I rescued her from
shame. Once when she was escaping from Tooljapoor;
once in separating her from those who have been slain.
Give her to me, for her shame to be hidden away for
ever."

"I will not go; I will not go!" cried Tara, entering
the door of the shrine, and clasping the feet of the
image. "Kill me if ye will, here,—I am ready; but
I will not go with him."

"I claim them both, sirs," cried Moro Trimmul
passionately; "her, and her sister Moorlee yonder. Beware, all of ye, how ye interfere with the family honour
of a respectable man. I will brook it from no one, not
even from Sivaji Bhóslay himself! Have I won a
victory to-day at the Mother's command, and am I to
be disgraced and humbled before her, by a deranged
girl and doting priests, ere it is closed? Come forth,

Tara !" he called, in a hoarse voice—" come forth, else
I will tear thee thence.   Away with her," he cried to
two of his attendants, who had seized Gunga, and were
holding her fast—" away with her to my house, and
bind her there ; I will bring the other.   Now, friends,
beware who stays me, for, by the Gods, he dies, be he
who he may !" and he drew his sword, and was advancing, when the Shastree stepped before him.

   " Madman," he cried, stretching forth his hands ;
" forbear ! put up thy weapon,—no one here dreads it.
We are Bramhuns, as thou art !   Fear not," he continued to Tara, who had stood up also by the altar, and
was trembling violently, but not with terror.   " Fear
not ; thou art under the protection of the council, and
he dare not interfere with thee."

   " Fool and dotard," exclaimed Moro Trimmul under
his breath, and from between his clenched teeth, " I
will settle with thee for this, one day yet.   As ye will,
sirs," he continued bitterly, looking round and panting
as he dropped his sword's point.   " My honour is in the
hands of a priest's council at last, not in my own keeping, and I am helpless ; but hasten what ye have to
do, for I will not leave ye till ye have decided in regard to her.   Look at her—harlot and witch, sorceress
and devil—who hath already destroyed men's souls,—
will ye believe the Mother protects such as she is ? "

   " Let it be so," said the Shastree.   " Tara, art thou
willing to abide the night, as the issue of the ordeal
suggested by thyself, to wait her coming ? If so, we
will stay here with thee."

" Mother," she said in a low voice, turning to the altar, and joining her hands in supplication before the image—" Mother, if I am thy child, tell me what to say to them ; or, if thou wilt, let me be another sacrifice to thee, and it will be well. Mother,—O Toolja Mata! dost thou hear ?—Tara is ready before thee—ready to come !"

Low as the words were spoken, they were heard by all ; and remembering the events of the day, and believing in the power of the Goddess, it was expected the girl would fall and die where she was, on the solemn invocation; but it was not so. For a few moments she stood gazing intently at the image, without altering her position of supplication; then she smiled, her hands dropped, and she turned at once and faced the assembly. Not even in her first office as priestess had her beauty been more glorious—the expression of her features more sublime.

" O priests and elders," she said calmly and simply, in her sweet musical voice, " hear my last words : I am an orphan and a widow, I have no one left on earth to protect me,—not one. To be in danger of that man's evil designs, is to die hourly. Did he succeed as he has tried, it would be to live in shame ; now I can die in purity. The Mother calls me ; she will not come to me, though I have asked her. She is far from me, yet she beckons to me ; look, there !" and she stretched forth her hand to the roof—" she calls me, and I come, pure, and purified by fire. Now listen, all

ye Bramhuns; I am true and pure, and I am Sutee*
henceforth. When ye will, and where ye will, I am
Sutee; and on his head be curses, and the vengeance
of Kalee, who forbids it. Let me die in the fire, and
I am happy! What she puts into my mouth, I say to
you truly. Let no one forbid it."

No one spoke, no one answered. The people before
her rose as one man. Many trembled, some wept,
and women screamed aloud; but Tara stood there un-
moved, her bosom heaving rapidly, and the glowing
beauty and rapture of her face unchanged.

"Jey Kalee! Jey Toolja Mata!" exclaimed the
Shastree; "let it be as she says, brothers. Henceforth
she is Sutee, and we accept the sacrifice, for the Mother
hath said it by her lips. Ah, the ordeal is fulfilled indeed, and to the honour of her votary! Fear not," he
said, "daughter: by this act is thy husband delivered
from hell; and all thou hast suffered in this life is
sanctified unto thee. Bring flowers, bring garlands,"
he cried to the people; "crown her here at the altar,
and let her be worshipped."

"Tara, Tara!" cried a husky voice close to her, entreatingly; "Tara, what hast thou done? Art thou
mad? O girl, why hast thou doomed thyself? Come,
there is yet time: come with me!"

"Begone!" cried the girl interrupting him; "I spurn
thee, Moro Trimmul, before all these elders: false and
cruel as thou art, I am at last beyond thy reach!"

"Come away, Moro," said Maloosray roughly, who

* Chaste, virtuous.

had just entered, and dragged him backwards with one hand, while he seized his sword and wrested it from him with the other; "art thou a child? dost thou fight with priests and women? Come with me; the Rajah calls thee." The Bramhun struggled to be free, but Tannajee's powerful arms were about him, in which he was borne away, helpless to resist.

Not in her first admission to the office she had held, not in the holiest of ceremonies at which she had before assisted, was greater honour ever done to Tara than now. Bedecked with garlands, with incense burnt before her, the priests present formed themselves into a procession, and, chanting hymns of praise, led her round and round the shrine. The temple court and its precincts were now filled with people, who took up the shouts of victory—"Jey Kalee! Jey Toolja Mata!" and as she passed before them, throwing handfuls of flowers among them, all who could reach her, touched her garments reverently, or prostrated themselves before her, with frantic cries for blessings; and so they led her forth.

How many sweet memories crowded into Tara's mind now, and urged her on. There was no fear, no irresolution—father, mother, Zyna, Fazil—all dead, as she thought, and a fierce and ruthless enemy persecuting her to the last. All she could think on was, that she was free, that no one could harm her now. Had they then led her to death, she would have gone, singing the hymns triumphantly.

Late that night Moro Trimmul returned to his place
of residence.   Long before, when Sivaji's power was in
its infancy, and the young men had taken possession
of the mountain-built fort, and led their bands forth to
plunder and destroy the Mahomedan villages around,
Moro Trimmul had fitted up a hollow bastion on one of
the angles of the precipice—in which the builder had
left a small room and anteroom—as his place of shelter.
The inside was rudely plastered with clay; and a sleep-
ing-place, also of clay, had been raised from the floor,
on which was placed a mattress and pillow.   In the
face of the bastion a small oriel window had been built,
which had a balcony projecting from the wall, large
enough for two people to sit in.   Seated there, you
looked down a dizzy depth upon the forest below; but
on all sides the precipices, the woods, and their deep
glens, and the varied mountains beyond, formed a combination of glorious beauty, which there, above all other
places in the mountain fortress, was most deeply felt.

Thither had Gunga been taken by the Bramhun's
servants on the morning of the battle.   He had charged
them to have the place swept and newly plastered with
clay, and Gunga, with having it done as he wished.
On its completion, she had gone into the temple to
worship for him in the exercise of her vocation, as the
signal was to be given, which they all told her of.   She
knew of his design.   He had charged her to watch
Tara, and, if she saw her, to give him information of
her actions.   He had told her that he should bring
Fazil's sister to the fort, for he felt sure she could not

escape him. Herself, Zyna, and Tara should be confronted at last. How long should the latter elude
him ? For the Khan, Gunga cared nothing ; for Zyna
and Fazil as little—they were Mussulmans, and must
perish,—but for Tara !

Ah yes, strange indeed, perhaps, yet not unnatural,
had been the revulsion. The jealousy which had urged
Gunga to hate the girl, and assist in plots for her ruin,
had strangely altered to love. Twice had Moro Trimmul been foiled ; twice had he fallen savagely upon
her, and beaten her cruelly. We know what he did
when Tara was last rescued, and how Gunga, relenting,
had not then abandoned him. But it had not ended
there. The fierce rage of disappointment had broken
out again and again, and he had vented it upon her
brutally. She had borne this patiently at the time ;
but she had now sworn to herself, in the temple of the
Goddess at Wye, not only to lend herself no more to
Moro Trimmul's design, but had formed the resolution
to assist Tara to escape—to carry her off by mountain
paths ; and she knew that if they could once enter the
forest near the fort, they were safe.

Day by day, as these thoughts passed through
Gunga's mind, the love for Tara grew stronger, till it
became an absorbing passion. Would she but trust
her—would she but believe her—they might yet again
see their beloved Tooljapoor, and she would work out
her forgiveness by devotion. It was not too late, she
thought : but . . . .

We have already told how she met her in the

temple; but it is impossible to describe her despair
at her failure to induce Tara to escape, or when the
man she dreaded, bid his servants seize and bind her.
If she could have remained with Tara—only near
her . . . .

Alas! it was too late now. She had scarcely been
carried, shrieking, from the temple, by the servants of
Moro Trimmul, when another man followed, and said
Tara had become a Sutee, and was to be burnt next
day beside the tank in the fort. Then Gunga felt the
heroism of the girl's resolution. At least Moro Trimmul could not injure her; she would soon be beyond
reach of his persecution. It was well—yes, it was
well. She could at least see her die; and then? . . .

The desire of death sat hard at her heart. At first
she shuddered at it; but once it had entered, it abode
there and grew stronger. If Moro Trimmul cast her
off now, it would be but to be haunted by the memory
of the girl she had wronged so cruelly, and the love for
whom, and the despair of whose forgiveness, had pur-
sued her night and day—night and day: but it seemed
to have reached her at last. " Yes, she touched me
kindly," she said to herself; " she parted the hair from
my face as a sister would have done: ere she spoke to
me she forgave me: and I will see her die, decked in
flowers, as a holy and pure sacrifice. I will worship
her as she goes to death, and then I will follow her.
O Tara, there, not here, I may be forgiven before the
Mother."

Moro Trimmul's servants had taken Gunga, and

literally obeyed the orders they had received; bound
her with one of her own garments, lest she should
do herself or them injury, and laid her gently upon
the couch in the inner room. How long she had
lain there she had no idea; but, as the time passed,
it only confirmed her resolution. She would die, no
matter how. There was nothing definite in her mind,
but that she would die: a dull despair blunting every
faculty—a reality of determination before which her
very senses seemed to refuse office.

She heard Moro Trimmul ask without where she
was, and the servant answer that she was within, lying
on the couch. A small lamp had been lighted and
placed in a niche; and as he entered and stood over
her, she feigned sleep. She felt him unfasten the
bandage round her arms, and then he dragged her
roughly to her feet.

"Devil!" he cried, "this is thy doing, and she is
gone. Lost! O Tara, how beautiful thou wast in
living death!" he continued, apostrophising her, "speaking thy own death-sentence—as I listened, I could have
died for thee."

"Thou art a coward, Moro Trimmul," cried the girl,
scornfully and desperately; "thou darest neither die
thyself, nor kill me. Thou die with Tara? she would
spit at thee, as I do."

He struck her brutally to the ground with his
clenched hand. "Lie there, witch! devil!" he cried.
"Thou hast been the cause of all this; alone, I could
have done it. Thou and she are one now, else why

didst thou not decoy her here? Did I not tell thee to do so? Speak!" and he pushed her with his foot as she lay.

She arose. "Moro Trimmul," she said calmly, but with desperation in her voice, "may the Mother forgive me what I have done with thee against Tara; that is all I pray now. Between me and thee all is ended, long since. Let me go. I will serve thee no longer. I spit at thee and defy thee; and in the Rajah's court, before every image of Kalee in the Dekhan, if I live, I will sing thy shame and her honour. Let me go out!"

She saw him set his teeth, as his eyes flashed with a wicked glare, draw a knife from his waistband, and spring at her. The glitter of that knife was the last thing, perhaps, of which she was conscious, except that she seized the hand that held it, instinctively, and then came a struggle for life. But only a brief one. A weak girl, before a powerful man, could not endure long,—sickened, too, as she was by his previous blow. Back—back, he forced her to the window, which was open; on the little balcony without, they swayed to and fro fearfully for a moment; but he wrenched his hand free by a desperate effort, and, striking her one heavy blow with the knife, where he knew not,—as the body dropped heavily in his arms, he pushed it forth into the dark air. He did not hear it fall, though he listened; but in the morning, the vultures, which lived on pinnacles of the precipices, were seen descending in hundreds to their hideous feast below.

CHAPTER XXI

FAZIL KHAN had followed the progress of his father
up the mountain-side with intense interest.. The little
pavilion on the knoll, the group of Bramhuns already
there, and the open and nearly level spot which had
been selected as the place of meeting, were distinctly
visible from where he stood with Bulwunt Rao, and a
few other of his trusty associates and retainers. Around,
the horsemen—now mostly dismounted—were dispersed
in picturesque groups, talking together or lying lazily
upon the soft sward holding their horses' bridles, and
shading their eyes from the sun.

In the town through which his father had gone, there
appeared no stir. A few men were lounging about the
gate, and upon the bastion near it, and thus were looking
out upon the Mahomedan horsemen apparently in idle
curiosity. The gate was open, and the townspeople,
and women with jars of water on their heads, were
passing to and fro unconcernedly as usual. There was
nothing to excite suspicion or apprehension, except in
the mode of reception of his father, and the strange,
unusual proposition, that the first interview should be

on the mountain - side, and alone ; but Bulwunt Rao
had explained this characteristically, and with a fair
show of reason, and Fazil, though uneasy, was obliged
to be content : there was no remedy now.

So the Khan's progress in his palankeen had been
watched with intense anxiety as he ascended the rugged pathway. At times the bearers could be seen,
and the priest holding the side of the litter to help
himself along : again the thick foliage, and turns in the
road, hid them from view. At length Fazil saw the
Bramhuns on the knoll rise and advance a few steps,
and the palankeen emerge upon the open space, where
it was set down ; and his father got out, adjusted his
turban and shawl, and stood with the rest. Then the
bearers and the priest moved a little aside ; and as the
two men from above appeared, his father advanced to
meet them, and embraced one.

It was but for a moment, and the fatal result was
at once apparent. With a cry of horror, which aroused
many around him who had not been watching the
proceedings above, Fazil saw his father reel and fall,
rise again, as his sword flashed in the air, and with the
Peer maintain the unequal combat we have already
described. No sound reached those below ; they could
only see the flashing of the weapons in the sun, and the
struggle of the combatants. Involuntarily, Fazil urged
on his horse. Alas ! of what avail now ? Others had
been watching as well as he ; and the blast of the
horn, which rose shrill and quivering as the Khan
fell, was answered by volleys of matchlock shots from

the woods around. The gates of the town were shut, and the walls and bastions manned as thickly as men could stand on them, whose fire on the horsemen below was hot and deadly.

The effect of the surprise upon the helpless cavaliers need not be detailed. Panic-stricken, and hemmed in on every side, they rode hither and thither, vainly seeking places of egress through the woods, or by the way they came, and were shot down in scores either where they stood, or as they gathered in groups and charged hither and thither in the vain attempt to reach a foe. Among these, Fazil Khan, with Bulwunt Rao and some others, had kept together; and, in the emergency, Bulwunt's clear perception, not only of the danger, but the best means of extrication from it, saved his young master. On the first perception of his father's fate, Fazil had seen that it was impossible to give help. The town and its walls stood between him and the ascent to the fort, and were utterly impassable. His next idea, in his grief and desperation, was to die with his men as martyrs to the faith; and he was about to dismount, and take his chance on foot, when Bulwunt stopped him.

"No, Meah," he cried, "not while there is hope. They who will be helpless indeed without you, will need you yonder in camp. If it must be, I will die with you, but not now. Follow me, and we will soon join them."

Well was it for Fazil Khan that in his retainer he possessed equally, a devoted friend and one who had

known the country as a youth. In his recent visit to
the fort, Bulwunt Rao had explored some of his old
haunts. One pathway, lying near that by which they
had come, was hardly visible from the plain, but if it
could be gained, it opened out afterwards into a long
glade, which joined the main-road below. It might be
guarded, and they could but fight their way through it
or fall. Certainly it was better than the way they
had come, before which, from the deadly fire maintained there, the horsemen had already fallen in a heap.

"Look," continued Bulwunt Rao, pointing to the
entrance to the main-road, "there is no hope there.
They have been at their old trick of felling trees across
it, and no horse can pass. The Abyssinians have fallen
in a heap, and if we try, we shall but follow them.
We need not be martyrs yet, Meah," he laughed cheerfully. "Now, set your teeth, my sons," he continued
to the men around, "and follow me. We may not all
get through; but, Bismilla! come, and let God take
whom he pleases."

There might have been fifty men; and others, as many
more perhaps,—as they saw these ride together in a
desperate race in one direction,—joined them. Bulwunt
Rao and Fazil were leading; and as they approached
what seemed a portion of impervious wood, Fazil's
heart failed him for a moment. "You are wrong,
Bulwunt Rao," he cried. "We cannot get through
this—let us turn."

"Madman!" exclaimed the other, seizing the bridle
of his horse. "By your mother and sister, I swear I

am right ! Follow me, my children," he shouted, looking back, while he again urged his horse to its
utmost speed ; " we are near now."

He was right. A portion of the jungle jutted out
beyond the rest, and made a slight shoulder, as it were,
behind which was the path. As they turned round the
corner, they saw a body of foot-soldiers drawn up across
it ; but ere these could raise their matchlocks to fire,
the impetuous horsemen were among them, trampling
some down, and hewing fiercely at others with their
long Spanish swords.* The attack was irresistible, and,
the first line of men forced, they encountered no others.
Straggling shots were fired at them from the sides of
the mountain, but without effect ; and after riding
nearly a mile down the glade at the same speed, the
pathway turned into the main-road, and they heard the
din of the fight die away behind them. Of the fifteen
hundred gallant cavaliers who had ridden that morning
from the camp at Jowly, they were the only survivors.

While Nettajee Palkur was finishing his bloody work
on those who remained after Fazil Khan's escape, by
closing up the pathway, and attacking from all sides
at once, such of the horsemen as remained in the field,
—Moro Trimmul was busy with his part of the general
slaughter ; and as the fugitives rode on, the din of the
fight behind growing fainter as they proceeded, they

---

* The Portuguese of Goa used to import large quantities of Spanish and Genoa sword-blades. They were held in high estimation
at Beejapoor, and they are still often to be met with in the country.
The Rajah Sivaji's famous sword Bhowani, with which he killed
Afzool Khan, is a Genoa blade of the first water.

were met by that of the greater work in front,—more
furious, and more terrible.

Yet they pressed on, until, reaching a rising-ground
which overlooked the field, they could see it all in its
hideous reality. The Mahrattas had seized the Beejapoor guns, and that point of defence no longer remained to the Mahomedans. Thousands of the enemy's
foot-men, in compact masses, were charging disordered
groups of men huddled together, who made a vain resistance. Great numbers of horses were careering
madly about, but, for the most part, the troop-horses
were still at their pickets, and were now protected by
the Mahrattas. It was evident that the surprise had
been as complete and irretrievable as at the fort.

Casting his eyes round this field, in sickening apprehension—indeed, in almost hopeless despair—the
young Khan looked towards the tents where he had left
his sister and Lurlee. The tents were standing, but the
outer enclosure walls were thrown down, and a crowd of
followers and soldiers were apparently struggling together in the plunder of what they contained. The place
was apart from the field itself, and Fazil pointed to it ;
he could not speak.

The men with him had had no time for thought. From
the moment the Khan had died at Pertabgurh till
they drew rein on the eminence over the camp, they
had ridden for life. But the worst was now evident ;
and what they had hoped to find, was gone. The conviction that all their companions,—those whom they
had loved in life, were dead, at once fell upon their

hearts; and Bulwunt Rao, and many another rough
veteran, burst into passionate weeping.

Fazil appeared calm, but it was the calm of desperation and of misery. "Why do you weep, friends?"
he said. "They are all dead; why should we live?
Death is better than dishonour! Come and see—
Bismilla!"—and he turned his horse's head in the
direction of the tents.

None thought of the risk. "Bismilla!" shouted the
men, as, with teeth hard set for a last struggle in life,
they rode a mad race to their old camp. Near it they
passed many a familiar face lying upturned to the sun;
and, hewing their way through a crowd of plunderers
which were upon the area that had been covered
by the Khan's tents, Fazil saw that their walls were
torn down, and that no one remained; and in the bed
of the rivulet which, lying low, screened them from observation, they drew rein. In his misery Fazil would
have dismounted, and again sought death on foot, but
Bulwunt Rao saw the intention, and prevented it, as
he had done before.

"No, no, Meah," he said roughly; "you are our
master now; and as the Gods have enabled me to save
you once to-day, so we will all try again. If they you
sought have been taken, they are in honourable safety
with the Rajah: if they are dead, there is no help but
in submission to God's will."

A shout from several of the men caused Fazil to look
round. He saw some persons running towards the
party who had emerged from the thick jungle on the

other side of the stream.   They were grooms who had
hidden themselves.

One of them clasped Fazil's knees. "They are safe,"
he cried; "Meah, they are gone this way with the
hunchback and Ashruf, who would not let us follow
lest we should be seen.   They went down the river;
and see! here are their tracks.   Come!"

What need to speak more now?   The new interest
absorbed all other considerations.   Several of the
grooms were good trackers, and the hoof-marks of the
two ponies could not be mistaken.   They knew them
well.

Late in the afternoon—often bewildered in deep
silent forests, often thrown out, often despairing of
success, often passing hard rocky ground where Fazil
could see no tracks whatever, but where Bulwunt Rao
and the trackers held their way with confidence, a
small group of people were discovered, from a knoll
where the trackers stood for a time uncertain, sitting
near a large banian tree, on the bank of a mountain
stream.

At a little distance, too, from them, sat a few men
armed with matchlocks, who were apparently guarding
the rest.

Fazil and the scouts approached, cautiously leading
his horse; and the first greeting was a rough one
from the guards, who raised their guns to fire; but the
next, a frantic cry of welcome from the hunchback
and Ashruf, who ran forward and prostrated themselves
before him.

"O Meah, they are safe—they· are safe!" cried Lukshmun, rising first. "Come and see," he cried, bursting into tears; "and the Gods have sent thee."

Hearing his cry, Goolab rushed forward, clasping his knees, and, unable to speak, was sobbing passionately.

Yes, they were safe—Lurlee and Zyna. A rude bower of leafy branches had been hastily made, with a screen of boughs twisted into stakes in front; and so concealed were they by the thick brushwood, apart from the grassy glade, that the little commotion which Fazil's coming had caused, had not been heard by them. Having dismounted, and preceded by old Goolab, who, in her uncontrollable joy, now ran before, screaming the news of his arrival, he entered the enclosure,—and the two desolate women, whose utter despair nothing as yet had soothed or alleviated, fell upon his neck and wept aloud.

How long they sat into the night they could not tell. Kakrey, the Mahratta officer who had followed the party by Moro Trimmul's order, had overtaken them; and, touched by the beauty and sorrow of the women, had not molested them. The nearest Mahomedan garrison was Kurrar, a town at some distance; but he had engaged to guide and protect them thither, and the reward promised by Lurlee was at once confirmed, and even enhanced by Fazil. Kakrey had already told them that the Khan's escape was impossible; and they were thus prepared for the sad news which Fazil brought.

Kakrey decidedly objected, however, to Fazil's horse-

men, and even to Lukshmun and Ashruf ; they were
strangers, and would be inevitably suspected. Fazil
and his men must take another road, he said ; and the
ladies must submit to hardships among mountain villages and rough tracks for some days. They had no
other chance of escape but in disguise, and alone with
him.   He had already procured rough food and coarse
clothes, and there was little time for rest ; ere the
morning he must take them away.

Poor Lurlee! All night while Fazil sat there, she
had pored over the book of astrological diagrams in a
hopeless puzzle of mind. Why should she have been
mistaken? Why should her husband have died who
had left her so hopeful in the morning? Were they all
wrong? was all this, the faith of her life, false?

It seemed so ; but one thing was at least certain,
that Tara's nature and Fazil's were alike ; and she appeared, in spite of her grief, to return to this discovery
with a peculiar zest. " I am not wrong," she said, " in
this; look !"—but we will spare the detail. She was too
much bewildered by far, to understand as yet the loss
that had befallen her, nor was she at all convinced that
she was a widow. No, the stars could not be wrong ;
and for all they could say, she only believed the more
that the Khan would return. "Who had seen him die ?"

Fazil was convinced of Kakrey's good faith. Bulwunt
Rao unhesitatingly answered for him. They were neigh-
bours, and had been boys together. Fazil's promises
of reward were too profuse to have aught in competi-
tion with them.   It was hard to persuade Zyna that he

must leave her again; but as they were situated, they could not remain together, and must separate. For Fazil would not leave his men, and he determined, with Bulwunt and the hunchback, to hover as long as possible about the vicinity of Wye. He might be joined by other fugitives, he might rescue many of his people, and even make head against the enemy; above all, perhaps he might get news of Tara, and assist her. He should avoid the Mahratta horse, and with a guide like Bulwunt Rao, and one of Kakrey's followers, who volunteered to accompany him, he could either conceal himself or advance as needful.

So, with many tears, and almost despairing, Lurlee and Zyna, dressed as peasant women in the coarsest clothes, left him ere morning dawned. Lurlee was not remarkable; but the fair skin and beautiful features of Zyna were often objects of wondering interest and admiration among the mountain peasantry, as they journeyed on.

.   .   .   .   .   .

Three days afterwards, Fazil and his men, who had been joined by other stragglers on foot and on horseback, were lying during the day in the place of concealment which had been chosen by Kakrey's follower, and approved of by Bulwunt Rao and the hunchback. In the depth of the jungle near Wye, there was a large banian tree, planted by a small temple now deserted, because of some evil repute. The tree had flourished while the temple had decayed, and was large enough, with its offsets, to have sheltered thousands.

The outside boughs trailed on the ground, screening everything within, where the bare, gaunt branches, and the naked roots falling from them, rose high into the air, covered above with a thick foliage.   A bright rill sparkled past the tree ; grass was abundant on the hill-sides, and a liberal price for grain had induced some villagers near, to supply the men's wants for a few days.   Every day, the hunchback and the boy Ashruf, disguising themselves as mendicants, had sung ballads in the town of Wye, in order to gain information of passing events.

They were lying concealed in this hiding-place when, in the afternoon of the third day, the hunchback broke in upon Fazil and some others sitting together.   " Bid them all go away," he cried excitedly ; " I have strange news, Meah, for thee,—for thine ear only."

The men rose and went to a distance.   " Can it be of his father ?" they said.

No, it was not of him ; he was beyond all hope now, and his bloody head festering in the sun above the gate of Pertabgurh.

"Meah," said the man, in a low voice, "Tara the Moorlee, is alive, but they are going to burn her to-morrow ; and I saw them taking wood to the river-side to make the pile.   They say the Goddess came to her at Pertabgurh, and told her, before the Rajah, to be a Sutee, and he is going to make a great show of her to the people.   I waited till I saw her come into Wye in a palankeen, and I would have told her you were here, but I could not get near her for the crowd—they were throwing flowers upon her. The people do not know her name, but I knew her: it is Tara. O Meah, you will not let the Bramhuns do this!"

"By Allah and the Prophet, no!" cried the young man, starting to his feet. "Dost thou know the place?"

"I—I can lead a Durôra* on the house," said Lukshmun hesitatingly. "God forgive me, it is not the first I have led, and I observed it all before I left."

"Where is Bulwunt Rao? Call him."

"He is asleep," replied Lukshmun; "I will go and bring him."

"Meah wants you; come," he said to Bulwunt Rao, after waking him; and when he joined Fazil, all was told him; and the three men consulted long and earnestly as to how the girl might be rescued.

"O were but Rama and a score of Pahar Singh's Ramoosees here," said Lukshmun, "we could go and bring her to you to-night, without waking her; but your Mussulmans would make but a poor hand of that work."

So, after discussing the subject in every way, there seemed no chance of success but in an effort to carry her off from the pile itself. The attempt might succeed or fail; but the men who would undertake it were at least desperate, and to abandon the girl to her fate without endeavouring to rescue her, was not to be thought of. In any case, they must leave their

* Gang robbery at night by armed men with lighted torches.

hiding-place on the morrow, or starve.   A long march
might take them at once beyond the disturbed country; and they were not, in their present mood, likely
to falter in their project.

Tara!   Her name aroused a thousand sweet memories.   The day after the interview with the Rajah, she
was to have been demanded as a subject of their King;
and, in the Rajah's apparently submissive mood, Fazil
had anticipated no refusal.   What had happened to place
her in the situation in which she was, he could not con-
jecture; but Bulwunt Rao and Lukshmun understood
at once that she was the victim of Bramhun intrigues
excited by Moro Trimmul, and rejoiced in the prospect of frustrating his intentions.   Finally, the whole
project was explained to the men; and in their hearty
acquiescence, and in the excitement of a new and
desperate action, the young Khan lay down that night,
and, for the first time since the slaughter, slept
soundly.

CHAPTER XXII.

MEANWHILE, the Shastree, Anunda, and Radha, were pressing on as fast as the nature of their travelling would allow. The Shastree had a palankeen, for he was still weak, and the women rode; but as he gained strength, he was able to ride in turn.

At first their stages were necessarily short, with frequent halts; but as they proceeded, they had increased the daily distance; and the news of the action at Pertabgurh, which had spread over the country with incredible rapidity, made them more and more anxious to reach Wye, and ascertain Tara's fate. All attempts to trace her on the road were fruitless. The army had passed, but in the confusion attendant upon its progress, individuals could not be traced or distinguished.

At the last stage before Wye they found the village where they rested in much excitement. It was understood that a Sutee would take place in the town the next day; and though it was not known who the person was, the certainty that such a ceremony would occur was beyond question; and it was evident that people from all the country round, would attend it.

Anunda had not been at Wye since her youth.   Her
parents, who had resided there, were long since dead,
and she knew, vaguely only, of some distant relatives.
The Shastree, however, in his professional expeditions,
had frequently visited the town which, from the number of Bramhun families residing there, was then, as
it still is, the seat of much learning, and, from its
many temples on the bank of the Krishna river,
esteemed sacred.

The chief priest of one of those temples, Vishnu
Pundit, was an old friend and antagonist in scientific
and literary discussions, and Vyas Shastree knew he
was sure of a hearty welcome, even if his coming were
not formally announced.   But considering that his
wives might be an inconvenience, he had sent a note
on by a messenger, who had engaged to deliver it by
daylight at furthest; and as they set out for their last
march, it was in hopeful, perhaps joyful anticipation
of news of Tara, by which their long suspense would
be ended.

Mingling with the parties, therefore, which thronged
the roads to the town, and hearing many speculations
as to the nature of the Sutee, but nothing definite,
the travellers passed on as rapidly as possible ; and a
fairer scene than the bed of the sacred stream, with
its hundreds of bathers in the sparkling waters, the
temples on its banks, and the broad flights of steps
leading to the river, could hardly be imagined ; but
there was one object in particular upon which all their
interest centred.   In the middle of a broad bed of

sand near the stream, some men were already piling
logs of wood into a square mass, and pouring oil on
them; fixing tall poles at the sides, and hanging garlands of flowers and wreaths of leaves to them. The
pile was large, and would soon be completed for the
sacrifice.

Vyas Shastree rode to the spot, and inquired of the
men—they were Bramhun priests—for whom the preparations were being made. They did not know they
said,—it was a state matter. When the Sutee came
there to die, she would be seen. Meanwhile she was
at Vishnu Pundit's house, and he might go and see
her, and worship her, as others were doing.

At Vishnu Pundit's house! The place to which
he was going! Certainly, then, he should see the
woman, whoever she might be, that was to be burned.
"Had her husband died, then, last night?" he asked.
If he had, the Pundit's house must be impure, and he
must look elsewhere for lodgings.

"No; the Sutee was in pursuance of a vow," they
said,—"not an ordinary one, and an effigy would be
burned with her."

The Shastree was puzzled, and rode on, musing
much at the strangeness of the act, and unable to
account for it satisfactorily. Such sacrifices, from such
motives, were no doubt meritorious, but they were un-
common.

He was not far distant now from their destination,
and, joining Anunda, who, riding a stout ambling
pony, was forcing her way through the crowd, followed

by the litter in which sat Radha, he bade her come on
leisurely, and himself urged his horse forward as
quickly as the crowded streets would allow, to his
friend's house. Vishnu Pundit himself was standing
at the door of the outer court opening into the street,
across which some men were tying garlands of green
leaves and flowers. Seeing the Shastree advancing, he
came to him, and, assisting him to dismount, embraced
him warmly.

"I received your note," he said; "but I have had
no time to reply to it. I have no room for you, old
friend, owing to the Sutee whom the Maharaja has
sent to me—that is, not till to-morrow; but meanwhile
my neighbour the Josee gives you one of the courts of
his house. Take the ladies there," he added to an
attendant, "as they arrive. But do you, Vyas Shastree, come with me. I must speak with you alone.
Ah, we had mourned you dead—yet how wonderful it
is that you are here, and to-day, too! Come, I have
much to say to you that is strange—most strange."

The Shastree followed him curiously into an inner
court—one like that in his own house at Tooljapoor,
where he taught his pupils. Numbers of people were
pressing through the outer court, bearing offerings for
worship; but in the place they went to, they were
alone, and the Pundit closed the door.

"Vyas Shastree," he said, looking at him intently
as they sat down, and speaking with irrepressible concern and grief in his voice, "O friend! O dear old
friend! I have dark news for thee to-day. Alas! and

woe to me that I have to tell it! Hast thou a daughter named Tara?"

"I have come to seek her—followed her thus far—what of her?" replied the Shastree, sickening with apprehension—"what of her?"

"She was a priestess of Toolja Mata at Tooljapoor, was she not?" asked the Pundit.

"She was so, friend, and the Mahomedans carried her off. But they spared her honour! O say they spared her honour!" he exclaimed piteously, and stretching forth his hands.

"She was an honoured guest with them, friend, and would that—— O how shall I say the rest?" he thought,—"how explain this misery? Alas, what evil fate hath sent him to-day!"

"Thou art keeping something from me," said the Shastree, striving to be calm. "If—if Tara—my daughter—What is it, O friend? we have suffered much suspense, much anxiety:—for her sake have taken this weary journey; and we hoped to have found her here among friends, perhaps with thee. What hast thou to say of her? Did they not give her up, as we heard they would? Have—they——"

"Yes, she is here," returned the Pundit hesitatingly, and turning away his head in a vain attempt to repress his tears. "She—she—is a widow, is she not?" he asked.

Then the truth flashed upon the wretched father with fearful rapidity. That crowd of people; that hideous pile of logs: the preparations and rejoicing

were for her death—for Tara's, and after all he was too
late to save her !   O, if he had only hurried on,—if he
had only left home sooner !   But thought now had no
definite form.   It was a confused and conflicting chaos,
utterly uncontrollable.   " Where have ye put her ? " he
asked, in a low husky voice, as, with a sickening pressure at his heart, his features assumed the haggard expression of weary age.

   " Friend," said the Pundit, passing his arm around
him and trying to raise him up, " come and see.   Such
poor honour as we can do to her on earth while she is
with us, we have already done and will continue.   Come
and see.   Arise ! If thou art a true Bramhun, hear
this, like a God on earth as thou art, and believe it for
her eternal glory.   How few are chosen for this sacrifice ! true jewels only are they—pure gold, to be purified in the fire ! "

   " In the fire," he echoed dreamily—rising, and supporting himself against a pillar in the room with
a hopeless gesture of despair — " in the fire !—I
tell thee, Vishnu Punt," he added presently, " it
cannot be : who has wrought this cruelty upon her ?
Who has done it ? Of her own act and will it could
not have been ; but if the council have dared to—
to——"

   " She thought you dead—you, her mother, and your
new wife," replied the Pundit, interrupting him.   " She
was suffering hopeless persecution and insult, and in
the temple at Pertabgurh she stood before the Mother's
image, and declared herself Sutee before the Bram-

huns. Could we recall the words? I was present. Had it been my own daughter I had been thankful. O Shastree! it was her glory!"

Vyas Shastree could not reply. "Let me see her and hear it from her own lips," was all he could utter at all intelligibly.

"Certainly, if thou wilt," replied the Pundit; "she is ready to go even now, but the hour is not come. And yet, Vyas Shastree, beware; would it not be better she believed you all dead, and so died happily looking for you, than, seeing you alive, be shaken in her determination? Will not the love of life come out of this, and rise defiant to all convictions? Alas! alas! my friend, it is not for me to come between your love and her mother's and that poor child; but beware! she cannot retract now and live, otherwise than in dishonour and infamy; and hereafter you will cry in agony to the Goddess Mother, she had better have died —and will be guilty of sin in having shaken her faith if she live. Did you refuse when she was called before?——"

The Shastree groaned, and his breath came as it were in broken gasps. He was trembling violently. "I— I—must see her," he said. "Let her decide;" and unable to stand, he again sat down.

"Drink some water, Vyas Shastree; it will refresh you," said the Pundit, bringing a vessel full from the end of the apartment.

"No, no, friend," he replied, putting it away, "I will not eat or drink till this is past, if it is to be. Let

us go. I am no less a Bramhun than thyself. If
the Mother whom she serves has spoken to her, it is
well—she will go to her. My child! O my child!"
cried the miserable man in his agony. "O Mother,
what hath she done for this to come to her—she, so
pure, to need the sacrifice of fire! O Toolja Mata, was
it needed? Come, Shastree, I am ready now," he continued, after a pause. "Do not delay."

The Pundit said nothing. He again passed his arm
round his friend to support him, and, leading him to a
door in the further end of the room, opened it. A small
court intervened between the place where they stood
and a larger one beyond, the door of which was open,
and showed a crowd of people, mostly women, struggling to approach some object beyond. All had garlands of flowers in their hands, and vessels wherewith
to pour libations. Suddenly, there was a shrill piercing
scream; and the crowd swayed to and fro, retreating
backwards before some priests who were putting the
people out.

"What can have happened?" cried the Pundit,
hastening on. "Come quickly."

Vyas Shastree felt instinctively that Anunda had
seen Tara, and he rapidly followed his friend. As he
entered the next court, he saw at a glance all he
yearned for—all that he most dreaded to see.

A bower as it were, of trellis-work, had been fitted
up in the large apartment of the Pundit's house which
was raised slightly from the ground, and it was covered
with heavy garlands of green leaves and flowers, as

though for a bridal. In the narrow doorway of this bower stood a slight female figure, richly dressed in a bright crimson silk dress, striving to put away the arm of a Bramhun priest,—who was preventing her from stepping forth,—and struggling with him. The face was full of horror and misery, and the eyes flashing with excitement and despair. Before her, without, lay an elderly woman senseless on the ground, supported by a girl and several other women who were weeping bitterly. Tara, Anunda, Radha!—how had they met? Alone, he could have met Tara firmly, but with them? Not now, however, did the Shastree's heart fail: no matter what followed, honour or dishonour, he would not leave his child. Darting forward past the Pundit, pushing aside some women, who, screaming senselessly, would not be put out,—Vyas Shastree leaped upon the basement of the room, and, dragging away the Bramhun priest, stood by his child. "Tara, O my life! O my child!" he cried passionately, "come forth, come to us!"

It was the effort of an instant only, for the attendant priests had seized him and drawn him back forcibly, while they held him up. "Thou canst not touch her now without defilement," one said, who knew him. "She is Sutee, O Vyas Shastree, and pure from thy touch, even; she is bathed and dressed for the sacrifice."

"Tara, Tara!" gasped the unhappy man, not heeding the words. "Tara, come forth — come; I, thy father, call thee! O my child, do not delay; come, we will go away—far away, to the Mother——"

To the Mother! Perhaps if he had not said this, Tara would have been unable to repress those last fearful yearnings to life which tore her heart; but the echo fell on her own spirit heavily and irrepressively. To the Mother! Yes, in her great misery, all she could see in her mental agony—what she saw in the temple at Pertabgurh,—all that she had dwelt upon since,—were the glowing ruby eyes of the Mother far away at Tooljapoor, glittering, as she thought, in glad anticipation of her coming. The same Bramhun priest who was preventing her egress when her mother appeared, had again crossed his arms before the door. As she saw her father advance, Tara staggered back affrighted; it was as though he had risen from the dead; and at his despairing cry the girl could not have restrained herself, had not the echo of his last words fallen on a heart which, though wellnigh dead to life, had rallied for a while to its purest affections; —but only for a while.

"Thou canst not move hence," said the Bramhun priest. "Cry 'Jey Toolja! Jey Kalee!' O Tara! thou wilt not now deny the Mother!—all else is dead to thee."

No, she could not deny her now—she would not. With that strange light in her eyes—that seemingly supernatural force in her actions, which the people thought the emanation of divinity, Tara's spirit was rallied by the priest's words. "Jey Toolja Mata!" she

cried, stretching her arms into the air; "I am true, O
Mother! I am true; and even these shall not keep
me from thee now!"

Strange enthusiasm! stranger fortitude, which, having no terror of a horrible death, has carried on its
votaries even to the flames with a constancy and devotion worthy of a nobler fate! In other cases, earthly
love—the desire to free a beloved object from the pains
of suffering for life's errors, and insure final and perfect rest to its immortal spirit—or a gratification of
the all-absorbing grief which looks on present death
as the only remedy for despairing sorrow—might exist;
but here was no such incentive. The spiritual portion
of the girl's nature was alone concerned in the question; and that, once excited by position and circumstance, had insured a more perfect observance of her
vow than earthly passion.

A strange enthusiasm indeed! Ah yes,—from the
period to which we can trace it in a dim legendary
superstition of the past, through the two thousand
years since the Greek philosopher stood on the banks
of Indus and Ganges and recorded it, to the time when
it was made to cease under the stern power of a purer
creed—how many have died, alike self-devoted, alike
calm, alike fearless! Women with ordinary affections,
ordinary habits of life, suddenly lifted up into a sub-
limity of position,—even to death,—by an influence
they were unable to repress or control—barbarous and
superstitious if you will, but, sublime.

Tara had conquered. Her father hung upon her

words with an absorbing reverential fear, as the last
sound of them died away and was drowned in the
shouts of " Jey Toolja Mata !" which burst from the
Bramhuns around, and were taken up by the people
without, whose frantic efforts to gain entrance were
redoubled.   He had heard her doom from her own
lips, and, believing in the inspiration which prompted
them, his head fell on his bosom ; then the men, feeling
his frame relax, let him go, and he fell prostrate before
his child, and worshipped her.

They had removed Anunda into an inner room, and
her senses had rallied under the care paid to her.   As
he rose with a despairing gesture, and turned away
from his child, the Shastree sought Anunda.   " There
is no hope," he said, " wife—none.   It is her own act,
and the Mother takes her.   She is doomed, and I saw
it in her eyes.   It is enough that we have come to see
it ; she is already gone far beyond us, and we dare not
recall her."

He closed the door, and within were Radha, Anunda,
and himself.   What he said to them — how he con-
soled them, no one ever knew ; but after a while they
came forth, bathed and purified themselves, and went
and sat silently near their daughter.

Now, they looked at her calm, glorious beauty as
she sat within the bower, decked for the sacrifice, with
heavy wreaths of jessamine flowers about her head,
and rich golden ornaments about her person,—their
faith, cruel as it was, bid them rejoice.   No more con-
tumely now, no more reproach, no more sin, no more

persecution. Her little history was told them by Vishnu Pundit, and believed. Tara was pure, and if the Mother had called her—even through the fire—she must go.

So they sat listening to her, as she recited those passages from the Holy Books which her father loved, relative to humble and yet glorious martyrs like herself,—men and women who had undergone the trial, and were at last free. Sometimes she spoke to them calmly—told them how she wished her ornaments to be disposed of—what charitable donations were to be given in her name—what messages were to be delivered to her friends, and the servants who had tended her; but she never spoke of the past, nor alluded to her parents, as though she had believed them dead. She never mentioned Afzool Khan or his family; she shed no tear, nor did any human weakness appear to mingle with the rapt devotion which it was evident filled her mind, and absorbed every other faculty.

So they sat—the girl within, the father and mother and Radha without, the bower—their eyes blinded by tears, their voices choked with sobs. Tara bid them not to weep; but that emotion could not be denied. No one dared to intrude upon that last terrible severing of earthly ties. And so the priests chanted, and the shadows fell eastwards, and lengthened.

CHAPTER XXIII

AFTER a while, they heard the sound of drums and cymbals, and of the rude Mahratta pipes, advancing up the street, playing a wailing, mournful air, and the musicians stopped at the door of the outer court. The people within fell back, and made a lane of egress, and Tara rose and came forth from the bower. Once she prostrated herself before her father and mother, and those with her saw a shiver—whether of grief, despair, or terror, who could say—pass through her body ; but she recovered herself quickly, and as she stood on the upper step of the basement, she asked for flowers, and, throwing handfuls among the crowd, descended the steps into the court.

Then slowly on through the people, who worshipped her as she passed; and out of the court into the street, where an open litter, such a one as she had sat in when they made her a priestess of the temple at Tooljapoor, awaited her. Carried in this, as in a triumphant procession, and with baskets full of flowers before her, she threw them among the crowd. As she proceeded through the streets, shouts from the people around her,

and from those on house-tops, trees, and terraces, were
redoubled; many women shrieked, and most prayed
aloud for the Sutee. The clash of the music increased,
and the march played, was one of victory; while companies of Bramhuns, bare-headed, joined the procession,
singing and chanting the hymns of death. So, on
through the town, past the holy temples, and into the
river bed, where thousands awaited her, and set up a
hoarse shouting as they saw her first. What was the
first honour of life as a priestess, to this glory of its
death?

She reached the pile, now covered with fluttering
pennons, and streamers,—orange, white, and crimson,
—and thousands of garlands, which the people had
hung or thrown upon it as votive offerings since the
morning,—and the litter was set down for her to alight.
It was with difficulty the crowd was kept back so as
to form a space round the pile which would admit of
her passing in procession; but it was cleared at last by
the Bramhuns, and the people hung back awestruck
and staring at the beauty of the victim.

Tara looked at the pile; but there was that strange
ecstasy glowing in her eyes which appeared to have
rendered her unconscious of its purport, or of all else
about her. Sometimes she cast up her eyes with a
strange bright smile, and nodded as if she were saying,
as perhaps she did, " I come, I come." Again she
looked round her dreamily. The roar of the people's
voices, the clash of cymbals, the shrill screams of the
pipes and horns, the hoarse braying of trumpets, and

the continuous beating of deep-toned drums, were
around her, drowning the sound of words, and the
bitter sobs and low shrieks of her mother and Radha
at her side.   Her father's spirit seemed to have risen
to the need of the occasion, for he stood near her, joining the solemn chant, which blended with, and softened, the rude music.

As she stood, the Bramhuns worshipped her, and
poured libations before her and on her feet, touched
her forehead with sacred colour, and put fresh garlands
over her neck.   Then the last procession was formed,
in which she would walk round the pile thrice, and
ascend it, as her last act of ceremonial observance.
Now, and before she had to take off her ornaments,
she turned her full gaze on it, and they thought, who
were watching her, that she seemed to comprehend its
purpose.   A huge platform of logs, black with oil
and grease that had been poured upon them, strewed
with camphor and frankincense, which had been scat-
tered lavishly by the people in their votive offerings,
and smeared with red powder.   A rude step had been
made for Tara to ascend by, and on the summit some
bright cloths were laid as a bed, where she might re-
cline, upon which a small effigy of a man, rudely conceived and dressed, had been placed.   Her marriage-
bed in the spiritual sense of the sacrifice, on which,
through fire, she would be united to her husband.
The whole was garish, hideous, and cruel.   Face to face
with death so horrible, so imminent, the girl seemed
to shiver and gasp suddenly, and sank down swooning.

Vishnu Pundit, and another old Bramhun, raised her up. "It must not be," they said to each other in a whisper ; "she must not fail now, else shame will come upon us."

Moro Trimmul was near her also, and had been one to seize her mechanically as she was falling. To him the scene was like some mocking phantasy, which held him enthralled, while it urged him to action. Since he had murdered Gunga, his evil spirit had known no rest ; no sleep had come to him, except in snatches more horrible than the reality of waking. Again and again he had felt the rush of the girl's warm blood upon his hands, and the senseless body falling from his arms into the black void of air, to be no more seen or heard—and had started up in abject fear. Day or night, it was the same ;—the short struggle, the frantic efforts of the girl for life, his own maddened exertions to destroy her, were being acted over and over again. Every moment of his life was full of them ; and nothing else, do what he might, go where he would, came instead. He had eaten opium in large quantities, but it only made the reality of this hideous vision more palpable, and exaggerated all its details. He had busied himself deeply in the arrangements consequent upon the victory and the distribution of plunder, but with no effect. Haunted by Gunga's murder on the one hand, by Tara's determination to die as Sutee on the other, the remonstrances of Maloosray and other friends only irritated him the more. They had endeavoured to restrain him from going to Wye to see

her burned, but with no result—he had broken from
them and ridden over alone that morning.

Soon after he arrived, he heard that Vyas Shastree
and his sister were already there, and he had sought her,
and in his former desperate manner, threatened and
persuaded in turn. It might be that, having experience of these threats, Radha no longer feared them, or
that the position she now occupied was so utterly hopeless as regarded Tara, that even he must see that it
was useless to persecute her further. As a last resource,
he had proposed to some of his own men, desperate
and licentious as himself, to attack the procession, and
carry Tara away; but, hardened as they were, the
sacrilege of violently abducting a Sutee, was an impossible crime against their faith, and his proposal
had been rejected.

He was there, therefore, alone. He had bathed and
performed the needful ceremonies with the other
Bramhuns, and the thought that he should at least see
Tara die, came, for the time, like sweet revenge into
his heart, feeding his evil passions and sustaining them.
Devils both, Tara and Gunga, witches and sorceresses.
What matter if both died horrible deaths ? it was the
penalty of their crimes; and in such thoughts a mo-
mentary consolation was offered by the mocking fiend
at his heart, to be whirled away to the chaos of despair, in which Gunga seemed writhing in her blood,
and Tara tossing her arms in the agony of the fire.

Thus he had walked with her, almost beside her,
from the house, through the streets, to the pile by the

river - side. In the litter, surrounded by chanting priests, she was unapproachable; but, sinking to the earth helplessly before him, she seemed once more fated to be his prey.

"Tara, Tara," he whispered quickly and sharply in her ear, as, helping her to rise, he passed his arm under her. "Come, O beloved! save thyself, even now— even now. I can do it. Come, O beloved!"

The words and his hot breath on her cheek roused the girl more completely than aught else could have done. She did not speak, but she arose, strong and defiant, and, shaking him off, pushed him away so violently from her that he staggered and fell backwards.

.   .   .   .

For some time past, a body of horsemen, with their faces tied up, after the fashion of Mahratta cavaliers, the housings of their horses weather-stained, and their arms rusty and unpolished, had moved about the bed of the river and the bank beyond, and as the procession advanced to the pile, pressed on nearer to the crowd. It might be a hundred men or more; and the leader, who was a Mahratta, spoke cheerfully to the people who addressed him, and told them of his pursuit of the Mahomedans, and the raid they had done into the Beejapoor country, from which they were only now returning in time to see the show before they went home to the fort.

Our old friend Bulwunt Rao had become spokesman and ostensible leader; and the hunchback rode with

him, and bandied words with the bystanders freely
but in good humour. With them, too, was Fazil
Khan, who joined heartily in the rough jokes which
were passing—many, at his own expense of ragged
clothes, rusty arms, and gaunt features; and thus the
band pressed on to the very skirts of the crowd, as
if to see the Sutee, but actually to take up the position necessary for their adventure. During the day
they had passed several bodies of Mahratta horse,
but had been taken for a similar party, and had as
yet been unchallenged; and in the crowd, their bold
confident demeanour, and the ready replies given to
all questions, with the certainty among the people
that every Mahomedan soldier had perished at Pertabgurh, or was a prisoner, prevented any suspicion of
their real character.

Bulwunt Rao had seen Sutee rites before. They
had watched the procession issue from the town, and
he knew Tara would alight from the litter when she
arrived at the pile. As she did so—as the litter was
carried aside, and before the procession around the
pile was formed—they had determined to ride in upon
the crowd and bear her away. They had no fear of
the result; there was not a doubt among them. They
knew that every horseman in the town would be present there, unarmed and on foot, and that miles would
be passed by them ere pursuit could be made. Their
old hiding-place was not known, and beyond was
open country; and if a long ride by night, what fear?
—the horses were fresh and well fed.

"Be ready, Meah," said Bulwunt Rao, in a low voice. "See, they are clearing a space around the pile for her to walk. Holy Krishna! how beautiful she is! 'Jey Kalee! Jey Toolja Mata!'" he shouted with the crowd. Then turning to the hunchback, he bade him go round the rear of the party and see they all kept together. "As one man, Lukshmun, when they hear our shout, let them follow."

So they advanced nearer and nearer, and the crowd on foot, unable to resist the pressure of the horses, gave way before them. The sword of every man was loosened in its sheath, and a few of the rear men, who had matchlocks with lighted matches slung over their backs, unslung them, and held them on their saddlebows ready for use. If any one had noticed Fazil Khan, they would have seen him smoothing a cushion, as it were, of cloths upon the pommel of his saddle, while he wakened his horse with an occasional touch of his leg, and kept him excited for a sudden rush.

He moved up close to Bulwunt Rao. "If I fall, dear friend, in this," he said, "tell them how it was, and take the men to them. Do not wait for me; let them do with me as they list."

Bulwunt Rao smiled. "Fear not, Meah," he replied. "Ride thou in to her, and trust to us for the rest."

Fazil's teeth were hard set, and his heart throbbed quick; but he was calm and cool. It was no time for chance work, and there must not be any mistake now. He felt his sword was loose in the sheath, and smiled to himself. The men had orders not to strike unarmed

people; but if any resisted, there would be some revenge for Pertabgurh he thought, and, looking round,
saw the rough faces of his followers in thick array behind him, holding in their horses as though for a race.

They saw Tara alight. Fazil was not a stone's-throw
distant, and perhaps she might see him, but she did
not. He was not in her thoughts now; the agony of
relinquishing him had passed from her in the despair
of life long ago. They saw her suddenly sink down,
and Vishnu Punt and Moro Trimmul stoop to raise
her up.

"Bismilla! Futteh-i-nubbee!" cried the young
Khan, as, pressing his horse's flanks, the animal
bounded forward. "Bismilla, brothers, Ya Alla! Ya
Alla!"

"Ya Alla! Ya Alla!" shouted the rest behind, as
they too gave their horses the rein, and all dashed
forward furiously.

Some men with poles and sticks struck at Fazil,
Bulwunt, and Lukshmun, as they came on first, but
none there had arms. It was as Tara, watching the
effect of her effort against Moro Trimmul, stood apart,
with flashing eyes and heaving bosom—belonging for
the moment to the world she had abjured—that the
hoarse shout of the horsemen fell upon her ear. She
looked at them for a moment; she saw people go down
before them, trampled shrieking, under foot, and the
weapons flashing in the sunlight. Then two men
stopped for an instant—she was between them: both
stooped towards her at the same moment, and one

threw himself off his horse, and lifted her to the other's saddle.

As it was done, a man sprang at Fazil's horse's bridle, with a frantic execration, caught it, and jerked it violently. The noble beast, urged on—for Fazil saw the danger—partly reared, but was held down by the bridle; else it had fared ill perhaps with the young man—for Tara was not sensible now, and he could only hold her up with difficulty—had not Lukshmun been nigh.

" I never kill Bramhuns," he said through his teeth, "but thou art a devil;" and he struck at Moro Trimmul's bare neck with all his force. As the wretched man sank to the earth under the terrible wound, the hunch-back sprang to his horse, clambered upon it like a cat, and flourishing his bloody sword, though he struck no one, rode by Fazil's side onwards, unharmed.

No one opposed them ; the action was too sudden and too desperate. The crowd, also, was not so thick towards the river, and gave way before them ; and, dashing through the shallow ford, the horses throwing up the bright water in a cloud of sparkling drops, they galloped up the bank, and even then, were be-yond pursuit. A few of the matchlock-men, firing their pieces over the heads of the crowd beyond, shook them in defiance, as they turned to ride after their party ; and a few shots in return, the balls of which sang shrilly in the air over their heads, were fired after them by people in the throng with harmless effect.

It was long ere the party drew rein, and no one spoke.

Tara lay easily, supported on the cushion by Fazil's arms, and he watched anxiously for signs of returning consciousness. It came at last, as he felt her cling to him, and she looked up to his face, as they crossed a small streamlet leisurely, with a pleading look which could not be mistaken.

"Ah, fear not," he said; " fear not, beloved! Thou art safe now ; and that hideous pageant is far behind. Didst thou think, Tara, I would leave thee to die that frightful death without an effort ?"

The beauteous eyes opened again, and closed softly as the tears welled from them. The rapt glittering expression of religious enthusiasm had passed away, and left the world coming back fast into them, with all its tender interests and love, a thousandfold more powerful than before.

That night, another pile was lighted by the river-side, and a corpse, never removed from the spot where it fell, was burned upon it; but the pile of the Sutee remained, grim and black, and the garlands of flowers had withered in the next day's sun ere it was dismantled.

There were a thousand rumours current in the town for some days as to who could have done so bold a deed, but no one guessed the truth. Had Moro Trimmul lived, he could have told; but he had never spoken after the hunchback's sturdy death-blow. So the people believed that some of the starving Beejapoor cavalry, wandering about, had determined to attack the people collected for the Sutee, and plunder them of what they could; and that the rich ornaments which the Sutee herself had worn attracted their attention, and they had carried her off for them.

Some days afterwards, too, near a spot where the fugitives had rested for a while, the remains of a young woman, so much torn by wild beasts as to be unrecognisable, with some shreds of silken garments about them, were found by the village people. It was clear that a murder had been done, and the circumstances under which Tara had disappeared, rendered it probable that these remains were hers. So they were taken into Wye: and the miserable parents, believing them to be their daughter's, had them burned by the river-side in all honour and respect, and thenceforth believed her dead. They did not leave Wye immediately. The excitement and fatigue had exhausted the Shastree, who required rest; and the ceremonies consequent on Tara's death, and necessary purification, occupied some days; so Vishnu Pundit's persuasions prevailed, and they remained with him.

CHAPTER XXIV.

KHUNDOJEE KAKREY performed his promise faithfully. By secret mountain paths known to few, and through the dense forests of the tract which lies between Pertabgurh and Kurrar, on the right bank of the Krishna, the Mahratta guided his charge safely, and with as much comfort as the nature of the journey would admit of. The two women maintained their disguise of peasants, and Zyna's ability to speak Mahratta, as well as Lurlee's to speak Canarese, assisted in aiding the deception. By night Kakrey sought shelter of villages where he seemed to be well known, for a decent house was always ready for them to sleep in, the best delicacies of country farmhouses cooked for them: and frequently, not only the matron of the house, but other women of the village, attended to bathe them, and otherwise minister to their comfort.

But for all this, those days were remembered as a time of bitter grief and sore trial; the more difficult for Zyna to endure, because Lurlee could not be brought to believe that her husband was dead, and preserved throughout, a demeanour of hope, if not, indeed, of actual joy. "No one saw him die," she would say, " his body was not buried by them. They dare not say he is dead, and I will hear no more of it. When we are at Kurrar he will return, and we will go home to-gether." Again and again, too, were the astrological dia-grams consulted : but the lady was unable to find any error in them, and for the present they were to her far more conclusive than the report she had heard from Fazil, and it was a happy thing for her, perhaps, that the delusion lasted even as far as the town to which they were journeying.

With Zyna, however, there was no delusion. She had at once believed her brother's report. Kakrey, too, had told her that there was no hope of her father's existence. Of Tara's fate he knew nothing. Mourn-ing for him, therefore, and in miserable anxiety about her brother, Zyna had had to endure a twofold trial, which her naturally buoyant disposition and innate piety only, enabled her to sustain. Possibly, too, had she remained in one place it would have been more severe ; but, the daily movement—in a manner before unexperienced by her—the sense of freedom from re-straint in the wild country they traversed, the beautiful and, to her, wonderful mountains, forests, and natural objects of all kinds, which, brought up as she had been in the seclusion of a zenana, she had had no chance of seeing before—served to divert her mind from the terrible reality of her loss, to fill it with hope, and to render the sense of danger they incurred

in their escape to be blunted by the excitement of perpetual change.

Of the servants who had escaped with them, and
who joined Fazil's party, Goolab alone remained to
attend the ladies by permission of their guide. She
had been divested of every particle of Mahomedan
attire, and, dressed in a coarse Mahratta saree, with a
dab of red colour smeared on her forehead, and mounted
upon a small ambling bullock, passed readily for a Mahratta farmer's wife. In this ride, the old woman was
in her element; now guiding the docile animal she
rode, beside Lurlee, now beside Zyna, cheering them on
when they were fatigued, and often dismounting and
supporting them in places where the ponies hesitated
and had to be carefully led. Unless near a mountain
village, their guide, Kakrey, seldom approached them;
he was generally in advance with some of his men,
while others remained behind, guarding the rear.
When in motion, the party was made to resemble, as
far as possible, the appearance of people journeying
upon a pilgrimage, and small orange flags, carried
by several of the men, and fastened to the pommels
of the women's saddles, assisted and maintained the
deception.

It was on the afternoon of the fourth day that,
emerging from a rugged pass in the mountains, they
saw below them part of the wide plain of the Dekhan,
the blue waters of the Krishna river sparkling in the
sun, and the town, which they had hitherto only hoped
to reach. Great numbers of white tents were pitched

upon the plain near the fort, showing the presence of a considerable force, and the royal standard fluttered lazily in the evening breeze from its highest tower. It was a pleasant scene of quiet soft beauty, and seemed a true resting-place for the now weary and almost exhausted travellers. The last march had been a longer one than usual; for some of the way they had passed through village lands, in regard to the people of which Kakrey was not without apprehension : the country was becoming more open, and the danger of detection greater; nevertheless, he had guided them safely and truly, as he had promised.

It had been no easy matter to sustain the lady Lurlee that afternoon. All the confidence she had displayed hitherto, false as it was, seemed to have suddenly deserted her as she drew nigh to her destination ; and while they rested during the hottest part of the day, under some cool shade by the side of a rivulet, Zyna saw that the old diagrams were laid aside for once with a heavy sigh, and seemed to afford no comfort. She thought the evident weariness might be the result of a longer and rougher ride than usual, and tried to soothe Lurlee. "Only a few cose more, mother," she said, "and we are safe with our own people : do not fail now, when the end is so near ! "

" It matters not—what is the use of it ? " replied Lurlee—"who will care for us, now they are gone from us ? "

" The Blessed Alla, and the Prophet, and the

saints," answered Zyna devoutly, "and there is Fazil
too——"

"He could not love me, now that Tara is not with
me," returned Lurlee, interrupting Zyna.

"Tara, mother?"

"Yes, his soul will be gone away to her and to his
father, Zyna. He is dead," replied Lurlee sighing.
"I know it now. All day long the old man's face
has been before me, gashed and bloody, and I think,"
she said, passing her hand across her eyes, "that I
am not deceived now—no, not now."

"We shall know the best or worst soon, mother; but
Fazil could not have been deceived," replied Zyna.

"And thou hast not wept, Zyna! O hard heart!
Was he nothing to thee? It is the old who cannot
weep—the old like me."

Zyna's tears were falling fast, but she checked
them. "I would not grieve thee mother, need-
lessly," she said; "when Fazil comes, he will tell us
all."

"If I could see her, the daughter the good Alla gave
me, Zyna—the girl who softened my heart,—and give
her to him—it would be enough! but they took her
away, and she, too, is dead! Once," she continued
mysteriously, after a pause, and catching Zyna's arm—
"once since we were out in these wilds, she came to
me in a dream, and mocked me. She said she was
going to die, and go to her Mother, but she would come
to see me first. Ah, she was very beautiful, Zyna, and
smiled lovingly upon me in her old way. Now, when

she said that, it must have been near morning, when
we were asleep in the village where they gave us milk
to drink, and about the third watch of the night; but
I cannot understand what planet ruled the hour. Ah
me! I used once to do so, but the more I look at the
tables now, the more I fail."

"Trust in Alla, mother, not in them," replied
Zyna.

"I have no trust in them," muttered Lurlee gloomily
—"none now in anything; all have failed me, and
she most of all. O Tara! why didst thou go? O
my child, my child, whom Alla gave me when I had
none, and when thy mother died. Alas, why was I
mocked, Zyna? why did Alla take him too, who loved
me, and leave me here? O daughter, this is unjust
oppression, this——"

"Hush, mother! else Alla will hear thee, and be
angry, and the saints too; and can any one resist fate?
O mother, be patient!" said Zyna soothingly. "Only
for their help we had not escaped the slaughter, and
worse—dishonour; and yet we are here, and our
friends now are not far off."

"Your friends and Fazil's, girl!" she returned
tartly. "I have been of small account enough already
among ye, and am not likely to improve."

"Do not speak bitter words, mother, I beseech you,"
cried Zyna entreatingly. "We are your children—
indeed we are, and will never leave you. If Fazil
lives——"

"Peace!" rejoined the lady, interrupting her, "do

not let falsehood come into thy mouth, girl. Enough
for me that Tara is not, and thou art."

Zyna could never reply to Lurlee's caustic speeches,
least of all under the pressure of their mutual bereavement; and as they sat there they broke forth
from time to time from her without tear or sob—old
grievances—old jealousies—old allegations of neglect.
Matters which Zyna had utterly forgotten, seemed to
have rushed back on the lady's memory like a flood.
They were hard to endure ; and yet not so hard, Zyna
thought, as the false confidence, the fearful mockery
of truth and reality, which had lasted till then—that
disbelief in her father's death for which she could not
account.

"Ah, if Tara can only be rescued from them, there
may be some natural revulsion yet," thought the girl ;
and yet what hope of that ? She could not deceive
herself into a belief that Tara would be given up, or
that she could escape from her family ; perhaps, on
second thoughts, she would not desire it—but if it
could be so ? And amidst such conflicting thoughts,
and the endurance of Lurlee's dogged, desperate state
of mind, the afternoon's journey into Kurrar, though
the last, was indescribably more miserable than any
which had preceded it.

They descended the pass, and were once more on level
ground. "Hence to Beejapoor," said Goolab cheerily,
as she was leading Lurlee's pony down the last steep
descent, "there are no mountains—a child might ride
thither without trouble. Keep a good heart, therefore,

O my Khanum! trust in Alla, and the Prophet, and
the blessed Peer Khaderi, and thou wilt see it. I vow
Fatehas to the shrine, and to feed——"

"They are liars like thyself," retorted Lurlee savagely: "Peace, for a prating old fool as thou art! Did
not the planets tell me Afzool Khan was alive, and
now men say he is dead! After that, can I believe?
O woman, thou art mad—so keep thy tongue silent!"

Goolab thought her mistress mad—perhaps she was
so in some degree. Excitement, grief as yet without
vent, and heavy fatigue in a blazing sun to one un-
accustomed to exposure, might easily cause temporary
delirium, and it was with difficulty that she supported
her mistress upon her pony over the ground which intervened from the bottom of the pass to the town.
Shiverings had come on, and it was evident that the
poor lady might be seriously indisposed.

Several of Kakrey's Mahratta foot-soldiers, who had
guarded them, had run on to secure a lodging of some
kind, and the travellers were met at the town gate by
one who had returned to wait for the approaching
party, and he guided them on. Other parties had
reached the camp from the fatal field, and more were
still coming in daily, so that the arrival of the travellers was unnoticed, and from their disguise their persons and rank were quite unknown. To those who
saw them pass, they appeared women of the country
who had made a long journey that day, and were
utterly wearied; for Lurlee, closely muffled, was supported by Goolab, who walked by her side, with her

arm thrown round her waist; and Zyna, even more
entirely concealed from observation, leaned forward,
supporting herself on her arm, as if hardly able to
maintain her place on the saddle. Kakrey and his
followers had closed round them so as to protect them
from the jostling of the people in the narrow street
and crowded bazar of the town, and all cheered the
ladies by the assurance that the house secured for the
night was a good one, which belonged to a respectable
Mahomedan merchant, who had given part of it without hesitation on hearing for whom it was needed. It
is doubtful, indeed, whether either of them could have
supported their fatigue much longer.*

---

* Khundojee Kakrey's escort of the ladies of Afzool Khan's
family to Kurrar became known to Sivaji, and he was tried and
beheaded for—as it was esteemed—the act of treason.—*Mahratta
Chronicle.*

CHAPTER XXV.

A few steps further on, and Kakrey turned the ponies into a side street, and stopped at the handsome gateway of a respectable house. The steps up to the entrance being easy, the active mountain animals scrambled up them in turn, and their riders were thus taken at once into the first court. Then, when the gates were closed, Goolab lifted them from their seats; and the men, who had remained without, took possession of the guard-room inside the first archway, which, while it afforded ample accommodation, enabled them to continue their protection to the last.

Once more in private, and their mufflings removed, and as Goolab led Lurlee into the second court, they were met by a lady of middle age, who, attended by several servants, advanced and saluted them cordially, yet with a peculiar reverence.

"The wife and daughter of Afzool Khan are welcome to our poor house. O lady! why did you not advise me of your coming?"

"Who art thou?" asked Lurlee faintly, "and who told thee of us?"

" My husband was at his office in the bazar," replied
the lady, " and some men came asking for shelter for
noble travellers who were very weary. He asked who
they were, and was told of you. O lady, your steps
are fortunate, and Alla hath led you here to do us
honour. Many benefits hath my lord received from
the noble Khan, and there is much to repay—very
much."

" Have you hot water for a bath, lady?" cried Goolab,
interrupting her, " and some decent clothes instead of
these, and some food that noble ladies can eat? They
will be better than fine words. Alas! that for the
last four days we have eaten dry parched pease, dry
bread, garlic, and porridge—unblessed food, O lady;
and my mistress, you see, is ill of it, and talking to her
won't cure her!"

" Fear not," replied the dame smiling; " we have
had scant notice, yet we may do something," and she
was as good as her word. Hot water to bathe with,
was quickly prepared, and clean refreshing clothes;
and the rubbings and kneadings of several young girls
relieved their weary aching limbs. Soft cushions were
put down to lie on; and there was a hospitable, grateful
hostess ministering to every want. Even Lurlee's
churlish humour was already softened by the attention
paid to her; and she remembered, with satisfaction, in
spite of her late disbelief, that the day was Thursday,
and that, as she entered the house between five and six
in the afternoon, the hour was ruled by Mercury, and
was propitious.

About the same time, a body of horsemen—there might have been from two to three hundred of them—were approaching the town from the other side, through the camp which spread out irregularly among the fields and gardens. Their horses neighed frequently as they passed tents where others were picketed, seemingly envious of their rest and comfort; and the appearance of the whole party, jaded and wayworn, indicated a long weary march in a hot sun that day, which had now come to a close.

As they passed the first tents, the men loitering by the wayside asked carelessly who they were, and being told, followed them eagerly; while the news that one remnant of the noble host which had been so treach-erously destroyed at Purtabgurh had arrived, traversed the camp before them. As men of the Päigah of Afzool Khan were recognised, many a rough heart swelled, many an eye filled with tears, as the horsemen pro-ceeded: while crowds followed them, greeting old friends who had escaped, or tendering their respectful salutations to the young Khan, and congratulating him on his escape.

Bulwunt Rao and the hunchback were in front, and as they neared the town urged their horses on. "Wait for us at the gate; we will not be long, and will bring the water," cried the latter; and when Fazil reached it, a litter—which had been rudely constructed of a bed-frame and stout bamboo poles, covered with some coarse sheets—by which he had been riding, was set down. The men who had carried it were exhausted, and as they placed it on the ground, lay down themselves at a little distance.

Fazil dismounted and approached it. "Tara!" he said, "Tara! art thou asleep? We have arrived, and there is now no more fatigue or danger. O Tara, awake!"

The girl turned mechanically towards him, but did not seem to recognise him; her eyes were much glazed, and her lips cracked and parched. "Water," she said faintly.

"Alas! I dare not give it thee, Tara," he replied. "O my life—O beloved, look up! wait but till they return, and all will be well!"

She shook her head, and a smile, very sad and sweet, seemed to pass over her face, but she did not speak. Fazil looked out among the people passing to and fro; perhaps there might be a Bramhun among them, who could give her a few drops of water to moisten her mouth, but he saw none. How wearily the time seemed to pass! With what impatience did he watch the gate whence Lukshmun or Bulwunt Rao, on their double errand, should return; and with what misery did he look upon the poor girl, lying in heavy fever, without the means of relieving her! How he longed for his sister or Lurlee! but it might be days ere they arrived, and till then he must trust her to strangers.

It had been a weary day, indeed—a day of intense anxiety to all who accompanied him. Under the excitement of release from imminent death, and in the

rapid ride of the afternoon of her rescue, Tara had
borne the fatigue wonderfully; and as night set in,
and they took some hurried rest among the corn-fields
of a village, Fazil hoped that she would sleep, and
be refreshed against the morrow; but it was not
to be so. During the night the girl began to speak
incoherently at times, and it was evident that she
suffered from high fever. Still they must proceed;
there was no delaying there. The tracks of his party
were distinct, and a force of the enemy's horse might
yet overtake them, and destroy them if they tarried.

So, after feeding their horses on green corn-stalks,
and themselves obtaining a rough meal from the green
heads of corn roasted in a fire, they again set forth.
They had no other food, for they dare not stay to cook
it, and they had avoided villages as likely to expose
themselves to collision with the surly people.   Once
or twice, straggling parties of cavalry had been met;
but they had passed without notice, and the farther
they proceeded, the less chance there was of interruption.   So far all was well; but Tara grew worse, and
could no longer sit the horse on which she had been
placed; so, in a village which was passed, a litter was
contrived, a drink of milk obtained, and the party again
set forward. Finally, they had arrived safely at Kurrar;
but Tara now knew no one, she could not be roused to
speak, and lay moaning piteously, as if in pain.

"When she gets water it will refresh her," thought
Fazil, as he sat helplessly by her, praying, in his own
simple fashion, that God would be good to him and

spare her. "Weariness and the terror of death have caused this," he said to himself, "and rest alone can cure it."

At last Lukshmun returned with a Bramhun and some water, and the man, looking into the litter, shook his head hopelessly.

"She is dying," he said; "let her be taken out and placed on the ground, that her spirit may depart easily."

Fazil flung him away angrily. "She shall not die," he cried passionately; "give her the water—as much as she will drink." But it was of little avail,—she scarcely swallowed any, and motioned the man away with her head impatiently.

Then came Bulwunt Rao. "I had much ado to find the merchant," he said, "and when I did, he told me strange guests were already with him, and that he could not find room for a Bramhun woman. Nevertheless he yielded at last, and we are to go. I rode by the house. The porch was full of men, so we must seek shelter elsewhere. The merchant said he would meet you at the door of the house, but he does not yet know who you are. I did not tell him. I only said you were a nobleman of Beejapoor."

"And why did you not tell him?" cried Fazil, with some impatience; "he owed my father a thousand benefits."

"So much the better, Meah," returned Bulwunt, "and he looks as though he would repay them. Come, it is close by."

The bearers again took up the litter and carried it on. Fazil accompanied it on foot, holding the side; and at the same door which we have already described, stood a pleasant-looking man, dressed in flowing Arab robes and a green turban, and several servants behind him,—who saluted Fazil courteously as he stood aside for the litter to go by.

"Meer Jemal-oo-deen, if thou art he," said Fazil, "will have forgotten one whom he knew long ago."

"I have forgotten your face," returned the man, "yet you are welcome, and the peace of the Prophet be upon you. Who are you?"

"Fazil, the son of Afzool Khan," was the reply.

"O great joy! O thanks be to Alla!" cried the man, lifting up his hands, "and blessed be the saints and the Prophet who have sent thee. Embrace me, and come in quickly, for thy mother and sister have also been brought to us, and are safe within."

"Then she will live! they will save her!" cried the young man excitedly. "They will save her! O Meer Sahib, where are they?"

"Within, in the zenana," replied the merchant. "Sorely exhausted, I hear, but already better; and she?" and he pointed to the litter.

"No matter, sir," said Fazil advancing; "all will be told you hereafter. She is much to them; but she is grievously shaken, and we lose time. She cannot speak, and is burning with fever."

"Ah, is it so? Then let her be carried in," and he clapped his hands. "Take that litter within at once," he said to the women who came; "then see to the lady who is in it."

Four stout women took up the litter, carried it into the inner court, and set it down.

Lurlee and Zyna were lying in an inner room, the door of which was open, and from whence the entrance to the court could be seen. "What can they be bringing in?" said Lurlee, as she saw the end of the strange litter entering the door. "A man following, too! Begone!" she screamed violently, hiding her face under the sheet; "begone! this place is private."

"Mother," cried Fazil, who heard her voice but did not see her; "it is I; and here is Tara. Come, O Zyna; where art thou? Come quickly to her."

O delicious joy! Lurlee, forgetting all her previous troubles, sprang from the bed on which she had been lying languidly, and Zyna followed; and they fell upon his neck with low whimpering cries, like dogs when they have found a lost master. Where was fatigue now?

Tara! It was far in the night ere consciousness returned to her. "No matter, Alla hath sent her again to us," said Goolab, whose ideas were always of the most practical description; "she is ours now, and we will bathe her." And some Bramhun women, who lived hard by, came and assisted. So, ere morning broke, Tara was lying on Lurlee's bosom sobbing gently: and, with her loving arms wound round her recovered treasure, Zyna was sobbing too.

CHAPTER XXVI.

SOME three weeks after the events recorded in the last
chapter, Zyna and Lurlee were sitting near the foot of
the bed on which Tara was lying, and two Bramhun
women—widows, as appeared from their shaven heads
and coarse serge garments—sat on each side of it.
One was fanning her gently. The bed was very low,
hardly a foot from the ground, so that the women
were seated on the floor, leaning against its frame.
They had watched all night in pairs by turns, and the
dawn was just about to break; but a small lamp, in a
niche of the wall, threw a faint light over the room
and the verandah beyond, and fell upon a figure lying
there, covered in a sheet, which appeared, from its
measured breathing, to be asleep. All four women
were weeping silently, and their faces had that worn,
haggard expression which is consequent upon long
and continuous watching.

"When did he say he would come again?" asked
Lurlee of one of the women in a whisper.

"They will both be here at dawn," said the woman
addressed; "but they said they could do nothing now,

unless she rallies of herself: medicine cannot help her;
and still she sleeps."

"Look," said Zyna, with a tone of awe in her low
voice, "if you can see her breathe. I have been
watching for some time, and I cannot see the sheet
over her move as it used to do. Mother! mother!
she is not gone from us!"

"No, daughter," returned Lurlee, "she lives still,
but she is near to death, fearfully near, and is in the
hands of Alla. If she wake up restless, as she was
before, we must put her on the floor, that the spirit
may pass easily; but, as it is, we may yet hope, for
there is rest now after her weariness, and she hath not
asked for water all night. You have given her none,
have you?" she asked of the women.

"No, lady," replied the elder of the two; "none
since she went to sleep. It is near dawn, and if the
soul had to pass it would be restless to go; yet she
sleeps. We cannot move her, nor is there need; she
breathes as gently as a child. Look!"

The woman took the lamp from the niche in the
wall, and, shading it with her hand, yet so as to suffer
a little light to fall on Tara's face, looked at it earnestly. "She smiles," she said in a whisper; "behold,
lady, but do not rise, else it might wake her."

Lurlee and Zyna leaned forward and regarded her
anxiously. Yes, the lips, though blistered with the
parching heat of fever, seemed fuller and redder, and, as
the sweet mouth was partly open, the light fell upon
moisture on the white pearly teeth which glistened

brightly. The cheeks were not so wan and sunken, and the eyes, instead of being partly open, with a dull glassy stare which, except when they flashed in delirium, had been their only expression for several days past, were now closed entirely, and the long eyelashes rested peacefully, as it were, on the cheek. One hand had been placed under her head, and the other lay across her bosom. Her breathing could scarcely be seen, and yet, if they looked intently, the arm across the bosom heaved slightly now and then, and as it were without excitement.

"It may be the flush of life which precedes death," said the woman; "yet then they do not often smile, nor dream. See, she is smiling again."

"Ah, there is no death in that smile, daughter! Look! O blessed saints, pray for her! O Prophet of God, she will be thy child soon; intercede for her, and have her spared! O holy Syud Geesoo Duraz! I vow a golden coverlet for thy tomb, and Fatehas to a thousand poor mendicants, if she be saved!" cried Lurlee, with clasped hands and streaming eyes. "O give her to me! All have children but me, and this one strange child I took into my heart when ye sent her, and she abode there. O take her not—take her not from me! What use would she be to ye now in her young life? Wilt thou not pray too, Zyna, for her?"

"Mother, I have prayed," replied Zyna earnestly. "Fazil hath prayed. We have vowed Fatehas to all the shrines, and to the holy Saint at Allund. Mother! I will send my gold anklets and her zone to the shrine there, if she but live, and will give her others."

So they watched and prayed, and saw the smile
playing gently and sweetly over Tara's mouth and eyes.
Was it to hear the whisper of the Angel of Death?
It might be so, and then the last dread change would
follow; the eyes would glaze and sink, the breathing
become shorter and more difficult, and they must take
her up and lay her down on the ground to die. Would
it be so?

For many days Tara had lain between life and death.
The great excitement she had passed through—during
which her mind, strung by despair and superstitious
belief, had sustained her—had passed away suddenly,
and left its never-failing result in the utter prostration
both of mental and physical power; and the exposure
she had been subjected to in that wild night-ride from
Wye, with the succeeding days of heat and fatigue,
in the midst of constant alarm, had combined to produce severe fever. As she was lifted from the litter
the evening she arrived by the women, she was entirely
unconscious; but in Lurlee she had at once a skilful
and loving nurse, and after a while she had recovered
sufficiently to distinguish with whom she was, and to
feel that the hideous insecurity of her life—nay, the
imminent peril of a horrible and violent death—had
passed away.

But after that short period of blissful recognition,
and with the sound of Lurlee and Zyna's passionately
endearing welcomes in her ears, unconsciousness had
returned, and she knew no more for many days. The
burning fever, accompanied by low delirium, continued

without intermission. Happily her mind retained its last pleasant impressions most vividly : and from time to time, Lurlee and Zyna heard her murmur to herself more of her deep love for Fazil than she would ever have dared to tell them, and they listened wonderingly to the strange mingling of his name with those of gods and demigods of her own faith, and to the impassioned expressions which broke from her in that wild, perhaps poetic, language, with which, from her own studies and her father's recitals, she had become familiar.

The doctors of the town were early summoned ; and there was an old Gosai, known to the merchant's wife, who lived in a village near, whose repute for curing cases of fever was very great, and who was sent for, when the doctors' period of nine days' illness had elapsed without any relief. He declared the fever would last three weeks : and that, on the twenty-first day, or thereabouts, Tara would either live or die, for the disease was dangerous and difficult to subdue, but— he would do his best. So they sat and watched her day and night ; life now seemingly trembling on her lips, and yet again rallying within her, and giving hope when otherwise there was none.

Now, too, under the long sleep, her features had re- laxed ; the skin had lost its unnatural tension and dryness, and a soft smile was there which looked like life ; and still they prayed and made vows.

" No," said the woman, holding the lamp and watch- ing Tara, " it is not death, lady—not yet. There is no change ; and see, the smile faint as it is, does

not pass away. Surely there are sweet thoughts below it—thoughts, perhaps, of life. Let us wait and
pray."

And still they sat, and, after their own fashion,
humbly prayed too ; and the morning broke, and Fazil,
who, wearied by watching, lay outside, arose, performed his ablutions, and, with Zyna, spread their
carpets, and performed the morning service. Then he
watched in turn ; and the doctors came, looked at the
sleeping girl, and one of them gently put his hand on
her pulse and felt it, and smiled, and nodded his head
approvingly. "There is life in it," he said gently,
"but it is very feeble. Wait till she wakes—that is
the crisis of life or of death ; but, perhaps—God knows
—it may be life."

It may be life! Ah, yes! Many who read these
pages will remember like scenes ; watching the fluttering spirit of one most beloved—parent, or wife, or
child—with an intense and wondering earnestness of
misery or of hope, mingled with prayer: incoherent
perhaps—no matter—yet going straight from the heart,
up to Him in whose hands are the issues of life and of
death, to be dealt with as He pleased. Is there none
of this among the people we write of? Why not as
much as among ourselves? The same motives exist
there as here, the same deep ties of affection, the
same interests, and the same hopes and fears—often,
indeed, more powerful as belonging to minds more
impetuous, and less regulated by conventional forms.
Then the hope is greater, the agony of bereavement

more bitter, and the suspense between the final issue, perhaps, more unendurable.

So they sat around her. The kind, hospitable merchant's wife, with whom they still resided, came forth from her own court of the house, and, smiling as she saw Tara, bid them be of good cheer. No one spoke afterwards, but they watched the tranquil face; and the expressions still varying upon it, under the thoughts passing within, gave increasing hope of life.

It had been a sore struggle; but life at last was suffered to triumph over death. From the time when the weary tossing to and fro ceased, and the parched lips refused to speak even incoherently, and the death-like sleep began, the exhausted frame had been gathering strength. More than a night, and nearly a day, had passed in hope and fear alternately to them, but in rest to Tara; and as the shadows were falling long towards the east, the sweet eyes opened to the full, and looked around.

They could see but dimly at first; but they read in the faces which at once turned towards her, now the most precious on earth, the assurance of that love, of which, as her spirit hovered on the threshold of the unknown eternal land, she had been permitted to dream. There was no fever now in those soft eyes—no glare, no glassy brightness: but dewy, and their deep brown and violet shaded by the long lashes, into an expression of dreamy languor—they seemed more beautiful by far than they had ever appeared before, and Fazil thought, as his creed suggested, that those of

a Houri of the blessed Paradise, or a Peri angel of the
air, could not be more lovely. None of them could speak
then ; but the tears were falling fast from their eyes
in great and irrepressible emotion, as they stretched
forth their arms to welcome Tara to life.

"My child! my life!" cried Lurlee sobbing, who
was the first to find utterance. "Now, God hath given
thee to me again, and I will never leave thee—never.
O do not speak; it is enough that we see thee come
back to us, more precious, and more beloved than ever!"

Tara attempted to reply, but was too feeble. They
saw her lips moving, but no words could be heard.
She tried to stretch forth her hand to Zyna, but she
could not lift it. Zyna saw the attempt, and threw
her arm round her. "Not now, beloved," she said—
"not now. Lie still and rest; we are all near thee,
and will not go away."

So more days passed, and Tara grew stronger, though
slowly. The shock to mind and body had been very
heavy, and needed long rest and much care; but she
was in tender hands, and gradually, but surely, they
saw progression to convalescence, and were thankful.
Lurlee could not restrain her pious gratitude; and
Friday after Friday, the poor of the town, Hindus as
well as Mahomedans, received a munificent dole of
food and money, and rejoiced at the widow's profuse
charity.

Dear reader, if you have ever recovered from such
an illness as befell Tara, you will remember, vividly and
gratefully, the pleasant languor, the perfect rest, and

the sensation of growing strength of life,—amid its weakness, such as you cannot estimate till you attempt to act for yourself. You long to speak, but your tongue refuses words; you long to rise and help yourself, but your members as yet decline office. If you can turn yourself about as you lie, it is all that is possible. Then, if you are ministered to by loving hands, and you hear sweet familiar voices around you, how often has your heart swelled, and run over at your eyes, silently, and in very weakness, as you have abandoned yourself to their sweet influences! How powerfully the new life which God has given you, grows under their ever-present care! Sometimes you can hardly bear the excess of joy, and tremble lest it should suddenly cease; and again, you find periods of rest possessing you—dreamy unrealities—incomplete perceptions—even vacuity, which is not sleep, nor yet waking—and still with all, a consciousness of increasing strength which will not be denied.

It was so with Tara. No one spoke much to her, she could not bear it, nor could she reply; but if Zyna sat by her, or Lurlee, and held her hand, it was enough for reality; and morning and evening Fazil was admitted to see her, and to satisfy himself that she was gaining ground. The past was never alluded to by any of them. At first she had only a dim and broken remembrance of it, as of some great ill-usage or suffering. As she grew stronger, the detail became more distinct: and they often saw her shudder, and draw the end of her garment or the coverlet over her face, as if

to hide it from observation, or to shut out some terrible
sight from her view.   Yet to herself there was an un-
reality about the whole, which she could neither comprehend, nor account for.   Most of all about her parents :
were they indeed alive, or was their sudden appearance
on the day of the Sutee, a reality, or a trick of imagination—was all she retained in her mind one of the
hideous dreams of her illness rather than a fact?
Who was to tell her the truth ?

All that Fazil had heard from the hunchback, he had
told to Tara as they rested here and there in their escape ;
but her own mind was then in that state of terror and
confusion that she could tell him nothing, nor, indeed,
could she find courage to speak to him at all.   Long
before, when they had been together in camp, she
had never dared to answer him.   It was enough for
her that he spoke, and that she listened.   Her mind, as
he rode with her that night before him—for he would
trust her to no one—was sorely unhinged.   That she had
escaped death she knew ; that she was with him she
knew also : that she feared pursuit, and might be
taken and burned alive, was an absorbing terror, which
shut out the shame of her flight ; and it was perhaps a
happy circumstance that the fever, which had so long
affected her brain, shut out all realities till she was
stronger, and calmer to bear them.

CHAPTER XXVII

DAY by day, as strength returned to Tara, remembrance returned also. It might have been with abhorrence of her present position—with dread of her broken vows—with terror of the Mother's vengeance, and with a sense of her own pollution as an escaped Sutee— which would have utterly overwhelmed her with remorse, and forbidden recovery at all; and in such a case, death would have been welcome. We will not say that there was no revulsion of feeling : it would have been unnatural in one with so fine an intellect as Tara possessed, had there been no struggle. Perhaps the new life to which she awakened, after the illness she had undergone, had blunted the perceptions of the old ; perhaps, as Zyna and Lurlee told her, that it was her destiny, which she could not resist ; and that, if she were to have died, as her creed had determined, could Fazil have prevented it ?—would she have been delivered at all? Had she not already undergone the pains of death in preparation for it, and been delivered from them ?

Then Lurlee again brought forth her books, and went

over all her old calculations, and there were the priest's
also with them, all tending to the same point. If
her faith had been shaken for a time, in the fact that
Afzool Khan had died, when the planets showed that
he should be victorious, might there not have been
some mistake? Here at least there was none; none
in the restoration of her child, as she called Tara, from
death to life—none in her having been rescued from
the evil idolaters and Kafirs, to be newly born into
the true faith, acceptable to Alla and the Prophet.
All this was very plain and incontrovertible.

Could Tara deny it? It was not clear that she even
attempted to do so : and ever nigh her, were anxious
pleaders against any justification of the rites of her own
faith, from the most horrible consummation of which,
she could not possibly have escaped. "Even your
father and mother could not have saved you had they
desired it," argued Zyna, "from dying in the fire before
them : they would have seen you burned, and shouted
' Jey Kalee !' with the rest, to drown the scream of your
dying agony ; but they would not have relented." No;
Tara's heart told her they would not have relented, and
she must have perished, but for Fazil.

And when he pleaded ?—It was long before he attempted it ; but it was at last irrepressible. More
than his sister and Lurlee, he knew what struggle
would ensue in Tara's heart if she were called upon too
suddenly to renounce her own faith ; for he had lived,
young as he still was, more in the world. On this
point, he had as yet forborne to address her at all. But

such love as his for the deserted girl, must be spoken
by himself. Lurlee and Zyna had told him all they had
said, and it seemed strange to both that he was silent;
but, he had judged rightly. What the girl could bear
from them, could not have been endured from him till
her bodily strength assisted her mind to bear it, and
he waited his opportunity.

It was the first time she had ever mentioned her
own affairs; almost the only time she had spoken freely
at all. She had reverted to the past, to the day of
the attack on Tooljapoor, and to Fazil's recovery of
her mother's ornaments; for the Bramhun women had
bathed her that day, and she had performed some
simple ceremonies of her faith for purification after her
illness, and charitable gifts had been distributed by
Fazil and Lurlee on her behalf. So she had suffered
Zyna to twist a garland of flowers into her hair as she
used to do in camp, and to put on her some of the old
ornaments which, while she was yet decked for the
Sutee, had been brought away with her: and when
Fazil, who had been absent all day in the camp, returned before sunset for the evening prayer, he found
her talking earnestly with his sister.

Still pale, but only showing the traces of illness in
the purity of her colour, Tara had perhaps never looked
more lovely than in the resumption of some of her
former richness and elegance of costume; and as Fazil
entered the court, for the moment unobserved by her
and Zyna who were seated together, he stopped involuntarily to regard her.

Tara would have fled when they saw him, but Zyna would not have it so.

" Look," she said, " brother, is she not like herself once more ?   See how I have decked her for her sacrifice of thanks to-day !   Surely all that is past is as a dream, and Tara is again what she was the evening she was taken away from us. Is she not, brother ?   She is not changed ? "

" Yes," he said, " changed, I think, in spirit in her new life, as we had hoped—that is all ! Tara, sit down : we will all remain together, and you must hear me now, with Zyna as witness.

" There is nothing new to say," he continued, after a pause—" nothing.   It is only the old tale, once told before, when you believed it: and it is not changed, only confirmed.   Ah ! we have both been tried since ; and if out of that trial you have come, like me, strengthened, then there is no doubt.   Tara ! in the deadly struggle by that hideous pile, with the crash of music, and frantic screams of the people in your ears, even then your heart bore witness to me that I was true.   Am I false now ? "

" O no, no, no ! " cried the girl, throwing herself uncontrollably at his feet, after her old Hindu fashion. " Not false, not false !   You are my lord and my saviour, and I worship you !   I will be your slave, your servant, for my life, and Zyna knows it ; but consider——"

" Not thus, beloved," he said, gravely but kindly stooping and raising her up, " will I hear that, but so, face to face. There is no shame in it now—none; for it is our destiny, Tara: let it be as honoured as, methinks, it is loved. Sit there and listen." And Zyna put her arm round her, and they sat down together side by side.

"I have to say hard words, perhaps, Tara," he continued, "but you must hear them. In saving you from death by fire, I have brought you into a living death from your own faith ; for you are an outcast now, as you know—you cannot return to it. You could not be received as a Brainhun, nor would any other caste assist you. Shaven, denied shelter, and even water, by the very mother who bore you—if she live—you must herd with the vilest, and enter that condition of abject dishonour and profligacy which Moro Trimmul intended for you, and from which God—your God as well as mine, Tara—has now delivered you. There is nothing else for you that I can see but death, and that is now gone from you, and will not return. Could you escape this, Tara? Is this a life for you?"

He saw the girl shudder violently, and bury her burning face in Zyna's bosom ; while Zyna, drawing her to herself more closely, said gently, "Listen, listen ; is he speaking the truth? You do not answer, O beloved!"

Tara could not reply, but she clung to Zyna the more closely.

"Or instead," continued Fazil, "there is, what was said once before, in presence of my honoured father—peace be with him!—which I now repeat, and Alla and the Prophet, who sent me to you, and you to me, are witness of its truth,—that all of honour, all of wealth, all of love and respect that I possess, I will share with you as my wife, till I die. You are not of us, nor of our creed : no matter, we can admit you honourably to both. It is no disgrace to quit the blood-stained belief of Hinduism to join the glorious ranks of the true believers ; but a blessed gain, for which, out of all these trials, Alla hath preordained you. Enough, O Tara : before Him, your God and mine, and before Zyna, answer to me truly and freely, once and for ever. He is witness that there is no constraint upon you."

Could she resist that earnest manly pleading—she, already won long ago ? she who, in all her trial, had carried about in her heart that image of glory and beauty, which she could only compare with the heroes and demigods of her own sacred poems—her highest standard,—and who, in putting it away, had done so, only to die in that horrible, calm despair, which preceded voluntary immolation ?   It was impossible !

As she sat there, and as he ceased speaking, there rushed through her mind a sudden flood of old memories which, had the love she bore for him been weak, or less deeply rooted than it was, had swept it away as the torrent sweeps dry straws from its bed, and they are seen no more. Father, mother,. Radha, the old pleasant memories of Tooljapoor, and the old people ; a happy childhood, a joyous budding into womanhood without care. Next, her service to the Goddess, and all that had come of it—terror, desperation, and living death. She could not serve her now, even did she desire it; and she could not see the image as before, nor the weird ruby eyes which used to follow her, and seemed to glint into her very heart. She remembered the fierce Bramhun, her foe—the glittering fly which she had seen in her little garden—and trembling, clung more closely to the breast on which she was lying; and, last of all, the hideous pile of black logs, the crash of gongs and drums, the shouts of the people, the fluttering pennons, the torches blazing around her to light her to death, and the agony of two women as they beheld it all, and of an aged man who had come to her and caused her once more to fear——

It takes long to write this; but all, ay more, rushed through the girl's heart as a strong flood in a moment, tossing and whirling fiercely; yet it shook nothing there. How true was it that, in that long unconsciousness and delirium, the old life had passed away, and the new one came with other obligations to be fulfilled. She was weeping passionately while Fazil was speaking, but when the rush of thought came, it was with awe, which repressed other emotion, and was succeeded by calm, inexpressibly sweet and assuring. Yes, love for him had resisted the fury of passion in its last attempt, and she could not control it now. Zyna felt her arms withdrawn from about her, and Tara, covering her burning face, on which the tears were glistening, with her garment, bent down before him, not in prostration, as before, but kneeling and bowing her head reverently, as she joined her hands in an attitude of supplication.

"Do with me as thou wilt, my lord," she said gently; "my life is thine, and I am thine henceforth till I die. I am helpless now—do not forsake me ; and God and Zyna are witness that I pledge my troth to thee, freely and humbly. I have no fear—none ! it is past now ! "

"Shabash ! Shabash ! Tara," cried Zyna exultingly, clapping her hands; "now thou art ours indeed. See, mother," she continued, turning round and looking up, as Lurlee entered, "he asked her, and she has agreed ; and you are witness of it as well as I."

"I am witness," said the lady; "I have heard all, and I am content. Alla and the Prophet have answered my prayers. Ah ! I shall have a precious child to give to thee, Fazil, ere long."

"Put her hands into mine, mother," he replied. "It will feel real, that she is to belong to me hereafter : it will be an earnest of the end."

"It is not one of the orthodox customs, Fazil," said the lady, gravely and hesitatingly : "and I never saw it done at any betrothment ; nevertheless, wait an instant—I will return directly."

She did so, while they sat as before, bearing a silver salver — on which there were some pieces of sugar-candy, and seated herself by them.

"Thou art still a Bramhun," she said to Tara, "but thou wilt take one of these from thy mother? There," she continued, as she put a piece into each of their mouths, repeating the blessing, " Bismilla ! It is done ; ye cannot go back. There should be rejoicing, and music, and feasting ; but,—Bismilla ! it is done, and ye cannot retract. O children ! O children !" she cried, bursting into a flood of tears, " I am a widow, and have suffered sore bereavement ; but ye are the light of my eyes and the only joy of my heart now ! Here are her hands, Fazil," and she took up Tara's, and put them into his—" thine, boy, till the end !"

Fazil stooped his head, and put his forehead upon them ; they were not withdrawn, and he fancied that the slender fingers closed on his confidently ;—was it fancy ?

" They should know of it, if they live," said Tara hesitatingly, and with a gasp in her throat ; " methinks they do live, mother, and that I saw them—there—at Wye—my father and mother ; but it is all confused now, and it may have been a dream during my illness."

" O no !" cried the lady, " let them not come between us now, if they live ; but they are not alive, Tara."

" Perhaps not," she said, with a sigh ; " nevertheless, if my lord would send some one and ask. They would be found in Vishnu Pundit's house at Wye ; and if they are dead——"

" Surely," said Fazil, interrupting her, " I will send Lukshmun even now. If they are there, they should come on at once ; there is no fear. Could you not send a letter, or a token, Tara ?"

"I will write," she replied; "and here is a ring of my mother's that she loved dearly; it would have been burned with me! Let them take it; and if my lord would write, too, to say—to say—I am alive, it would be enough."

"It shall be done at once," he said rising; "O mother, surely thy science told thee this would be a happy day!"

"See!" exclaimed the lady triumphantly, taking her tablets from her bodice, "you mock the planets sometimes, son, but see; while you were speaking I looked. Is not this Wednesday? and, see, here is Venus ruling the hour as you sat and plighted your faith! O children, this cannot be wrong, for the sun is just setting, and the work is finished."

As she spoke, the last gleam of its rays, as it sank in a glory of gold and crimson, flashed into the apartment, lighting up the girls' radiant faces, and sparkling upon their rich dresses and golden ornaments.

"Beautiful as thou art, Tara," continued Lurlee, "thou wilt be lovelier still when we deck thee as his bride; and so may the blessing of thy new mother rest upon thee, and the evil I take from thee now,"—and she passed her hands over the girl from head to foot,— "depart to thine enemies!"

"Ameen! Ameen!" cried Zyna, as Tara, falling upon her neck, again wept silently those tears of joy which she had with difficulty repressed.

CHAPTER XXVIII.

" WELL sung !" cried the young Khan cheerfully, and joining in the general applause which followed a pretty Mahratta ballad which the hunchback and Ashruf had just sung, to the accompaniment of a lute played by the former and a small tenor drum by the latter— " well sung ! Where did ye learn that ?" he continued, advancing from the entrance to the court where he had paused as he came out. " It is something new."

The men, who were seated or lounging about the entrance hall to the house, rose and saluted Fazil. It was evident at a glance to Bulwunt Rao that something had occurred to remove the sad expression which his lord's face had worn so long ; for it had given place to one radiant with joy, and he exclaimed cheerily,—

" Thanks be to the Gods ! it is gone at last, Meah ! Never, since we rode together to Pertabgurh, have any of us seen a smile on your face that was worth looking at, or one which was not followed by a sigh, as much as to regret it had ever been there ; so I cry, with thanks to the Gods, the grief is gone at last. What say you, brothers? look at him; did I speak truly?"

Amidst the hearty responses to this congratulation by his retainers, Fazil Khan sat down among them, and the hunchback and Ashruf, stepping forward, assumed the positions of professional ballad-singers, and saluted him.

"Shall we sing it again, Meah?" asked Lukshmun; "you did not hear it all. 'Tis a fancy of my own, about a damsel waiting for her lover, who passes her by with another, and so she goes and weeps."

"And we have all been crying over it, Meah," added Bulwunt Rao; "'tis so sad a tune too—so plaintive."

"But as I am not in a crying mood, friend," returned Fazil laughing, "it would hardly suit me now, so another time—meanwhile there is something to be done which is urgent."

"Are we to meet a new army, and take our revenge, Meah?" cried several of the men. "Ah, we know the country now, and should not fall into another trap like the first.

"No, no, friends," said the young man sadly, "there is no such good news as that; 'tis but a private matter of my own, which our ballad-singers may help, perhaps."

"We, Meah?" exclaimed the hunchback; "thou well knowest, that if we were bidden to leap into the flames for thee, we would not hesitate. Speak, that we may hear and do."

"It is somewhat private, friends," said the young man, looking around. "If I might be alone with these and our old friend for a little, no one may take offence; you will know all by-and-by."

"Surely not," cried several, rising and going out, followed by the rest.

"Stay, Bulwunt Rao," said Fazil, putting his hand on his arm, "your counsel may be of use;" and when they were alone, he continued, "She will not be content unless she sees her father and mother; and she declares they are at Wye, and came to her the day she was to be burned."

"Impossible!" cried Lukshmun; "they are dead, and this must be some device of the Evil One—of that old Mother on the hill there, who wants to get her back; and she has sent spirits in their guise to mock her. She does such things very often, Meah Sahib, and I don't like to hear of this."

"Well, they must be substantial spirits," returned Fazil laughing, "for she told us that she had heard them speak, and that she thought her father had lifted her up once. They must be alive."

Lukshmun shook his head. "I did not see him, or hear of him, at Wye," he said; "and as I know them well, I should have recognised him and his wife anywhere. And, about the witches—if I were to tell you what I know about the Mother's devices," he continued solemnly, wagging his head, "I should not be believed. Nevertheless——"

"Nevertheless," said Fazil, interrupting him, "thou

art to go and see—thou and Ashruf. Wilt thou go, lad, if he is afraid of the witches?"

"To the death," cried the boy cheerfully; while Lukshmun, leaping up into the air, turned a somersault, and came down where he stood. "Go!" he said; "yes, Meah. I have a spell against the Mother and all sorcery, and his majesty the devil to boot, which Pahar Singh taught me. Where are we to go, Meah, and when?"

"Now," replied Fazil; "take two of the ponies and ride straight to Wye. Her parents will be found in the house of Vishnu Pundit, or he will direct you to them. If they are gone home, or to Poona, or anywhere else, they must be followed up and brought back; and they will come when that ring is given to her mother—so she says."

"They may need money," said the man musing. "Bramhuns never move without coin. Something for expenses, is the first thing they ask of one. Is it not true? Nevertheless, Vyas Shastree is rich enough. O yes, he knows me, and I can get into Vishnu Pundit's house, too. Come, lad, we must put on the Byragee's dresses."

Ashruf followed him. While they were absent, Fazil wrote the letter they were to take, which ran as follows:—

"*To the respectable and learned in the Véds and Shastras, Vyas Shastree, of Tooljapoor, who is kind to his friends;*

" From Fazil, son of Afzool Khan, with greetings, and the peace and salutation of God ; and after wishing you health and prosperity—

" You are to know that your daughter Tara is here, with my mother and sister, in honour and health; but she hath been ill unto death, and being, by God's favour, restored to life, wishes to see you and her mother urgently, and sends a token, by which you may be assured she is here.

" You will learn more from the bearer, my servant, who is to be trusted ; and I pray you to lose no time in setting out, for we await your coming. I have sent money for your expenses by him, which you are to be pleased to use freely."

The hunchback and Ashruf reappeared after a while in their new costume, which was that of Jogies, or religious mendicants of that part of the country. Orange-coloured turbans and garments, purposely torn and ragged, yet withal scrupulously clean ; large strings of wooden beads about their necks, wrists, and ankles ; black blankets, to keep out cold or heat, thrown over their shoulders after a graceful and picturesque fashion ; and the lute and small drum they had used before. The faces of both were smeared with whiting, and the broad trident of Vishnu was drawn in red and white paint upon their foreheads. The hunchback would perhaps have been known by his figure ; but Ashruf, from the smart Mahomedan boy, gaily dressed as became his master's favourite attendant, was utterly transformed, and could not possibly have been recognised.

"Shabash!" cried Bulwunt Rao and Fazil involuntarily; "it is complete—no one could know you."

"Except by this hunched back of mine," said Lukshmun, "I would wager that I went anywhere as anybody you please, Meah,—from the holiest Syud down to the lowest Kullunder—from the Secretary of Ramdas Swami himself, to what I am now,—and was not discovered. Hindu or Mussulman, 'tis all the same—only I must have a religious garb on, Meah Sahib : for my mind, you see, having that turn naturally, I am most at home in one. Did any one suspect us when we sang ballads in the ambush at Jowly, and found out what Moro Trimmul wanted to do? or in Wye, when we saw Tara? O Meah! this is a joyful errand, for I shall pay a rupee to a Bramhun, and get bathed in the river—just where they were going to burn Tara Bye—to wash away my sins, and be absolved from shedding a Bramhun's blood. The Gods forgive me if I killed him!"

"I hope you did," returned Fazil laughing: "and now, here is a purse of gold, tie it round you, and use what is needed; and here are the letters which are to be put into Vyas Shastree's own hand. If he cannot get mine read, this ring and her letter will be enough. If they are gone to Poona, or back to Tooljapoor, send Ashruf back to me, and go on thyself."

"To the top of Mount Méru, or the lowest deep of

Nurruk," * cried Lukshmun, snapping his fingers. "Fear not ; we will bring them, lad—won't we ? and, master, if I have to go on, and can send thee a letter by a sure hand, may I take on my son here ? I cannot sing ballads without him."

"Ah yes, my lord ! " pleaded the lad, joining his hands, " to bring them to her."

"Good," said Fazil ; " I trust you both. Go, and be discreet, and God's blessing and mine be with you."

"And now, my lord," said the hunchback, " let us sing one ballad before we depart—one that she must know well ; it will give her hope. Go and tell her that some singers are here who know the ballads of the Bala Ghaut, and will sing her one. She will recognise the tune, for I have heard her father sing it, and they say he wrote it for her, for her name is in it. We shall sing it before Vishnu Pundit's door at Wye."

"As thou wilt," replied Fazil ; " I will tell her ; " and he arose and went to the inner court door. "Do not follow me," he said to them—" she can hear from hence, and there are women within—it is private."

Fazil had watched Tara as the prelude began, and he beckoned her to the door. " Come and listen," he said ; " they are singers of your own country, and I have brought them to sing a ballad to you." She arose, and Zyna followed her.

The hunchback and Ashruf stood at the doorway without, and, after a short prelude, sang, as nearly as we can translate it, as follows :—

* Hades.

1.

" Fast her tears fell—faster, faster,
    As the days pass slowly by,
And her heart is sorely laden
    With the dreary, hopeless sigh.
O that cruel, ceaseless sighing !
    Weary tears which sadly fell,
All unheeded as she wept them
    Daily by the garden well.

2.

" Mother ! Mother ! oft she pleaded,
    Toolja Mata ! hear my vow !
Hear thy daughter's cry of sorrow—
    Why shouldst thou forsake me now ?
Not less thine, O Mother holy !
    If my lover come to me ;
If he come, a golden necklace
    We, thy children, vow to thee !

3.

" As she went for water daily,
    Raised alone the pitcher still,
She repeats the prayer and promise,
    As with tears her soft eyes fill !
The Goddess watched the weary maiden,
    And her daily burthen borne ;
' Faithful,' she cries, 'in earthly sorrow,
    Daughter true, no longer mourn !'

4.

" Then next morn, with anklets tinkling,
    The maiden tripped, and ceased to sigh ;
As she stooped to raise the pitcher—
    Light she felt it lifted high.
And sweet words he whispers to her—
    ' Tara, all thy sorrow past !
Faith and hope have won thy lover.'
    And the vow ?—'Twas paid at last."

It was one of those plaintive Mahratta airs, at once so musical and tender, and whose character is so original, as to deserve the rank of national music. How often Tara had heard it! Her father had written the words, and composed the air, to amuse her when she used to be sad; but she had no lover—no one then to take the burthen, to help to lift the pitcher, which was so heavy! Ah yes! she remembered it well, and that her father had said afterwards, it should not be sung in the house because it made her sadder, for there could be no lover.

So she listened, and the melody seemed to strike some new and tender chords in her memory, which as yet had been untouched; and they looked at her wonderingly, and in silence, as the features softened into a smile, and the eyes gradually filled with tears, which flowed as from a fountain within, and rolled silently down her cheeks. As the vow was named, they saw her hand rise to her neck and unclasp the heavy gold necklace she wore, and when the last words were sung she put it into Fazil's hands.

"Let the Mother have it," she said, "as our vow— she is not angry with me. You will not deny this, my lord, to Tara?"

Before they could answer her, a strange brightness seemed to come over her face and eyes, as she looked upward as if following a vision. "It is enough," she said gently, after a silence which they did not break; "the Mother is not angry with me—it is accepted, and

I am free; for when the trial came, she says, and
Gunga called me, I did not leave her."

They did not understand then, to what she alluded;
but it was evident that the excited spirit had again
wandered into the past, and had returned, more at
peace than before.

"Yes," said Fazil, " as thou wilt, beloved — thy
vow shall be truly paid, at last."

CHAPTER XXIX.

On the second morning Fazil's messengers reached Wye, without interruption, tethered their ponies in the courtyard of a temple, where they obtained shelter, and set about the work they had to do without loss of time. Taking their instruments, they wandered into the bazar, and sang their ballads to willing listeners; for the hunchback was a master of his art, and had a willing and skilful pupil in the boy.

"Wast thou not in the camp at Jowly?" said a man coming up to Lukshmun, "and this lad too, before we attacked the Toorks,—and we let thee go? Ah yes, and you promised to sing the hymn of the Goddess at Tooljapoor, and did not return when we were victorious! Ill for you, for you would have had a share of the gold. By the Mother! you shall sing it now. Come with me!"

"Not so," said Lukshmun; "we are engaged to sing at Vishnu Pundit's house—where is it?—and shall be free in the evening only : and if thou canst direct me to one Moro Trimmul, a Bramhun, and let me go

VOL. III.

now, we will sing an hour at night for as many as you
choose to bring to the Temple of Ballajee, where we
have put up, and take what you have to give us."

"Moro Trimmul!" cried the man laughing, "thou
wouldst have to go deep into hell for him. Where
hast thou been, friend, that his fate did not come to
thine ears?"

"I was afraid," replied the hunchback; "I fear
fighting, sir; and if a drawn weapon is flashed in my
face, I faint. So we ran away from Jowly—did we not,
my son? and have been travelling about the country
ever since, getting what we can. But what of the
Bramhun, sir? was he killed in the fight at Jowly?"

"No, no—not there," replied the man; "but he is
dead, nevertheless. Some one cut him down the day
the Sutee was carried off."

"Ah, yes, I have heard of that, sir; the people have
strange stories about it; but who carried her off? and
who killed the Bramhun? A Bramhun slain! O the
impiety!" continued Lukshmun devoutly; "think of
that, my son! A holy Bramhun!"

"I don't know; I was not there," replied the man;
"we were still out at Jowly, or it would not have
happened: but they said some of Afzool Khan's men,
who were starving, made a Durôra on the Sutee, and
carried her off; as to Moro Trimmul, he was no loss—
a bad man, my friend, though a Bramhun. They
might have spared the girl, however, for all the use she
was to the Bramhuns afterwards. I wonder no one
kept her, for she was very lovely they say."

" O sir," cried the hunchback innocently ; " and did she not live ? Who killed her ? "

" They say not," he replied ; " and that the cruel men killed her for the ornaments she wore. There was a woman's corpse found some days afterwards on their track, and the remains were brought here, and her father was told of it. They say he went mad after that, for he believed they were his child's. He married Moro Trimmul's sister, you know. Ah, it's a curious story altogether."

" Indeed," returned Lukshmun simply ; " I should like to hear it all. If I sing for you to-night will you tell it to me ? "

" A bargain !" cried the man joyfully ; " come to us without fail ; we are a jovial lot, and there may be good liquor, and some of the dancers too. I will come for thee. 'Faith, the story of the Moorlee's murder by Moro Trimmul is as good as a scene in a play."

" What Moorlee ? "

" Oh, the Tooljapoor girl, Gunga, who was with him. They found her body under the window of his room at Pertabgurh, hanging in the trees below the precipice, and so the whole came out ; but he was dead before then. One of those dare-devil Mussulmans had killed him, and they took some of the Sutee wood, and burnt him there, by the river."

" Ai Bhugwan ! O Lord, forgive me for having slain the Bramhun," ejaculated the hunchback to himself ; " and I did it too. Well, I can't help hitting hard when I do hit ; and truly he had murdered some

one, it appears, so it was only justice after all. Yes,
sir," he continued, "I understand. And the Sutee's
father ?—her name was T—T—T——"

"Tara," said the man ; "and her father is Vyas
Shastree of Tooljapoor. He is better now, and I saw
him a while ago sitting by the porch of Vishnu Pundit's
door, weak, but better ; people pity him very much.
Now I must go. You will not forget ?"

" No," said the hunchback ; "you will find me at the
temple after the lamps are lighted ; till then we must
sing about the streets. Come, my son. Let us hurry
on, boy," continued Lukshmun. " I know the house.
Do not pretend to notice any one ; we will sing the
ballad of the Vow, after the first invocation."

They passed on rapidly : up a few cross streets and
alleys, till they reached that in which was the house that
they sought. In the covered alcove, beside the outer
door, sat several Bramhuns, apparently talking together ;
one elderly man, covered with a sheet, was reading.

Lukshmun and Ashruf began to sing their ballads
at the doors of every house as they advanced, and
women from within, came out and gave them handfuls
of flour or rice, which were dropped into the bag
which Lukshmun carried. Gradually, as they came
nearer, the hunchback changed the songs to those of
his own country, Canarese and Mahratta in turn, and
he was sure there must be some, with which the Shastree was familiar.

Yes, it was he, reading, while the others sat near
him, and conversed among themselves ; thinner than

when the hunchback had last seen him, and looking
weak, yet still remarkable and unmistakable.   Once or
twice the Shastree had looked up at the singers, not so
as to seem to care about their performance, but as if
a familiar sound had reached him.   Now, however, it
came to the turn of the Pundit's house, and the hunchback and Ashruf stopped before it.

"Go on," said one of the Bramhuns impatiently ;
" you have been bawling all down the street, disturbing
our meditations, and the Shastree there is weak.   Go
on, and make no noise."

"Maharaj," said Lukshmun, humbly putting up his
hands, "we are under a vow, made before the Holy
Mother at Tooljapoor " ('May she forgive me for telling the lie!' he thought parenthetically), "to sing before every house in Wye, and bring her what we get;
'tis a good work, learned sirs, and we are poor people,
—do not hinder us ; 'tis a long way to go, and we are
weary.   Let us sing you a ballad for our vow, or only
a verse, else we cannot go on."   •

"Make haste then," said the first spokesman impatiently.

Lukshmun retuned the lute ; and as he played the
prelude which Tara had heard, he saw Vyas Shastree,
who had not noticed him, look up.   His large eyes
were opened to the full, and he leaned forward with
an expression of intense curiosity.   Then the singers
broke at once into the ballad :—

> "Fast her tears fell—faster, faster,
>   As the days pass slowly by."

"Hold!" he exclaimed, waving his hand; "who are
ye? and whence come ye?"

"From Tooljapoor, O Pundit!" said the hunchback
humbly.

"Who taught you that ballad?"

"No one taught it me. I heard it, and have remembered it. They say one Vyas Shastree composed
it. Maybe you have heard of him, sir. He had a
daughter named Tara. She was a Moorlee. I have
heard they are all dead now."

"Ye belong to Tooljapoor?"

"No, Maharaj; I am from near Allund—a long
way from this; but the vow I made is for" ('The Gods
forgive me if I tell another lie!' he said inwardly)—
"for a—child—O kind sir; if the Mother will send
me one. Your worship speaks Canarese?"

"Yes," said the Shastree, replying in that language;
"who art thou?"

"Do they understand it?" asked the hunchback.

"No," he replied, "none but my wife, and she only
a little. Why dost thou ask?"

"Can I go into the court? I know all the ballad,
and can sing it sweetly for the women; they always
like it," returned Lukshmun. "Will you listen,
Maharaj? 'tis not very long;" and, as they went in,
they sang on more loudly and confidently than before.
Some women of the house came and looked at them,
and listened, and among them were Anunda and
Radha. The hunchback looked from the Shastree to
his elder wife, and saw the tears falling from both

their eyes; at last the Shastree rose and went in to her, and when Anunda saw him, she burst into bitter weeping.

"Grieve not for one at rest," Lukshmun heard him say; "at rest in the peace which was denied her here. Yet the old ballad moves me strongly, wife. Come hither," he cried to the singers; "take this for the sake of . . . No matter now; I am Vyas Shastree, and what strange chance hath sent you I know not, but take this," and he offered money.

"The Gods be thanked! No; not from you," exclaimed Lukshmun, in Canarese. "Come aside," he continued in the same tongue, "for I have that to tell you and her, which will give you new life and strength. Listen," and he whispered in the Shastree's ear; "Tara lives, well and in honour. I bear a token and a letter which she hath sent you. Come, and I will give it; 'tis for her mother, and this letter for thee," and he took it from a fold in his turban.

"Anunda! O wife!" cried the Shastree, trembling and gasping for breath, as he leaned on her, opening the letter. "She lives—our Tara. Come—he knows of her; see her own writing, the holiest and most secret Muntra* I taught her; she hath written it."

"Away with ye!" cried Radha to the other women about, "this is not for your ears;" and the group were left alone; for Radha, advancing, shut the door of the court, and stood there with them.

* *Muntra*—a spell, a holy text.

"Do ye know this?" asked Lukshmun, when he had disengaged the ring from his inner garment. "Lady, it was to be given to thee, if thou art her mother! She is well who gave it to me, three days ago."

Her mother! Who could doubt it who saw Anunda then? The piece of gold spoke a thousand loving greetings to her. She laughed and cried by turns. She could speak nothing intelligibly. She kissed it rapturously, and hugged it close to her bosom, then looked at it till the tears rained from her eyes, and again did the same. A new life! a new daughter! born again, as it were. Anunda could not believe it.

"Thou art mocking us," she said at last, as a revulsion of feeling appeared to possess her. "This was among the jewels given to Janoo Nüik, when . . . she never got it."

"True," replied Lukshmun, "and she has the rest," and he enumerated them; "and here is a letter about her from my master, with whom she is. Listen to me, I can tell you better than that writing."

Listen? ah, yes, to the sweetest tale they had ever heard, did they listen for hours. The Bramhuns at the door wondered, and the people from within came and looked and wondered too, why the Jogies sat here talking to the Shastree—but, still they sat. Once, for a moment, the Shastree's cruel belief rose up against him, and forbade him to see an outcast; but nature asserted its own. "They dare not meddle with me," he thought, "and we cannot be as she is. But no matter, we will go to her, wife; yes, we will go to-morrow. Get the things ready. Thou wilt guide us, friend?"

"And guard ye, too, with our lives," said Luksh-mun. "Yes, to-morrow early, we will set out."

And so next day Vishnu Pundit and his friends marvelled that the Shastree and his family left them so suddenly, and knew not why they went, or whither.

CHAPTER XXX.

WE need not relate how the hunchback was washed
clean from his sins, how he and his companion en-
tertained those who came to them that night, nor
how he resisted their temptations to stay and sing to
others, who, they told him, would load him with gold.
Those he was taking to his master were more precious
than gold; and the same anxiety to present them to
him in safety, was shared equally by Fazil and by Tara
while awaiting their arrival.

Five days,—two to go and three to return—perhaps
more : never had time appeared so interminable to
those who remained at Kurrar : never had journey
appeared so wearisome to the Shastree. The spirit
within him was strong and earnest, but he had suffered much; and till roused by the hunchback's tidings,
Anunda and Radha feared that he had sunk into that
lethargic apathy which often precedes death. He could
not be awakened from it. Had Tara died a Sutee, it
might have been endured. Excitement and religious
enthusiasm, even the glory of the voluntary sacrifice,
would have deadened nature for a while, at least, in

both her parents ; but the attack upon the sacred procession, though but one had died in it, by, as they
supposed, lawless robbers—and the subsequent murder, as they believed, of their child—had produced a
revulsion which, to the Shastree, had wellnigh proved
fatal, and for many days those about him gave up
hope of life. The remains, as they supposed, of Tara
had, as we know, been brought in, and burned by
the river-side with all due ceremony ; and after the
period of mourning and impurity had passed, the
Shastree and his wives were to have set out on their
return home. Still, however, they lingered ; for the
climate had not agreed with Anunda, who had, in
her turn, fallen ill with fever, and they could not
travel.

During this period, they had heard from friends much
of what had befallen Tara: and yet not all of Moro Trimmul's share in her misfortunes. The only person who
could have told them truly was Gunga, and she was
dead. Radha had her own suspicions of her brother;
but beyond his wild attempt on the day of the Sutee,
to induce her to put Tara into his power, she had not
seen him ; and his violent death, while it affected her
mournfully, ended her anxieties ere the murder of
Gunga was discovered.

It was with difficulty that the impatience of the
Shastree and Anunda could be restrained. They
reached and passed Sattara the first day, and would
fain have travelled by relays of men without resting,
but the hunchback and Bulwunt Rao, when they joined

him, would not hear of increased exertion. "I will write by a speedy messenger that you are safe," he said; "but if I do not bring you in well to them, my lord will be angry, therefore submit yourselves to necessity,"—as, indeed, they were obliged to do.

Of his master's intentions, the hunchback had said nothing. Who was he, to know anything about them? The lady Tara was in honour as a guest; that was all he knew. Yes, his master had carried her off. Could he know that one who had been his guest, and had truly eaten of his salt, was to be burned alive, and not make an effort to save her? and she was still a Bramhun, and had Bramhun women attending upon her.

But Bulwunt Rao, who waited their coming at a village on the road with an escort of the Päigah, had no such discretion, and told what he believed—that Fazil and Tara had been privately betrothed. The lady Lurlee, he said, had one day distributed sugar-candy and pân to all the household, and to the mosque and other holy places in the town: and some had been sent to him on a silver salver covered with a cloth of brocade. What did that mean? And when the Shastree remonstrated, with a natural horror, at the idea of a Bramhun girl marrying a Mahomedan, Bulwunt Rao replied curtly—

"What could you do with her, Shastree, if you had her? You see she is no longer a Bramhun, but an outcast. You could not even give her water; and the two old Bramhun women who attended her in her illness, and the one who now waits on her, will have to be purified with plenty of ceremonies—and plenty to pay for them, too, will be needed ; but do not care for that, Shastree, my lord is very wealthy. So, you see, we must give her up as a Hindu, and even let her go into the other faith."

The Shastree would groan at these home-truths, but could reply nothing. As to his wife, she rejoiced heartily, and had no misgiving. The expression of a mother's nature would not be denied to Anunda ; for there is no mother with the experience of a life's love grown into her heart, who does not rejoice in the thought of a wife's useful happiness to her daughter, and in the expectation of its fruits ! All that had been done to soothe Tara, to distract her mind, to fill up the vacant place there with other interests—learning, religious exercise, and devotion to the service of the Goddess—had been tried in turn, and were, as Anunda felt, but a mockery.

Possibly, most probably, indeed, under other circumstances, Tara's pure mind would eventually have taken refuge in asceticism, and those severe penances, in which the woman who had persecuted her at Pertabgurh, had grown to take delight ; but, knowing the too frequent condition of the indulgence of lawless love by women situated like her daughter, and exposed to the same temptations, Anunda had often trembled for her safety ; and yet owned to herself that, to doubt her, was profanation.

No, she could not object. Had she been simply

asked the question previously, as a proud Bramhun woman, she must have refused. Now, circumstances had put that far beyond her reach. To object, would not retard the final issue, or influence it in any way; but to consent joyfully, would add so much, and so supremely to Tara's happiness, that opposition quickly grew to be an impossibility in the good lady's mind: and before she came to the end of the first day's journey, Fazil himself, could not have desired a warmer advocate.

A good deal of this fell out from being left to herself. Palankeens had been hired; and as the three travellers were carried on singly for hours together, each had fallen into the train of thought most congenial. Radha had certainly no voice in the matter, but was delighted. Anunda, between joy for her recovered child, and her new prospects of an honourable life, had been well-nigh beside herself at first, and the quiet soothing motion of the litter was of all things the best, perhaps, to calm her, and bring her practical mind into perception of the true realities of the position. "We have mourned her as dead," she said to herself, "we have performed all the ceremonies, and distributed all the charities necessary for the occasion; now she is alive after all, and born again into a new faith; so the death which we believed in, was a type of what was to be fulfilled. I see it all now," she said to herself, "and so it has been ordered for her without the pain of burning. Strange, my husband does not see this, but I will tell it to him when we arrive."

And so she did. Radha, too, caught up this tone of argument as best suited to her husband's mind, and the two women agreeing, left him little to say. It did not appear he had anything to urge or to object. "This ` is some punishment for her sins in an earlier life," he said to Anunda; "and 'tis well it is no worse."

Anunda and Radha could not see the punishment, except that Tara would have to eat unclean things; otherwise, what was left to be desired?

If this was their deliberate opinion at the close of the first day's march,—the second day, and the quiet jogging motion of the litters, the change of air and scene, and the peace which had settled gradually into their hearts, had much more than confirmed it. Whatever there was of objection, was dealt with on the first evening; and on the second, as they rested for the night, impatience to see their child once more, an irrepressible yearning to place her happiness beyond doubt, or chance of mishap, had driven out all other feeling. So, on the third morning, as they entered their litters for the day's journey, and knew they would reach Kurrar before sunset, Anunda, who laughed and cried by turns in a strange manner, as she dressed their morning meal herself before they set out, saw, with a thankful heart, that the heavy care which had sat on her husband's spirit for so long had passed away, and his old placid, benign expression, had taken its place.

That afternoon, as the sun's rays lengthened, and were filled with that golden radiance which clothed

the meanest objects with glory, and lighted up the
town and fort, and the camp beyond,—the little procession of the three palankeens, and the small body of
horsemen, approached the town gate. Bulwunt Rao
had timed their arrival to suit the lady Lurlee's desire,
for the astrological tables had been once more consulted, and the Moollas of several mosques had been
obliged to declare the most fortunate hour for the
entry of the party into the town. Messengers, too,
had met them, enjoining care in this respect; and
Bulwunt Rao and the hunchback were both relieved
by the appearance of a last emissary at the gate to
express approval of their arrangements and to urge
them on.

No need of hastening now.   The bearers themselves
were in hurry enough; for Bulwunt Rao's promise had
been liberal, and they had kept the horsemen at a brisk
canter for the last few miles of the journey. Now, therefore, shouting and hallooing to each other, the men
who carried the litters, rushed through the gate of the
town, and up the main street at their utmost speed;
and there was a race between the three sets, in which
Anunda's were victorious, and clamoured for largesse
as they set down her palankeen before the door of the
kind merchant's house where Tara still was. Much
the good lady had deliberated in her mind whether
she could ever be touched by Tara without pollution,
and whether it could be avoided; and we believe we
are correct in saying that she had determined, if it were
to cost her half, or all the money she had left in the

banker's hands at Tooljapoor, she did not care, but she
must hold her child once more to her heart.

Could she have repressed it? Ah no! a very outcast in shame, in misery, in misfortune—no matter
had it been so—the loving mother's heart would still
have been open, as her arms, to receive her child; but
in Tara's renewed life, as it were, in joy and in honour,
what signified the temporary impurity of contact with
one only impure by the hard rules of their sect?
Anunda trembled very much, and scarcely knew how
she got out of the litter; but as she emerged, a figure
she could hardly see for the tears which blurred her
sight, and which seemed to swim before her, bowed
down and kissed her feet, was raised up, and, falling
on her neck, wept aloud. Then it was strained to her
heart with a face buried in her bosom which dare not
look up, till her father and Radha entered, and Tara,
prostrating herself before him, clung to his knees
sobbing. With him, too, some scruple about touching
her, had remained; but his emotion on sight of her
could not be resisted, and he raised her up and blessed
her as of old. I do not think any of them could
speak, and if they did say anything, it was not intelligible enough to be recorded, and is better imagined.

Then Anunda sat down, for she was very dizzy:
and Tara saw the loving arms stretched out, and
went and lay down in them on the soft bosom in
her old place, and hid her face there, and felt her
mother's tears fall hot and fast upon it, while her
own were wiped away by the dear hands that had often

wiped them before. By-and-by she looked up, and
her mother saw in the clear soft eye, in the ineffable
expression of her countenance, that all trouble and
anxiety was past. No more excitement now, false
and mocking, even though sustained by religious fer-
vour ; and the peaceful calm which had grown upon the
face since her recovery, was a new expression to her
mother, which she felt could not change again.

Then Lurlee came with Zyna presently, when the
Shastree had been sent away, and, putting Tara aside,
Anunda arose and bowed before her, kissing her feet,
and embracing her knees. "She is thy child now,
lady," she said; "take a mother's thanks and gratitude
for her honour and her life. In our simple Hindu fashion
we know no other salutation, else it would be given."

"Nay, not to me, but to Alla, who hath preserved
her—not we," replied Lurlee. "Noble ye are, though
of another faith. Let us embrace as sisters, to whom
our mutual God hath given one daughter."

"It must be done, sooner or later," said Anunda to
herself, as she withdrew from Lurlee's arms, "and better
at once. Come hither, Tara : see how soon I give thee
away, my child, after I have recovered thee. Wilt thou
forgive me ? Take her, lady," she continued, putting
Tara into Lurlee's arms ; "thou art more her mother
now, than I. She hath been born to thee in a new life ;
be it as thou wilt unto her."

"I take her," replied Lurlee, "as she is given, freely
and truly. I had no child, lady, and often had prayed
for one, and Alla and the Prophet gave her to me long

ago, before all this misery, and when my lord lived, who would have rejoiced with us to see this day had he been spared. Yes, believing you dead, we took her to be our child, he and I. Now you have given her to me, and the gift is precious and is accepted : but I will not take it yet ; we are proceeding home, and you will come with us,—we will travel together. When we arrive, I will receive her ; till then, let her remain with you ; as yet she is pure from us——"

"Yes, mother, I am pure, I have transgressed nothing," said Tara gently. "I know," she continued, interrupting Anunda, "I am not as before ; but you can give me what I need till—till . . . . and there is no help for it now." Anunda and the Shastree did not object, and so it was settled among them.

How much they had to learn of each other's acts ! Nor was it till Tara told all, and they understood what the infamy of Moro Trimmul's conduct had been, that they felt the true honour of Fazil's character, or the deep loving kindness of the lady Lurlee and his sister. A grateful subject was this, now that she could speak unreservedly with Radha and her mother, and Tara had to repeat her tale again and again to willing ears. Sometimes her father, too, listened wonderingly ; and there was no part of it upon which he dwelt with more pride, even to rapture, than Tara's simple relation of the ordeal, and her devotion of herself to a cruel death rather than to dishonour.

"A true Bramhun thou," he would say, passing his hand over her head as she read him the old lessons, "and thou wilt not forget these, nor the Mother. If thou hadst failed, even to death, she had not released thee from thy vow.   As it is, see, she would not be denied a life! He used to scoff at her, and she drank his blood—not thine, my faithful child, not thine—and gave thee a new life, which will be happy.   Yes, the Khanum's skill in astrology is good, for my own calculations confirm her results, and, comparing his scheme of nativity with thine, Tara, there is no discordance."   But, nevertheless, the fact of Fazil's being born a Mahomedan and Tara a Hindu, often puzzled Vyas Shastree more than his science could explain, or than he cared to acknowledge.

CHAPTER XXXI.

THERE were many cogent reasons, public as well as private, why Fazil Khan's presence in Beejapoor was urgently required. Soon after his arrival at Kurrar, he had received the King's letter of condolence on his father's loss, with confirmation of all his estates and privileges, and with them a private letter in the King's own writing, urging him to come on without delay. The full effect of the destruction of the army had as yet, perhaps, hardly been felt, and the means of retrieving the disaster, or repelling the invasion which was likely to follow, were difficult to devise. As usual, the royal councils were much distracted; but, young as he was, the character which Fazil Khan had acquired among the soldiery during the few short months of this campaign, had raised him already to a rank far beyond that of his contemporaries, and even many of his elders. Only for Tara's long illness he would have proceeded to Beejapoor immediately after his arrival at Kurrar, and left the duty of collecting the fugitives to others; but that had rendered delay unavoidable, and all those who had escaped slaughter had joined him. On the other hand, Kowas Khan wrote that his preparations for the fulfilment of his marriage-contract were complete, and protested against further delay: and when the days of mourning for his father should expire, Fazil had no valid excuse for procrastination. In this the lady Lurlee agreed perfectly, and her idea of a double marriage in the family was by no means unacceptable.

In truth that long-desired event much occupied the good lady's thoughts, almost, indeed, engrossing them. What preparations would not have to be made! and all by her. There were Zyna's clothes and Tara's to be put in hand immediately; there were stores of flour, and butter, and spices, and sugar to be laid in, flocks of sheep to come from Afzoolpoor, all the dancing women in Beejapoor to be engaged, fireworks to be made, and sweetmeats without end. All the new bridal ornaments had to be designed and executed, and this was no easy matter. Inshalla! however, she was determined it should all be done; and when Lurlee Khanum took anything into her head, there was less difficulty, perhaps, in doing it, than with others who talked more.

They did not tarry now. An express was sent to the capital that they had determined to leave Kurrar on the ensuing Monday, and Lurlee was more than ever particular that on this, their last voluntary journey, all that could be done to insure its being propitious, should be observed. They were to travel south-eastward, and Monday was the sixth day of the month, so that the mysterious "Murdan-ool-Ghyb" (the invisible being) was behind them, as he ought to be. The old tablets showed, too, that Venus ruled the hour before noon, which was a very convenient time for starting, because every one would have bathed and eaten, and they could travel on till evening without difficulty. Now, too, the weather was cool, nay, the air was positively cold in the early mornings, when exposure to it was not wholesome, and all their preparations were made accordingly. As they were about to enter their litters, the good lady made both the girls and Fazil look at themselves in a glass, which was the crowning ceremony of all ; and we believe that there never were merrier faces, or a journey begun in truer hope, and with more thankful hearts.

True, Lurlee missed the familiar countenance which, though sometimes it used to look kindly on her, and sometimes was impatient, was in the main a loving one—sadly,—very sadly ; and as the city grew nigh, she had a dread, shared by Zyna and her brother, that the first days in the old house would be inexpressibly painful. So, also, when remembrances of the dear old Khan came over her, the good lady would weep plentifully and be the better of it ; and Goolab and the cook Kurreema, who, having escaped the Mahrattas, rejoined her mistress at Kurrar, and had shared all her trials, were ever ready with pithy consolations, and practical expectations of the blessings in store for her which, indeed, she was well inclined to believe.

We may say, too, as perhaps hardly unnatural, that Zyna's approaching marriage was by no means terrible

in contemplation : and the eagerness of her betrothed to
have it concluded, gave earnest of the happiness which
she hoped for, indeed felt assured of. We feel that we
do not know much of this young man, and that, if it
had fallen to his lot to accompany the Khan's army,
he might have become a prominent character in this
history, and displayed that devotion for Zyna and his
friend Fazil, which we believe he really possessed. But
after all, perhaps, it was better as it was. Who can
say, for instance, whether he would have escaped the
bloody field at Jowly, or the massacre in the ambush
at Pertabgurh,—or the deadly fever of the forests and
jungles, which had destroyed so many who had escaped
the sword ?

We have no doubt, too, had the lady Lurlee set
herself to work to find out astrological reasons why
he did not accompany the Khan, that they would have
been discoverable ; but as she had agreed with her
husband that, for the present, he was better away, so
she had left these mysteries unsolved, and the issue to
the young man had been favourable. Not only had
his house been put in order in all respects, and the
ceremonies after his father's death completed, but those
preparations begun in which Zyna was so deeply interested, and of which our friend the Lalla, who, as we
know, had been attached to the young nobleman by
Afzool Khan as secretary, wrote minute and eloquent
accounts.

According to him, never had such preparations been
made : while the accomplished scribe exhausted the Gul-

istan, the Mejnoon-i-Leila, and other love-stories, for the choicest couplets to adorn his letters, he not unfrequently composed other verses himself. Most frequently, too, in the bold rough hand which Kowas Khan wrote, there would be a postscript to say Fazil (which meant Zyna) was only to believe him as devoted as ever in all respects; and whenever Fazil gave these epistles to his sister to read, and directed especial notice to the postscripts, we are strongly inclined to consider that she found them by far their most acceptable portions. Under the constitution of Mahomedan society, even had her lover been in camp, he could have seen nothing of Zyna, and she would have been in stricter seclusion from him, perhaps, than others. As she was content to take him upon hearsay, and to trust, like all her people, to after-life with him, to know him as a lover and husband too, we do not see what business we have, to discuss the matter at all in this narrative.

So the journey was soon over, and little more than a hundred miles, with a light equipage, was quickly traversed. Lurlee had written to her old friend, the Moolla of the ward in which they lived, to send a special messenger to inform her at what hour it would be lucky to enter the house with two expectant brides in company; and that worthy, in conjunction with other friends, had duly solved this knotty question: and sent a return express to meet them at the last halting-place, wherein all the particulars were duly disclosed, and, we need not say, most scrupulously observed.

Fazil had wished to ride on several stages in advance and get to court, where the King looked anxiously for his coming ; but Lurlee would not hear of it. " Who could tell," she said, " what might not result from so incautious a proceeding ? They had met with great misfortune, which was happily past ; were they to risk more ? No ; she was positive ;" and we believe fully, that they were all much too happy together, to wrangle with her.

Fazil saw Tara daily ; and she and Zyna were little troubled by Lurlee, who was now busied in consultations with her domestic advisers, which appeared to be delightfully interminable. Every now and then, however, she would come into the tent where they sat—for Zyna was teaching Tara the pretty embroidery-work she practised herself—and, looking at Tara and saying nothing, would pass her hands over her, and press them against her temples, to remove evil, and then go away smiling.

Ah yes, she was very precious now. If Zyna or Tara laughingly asked how much evil could have accumulated in those short intervals, the good lady would shake her head, and once shocked Zyna by saying, that she should not think even, of Tara's beauty, lest it should altogether depart. We believe, however, that Zyna did not fear such a catastrophe. It was growing much too palpable and real to be doubted, or to be in danger of fading away : and became only the greater when, as Zyna looked at it, and whispered something which was probably a secret between the girls, though

Anunda guessed it as she sat with them, Tara covered her face, or hid it in Zyna's neck, or in her mother's bosom.

But the first few days after they arrived—in spite of congratulations of friends—of kind messages from the palace—of piles of Nuzzurs, or offerings of various kinds—were melancholy ones to all, yet tempered with grateful acknowledgments of providential care. Immediately on arrival, the requisite offerings were despatched to all the holy places of the neighbourhood and the city itself, as they had before arranged. The old Moolla, as almoner, collected a strange tribe of vagrant Fakeers, who were fed to repletion in the large courtyards ; and the Shastree and Anunda, made their offerings after their own fashion, at Hindu temples.

The journey, and the constant association with Lurlee and Zyna, had done much to reconcile Anunda to Mahomedan ways ; and, perhaps, in such matters women are more facile than men, for she was prepared for the evidences of wealth and rank which she saw on her arrival ; but her husband and Fazil did not make much progress. The simple Hindu priest could not bring himself to be on an equality with the young Mahomedan noble ; but he admitted the respect of Fazil for him gratefully, and a sincere affection sprang up between them out of it, which, if undemonstrative, was not the less permanent.

All Vyas Shastree now wished for, was the unavoidable termination. Till it took place he was not in his proper position. Few, if any, Bramhuns

knew the history of Tara in the capital; but he did
not feel justified, being impure, in visiting members of
his own sect, till he had performed expiatory ceremonies, and so, with his wives, kept himself secluded
in a court of the house specially allotted to him, and
the garden we know of, the shade and quiet of which
suited him. Radha, too, required rest and care; and
so a month passed, for Lurlee would not be hurried.
She had much on hand, she said, and must do it after
her own fashion; and no one interfered with her and
her assistants.

Perhaps we need not follow the good lady to the end
of it; but as all matters of this kind, when loving
care directs them, have an inevitably happy conclusion,
so we are bound to relate that nothing was wanting
here. Tara said that Zyna's marriage might be as
splendid as it could be made, and suited to the rank
and condition of two noble houses; but with her it
should be different, and so it was. If there was a
shade of disappointment upon the old lady's brow,
because the son of Afzool Khan was not married with
the same splendour as the son of the late Wuzeer, who
had no family to boast of, it passed away when Fazil
himself declared it could not be otherwise, and the
wistful pleading face of Tara confirmed it.

So, as part of the magnificent ceremony which united
Zyna to her betrothed—the like of which had not been
seen in Beejapoor for years—Tara was admitted to the
Mahomedan faith, and the blessing of God and the
peace of the Prophet said over her as she repeated the

new creed, received her new name of Ayésha, and was
received into her new home. Then the chief Kazee,
who had conducted the prayers, blessed all, and cried
with a loud voice, solemnly—

"O Lord God! grant that such love may live between these couples, thy servants, as was between
Adam and Eve, Abraham and Sara, Moses and Sufoora,
his highness Mahomed — on whom be peace—and
Ayésha. Ameen and ameen!" and all the assembly
repeated solemnly, "Ameen and ameen!"

Some of the old Khan's friends wondered, some
sneered, some blamed the young man's choice, but more
congratulated him; for, as they said, "though she was
once an infidel, she is now a true believer; and, after
all, was he not free to choose what would best insure
his own honour and happiness?" We are bound to
record, however, that those matrons who, being privileged friends and guests, were indulged with a sight
of the bride's beautiful face—as Tara's veil was raised
from amidst the cloud of gauze and silver tissue in
which it was enveloped—did not wonder at all that it
had been irresistible; and there might have been some
envious also, regretting that daughters of their own had
lost their chance in the choice which Fazil had made.
So, to prevent any evil consequences, Lurlee, with her
own hands, waved over Tara's head in succession, tray
after tray of lighted lamps and certain condiments which
would infallibly avert evil glances, and ended by passing
her hands over the bride and blessing her. "Mayst
thou be fruitful," she said, embracing her, "and remain,

with beauty undiminished, the joy of thy lord; and
may his love for thee increase till it is fulfilled and
perfected in Paradise. So be thou blessed, O my
daughter, altogether !"

Even more fervently did her mother bless Tara.
Although Anunda had cheerfully taken part in those
portions of the ceremonies that were possible without
clashing with the observances of her own faith, yet for
the most part they were strange, and she had felt out
of place. But she and her husband were thankful
they had witnessed all to the close—thankful that Tara
had been with them to the last. Henceforth their lives
must be divided, but there was an assurance of honour
and protection to their child which soothed the inevitable separation, and filled their hearts with hope
and trust.

Long she sat alone with them, and they spoke of the
future calmly and joyfully. There had been no misgiving from the first ; and while they could not, if they
would, have recalled Tara to their own faith, they saw
in her future life as much of true happiness as they
could have wished for. So they blessed her; and after
their own simple fashion put her hands into Fazil's:
and he took her from them, and, touching their necks,
vowed to be faithful, and they believed him.

"They have given thee to me, O beloved," Fazil said
to Tara, as her parents departed on their journey home-
wards. "Now fear not. As sacred to me as my vow
before the priest, was the last vow to them. Fear not
now, Ayésha!"

"I would rather be Tara to thee, my lord, for ever," she said shyly. "The little maiden who, once rescued by thee from dishonour, has lived in thy heart since then, cannot change to thee, even in name."

"Be it so," he replied. "To thy new people be Ayésha ; to me, Tara—so be witness, my God and thy God—evermore!"

CHAPTER XXXII.

EPILOGUE.

PERHAPS I ought to have told my fair readers more
of the particulars of this double marriage, but I
am afraid they would have found them as tiresome in
the relation, as Zyna and Tara did in actual sufferance
of the nine days of their continuance.   We can at
least imagine that, with unlimited means, the jewels
and trousseaux provided for both brides by the lady
Lurlee (and these things are as indispensable there as
here) were—perfection.   And we may also state thus
much in confidence, that particular friends were admitted to private views of them.   The young to be
envious : the old to be congratulatory—envious too,
perhaps, who knows ?—for such things happen there as
well as here.   Then, as marriage gifts were presented
by friends, there were trays upon trays from the Queen
to both of jewels, brocades, and muslins, which need
not be specified ; and the royal lady availed herself of
her privilege to see the brides, and put sugar-candy into
both their mouths, wondering at Tara's beauty, and

heartily wishing them both God-speed on their life's journey.

Did not also the poets of the city write verses, and the singers sing them; and are they not sung there to this day? Were there not poor folk fed by hundreds, Hindus as well as Mussulmans, and clothed too? and was there one of the sixteen hundred mosques in the city, where alms and thank-offerings were not distributed in proportion to their importance? "No one else remained to be married," said the lady Lurlee, when she had collected all the poor couples she could hear of, given them clothes, and had them married with her children. And, Mashalla! of what had been done, she was in nowise ashamed. No, indeed; and plenteous were the congratulations and blessings showered upon her, and upon them all, by high and low.

Vyas Shastree, Anunda, and Radha, remained long enough to see Tara reconciled to her new station in life, and to appreciate, how irresistibly charming the quiet natural dignity of the Bramhun girl became, among the new society into which her destiny had thrown her. But, beloved as she was by many a sincere friend among her new faith—as years passed, the devotion borne to her by the retainers of the house, the farmers on her husband's vast estates, and the poor everywhere, was most affecting to witness, and increased with time; and her parents heard with joy and pride, far away in their own home, of the bounty of the good lady, Ayésha Khanum.

They left their daughter, then, at peace ; and her last connection with the temple, where her father served, and where she was long remembered, was the presentation to the shrine, of the necklace she had vowed to it, which was taken there in solemn procession, and hung round the neck of the image. Some time afterwards, and when all expiatory ceremonies were completed, Radha's first child was born—a son, which Anunda adopted as her own : and in her care for it, found love and occupation to fill her heart and her time, and to supply, in some part, Tara's absence.

Mother and daughter met, however, frequently. No entire year elapsed without a reunion, and in the course of time came children too, who climbed in turn about the good dame's lap and called her grandmother. Then her heart clave to them—strangers though they were in faith—and after her own simple fashion she lived much among them during the latter years of a tranquil and happy life. Sometimes the Shastree came with her to Beejapoor, but not often.

Fazil Khan lived in stormy times and bore his part in them. The destruction of the force under his father's command had not only been a sore loss to the King's army, both in *matériel* and in men,* but a vital blow at the very existence of the kingdom and of the Mahomedan power in India. Treacherously as it had been gained, the Rajah Sivaji did not slumber on his

---

* The loss of the Beejapoor army at Jowly was 4000 horses, with all the guns, elephants, camels, *matériel*, and treasure of the army.

victory. His people were assured it had been suggested by divine counsel, and carried out by divine aid, and that their prince thenceforth was an incarnation of divinity. He, perhaps aided by his mother, believed this of himself, propagated the belief, and acted upon the effect of it. He was everywhere active and persevering: now invading the kingdom of Beejapoor, plundering up to the gates of the capital, and inflicting rapid and terrible blows in all directions : now attacking the Mogul posts and forts, and extending his authority until, though professing subservience to both, he became virtually independent equally of Dehli and Beejapoor, and finally assumed the state and insignia of a sovereign.

Fazil Khan had not long concluded his marriage ceremonies, ere he was called upon to take the command of part of a new army, with which the King took the field in person. Tara would not leave him, and shared the fatigue and peril of the new campaign in a manner which called forth the lady Lurlee's warmest approbation. She had not been more, she said, to his father than Tara was to his son, and she always contrasted her practical usefulness and endurance, with the behaviour of other ladies who could not leave luxurious palaces, and the state and splendour which had greater charms for them, than the rough vicissitudes of camp life.

For a time the royal forces succeeded in checking the Mahratta incursions and restoring tranquillity on the borders, and Fazil Khan continued, like his father, to render service as a commander whenever he was

called upon ; but he could not be induced to take office
in the administration, and as disquiet and intrigue at
the capital became more formidable, retired for the
most part to his estate of Afzoolpoor, near the Bheema
river, and usually lived there, visiting Beejapoor only
on occasions of ceremony. He never married again, as
the law would have allowed, and at his death was
buried beside his wife in the mausoleum which his
father had built at Afzoolpoor, and where such of the
remains of the old Khan as could be afterwards recovered, had been deposited. The mausoleum still
exists as perfect as when built, and on the several
anniversaries of their deaths, flowers are strewn by
the Mahomedan priests of the town and by the people
over their graves, and prayers are said for the repose
of their souls in Paradise.

We have said that the Mahomedan power in India
received its first material check in the massacre at
Pertabgurh, and we state this advisedly. That event,
in 1657, led as directly to its ruin, and the steady rise
of the Mahratta predatory power, as did the English
victory of Plassey, in 1757, to the destruction of the
Mahratta and Mahomedan powers of India. For
though, by the conquests and subversion of all the independent Mahomedan kingdoms of the Dekhan by
Aurungzeeb, the empire of Dehli culminated to its
highest splendour,—it was not maintained: and rapidly
fell to pieces under the effects of disastrous civil wars
on the one hand, and the increasing power of the
Mahrattas on the other. In 1689, Beejapoor was

again attacked by the Mogul armies under the Emperor
in person, and, surrendering by capitulation, ceased to
be an independent kingdom.   The rest is matter of
general history, with which this particular chronicle
has no concern.

Sivaji died in 1680, after a life which was a stirring
romance from first to last, but not before the power he
had aroused and created had become for the present
invincible—fulfilling his mother's prophecy, that the
Hindu war-cry, "Hur, Hur, Mahadeo!" should be
shouted in victory throughout the land of Hind, in
triumph to the Goddess who led it on, from Dehli to
Raméshwur.

It was singular that Kowas Khan, with his father's
tragical fate fresh in his memory, should have been
unable to resist the same temptations to treason and
treachery.   Though he had ceased them for a while, the
Emperor Aurungzeeb renewed his intrigues at Beejapoor; for Kowas Khan, who became regent of the
State after the King Ali Adil Shah's death, entered
into negotiations with the Mogul general, Khan Jehán,
who commanded in the adjoining provinces, to give a
daughter of the royal house in marriage to a son of the
Emperor's, and as the price of this, to hold the kingdom of Beejapoor himself in dependence, which had
been his father's aim also.   The plot was discovered,
however, and Kowas Khan was assassinated in 1675,
eighteen years after the events we have recorded.

Some of his lineal descendants still survive, and
the memory of the lady Zyna and of her beauty lives

among them.   There is a noble mausoleum on the west
side of the town of Suggur, in the province of Shora-
poor, which, at the period of which we write, belonged
to this family.   It was begun by the "Wuzeer" of
Beejapoor, and finished by his son Kowas Khan : and
in it the remains of the lady Zyna and her husband
rest, under the care of their descendants who, now reduced in circumstances, have preserved a small village
with its lands, which adjoins the tomb, as the only remnant of the once princely estates which were held by
their ancestors ; and the revenues of this village, which
had originally been assigned in payment of oil for the
mausoleum, are now their only support.   They are,
however, most respectable.   The soubriquet of Wuzeer
is still attached to them ; and the head of the family,
Sofee Sahib, still preserves much of the "aristocratic"
dignity of descent.   The family palace at Beejapoor,
though deserted, is still standing, and is, or was, one
of the very few private buildings there of which the roof
is entire.   Perhaps by this time, however, its owner
may have been unable to resist the price he could obtain for its massive teak timbers.   The roof may have
been sold, and the handsome rooms and courts left
open, to decay rapidly under the influence of the
seasons.

A few words in relation to some other characters in
our history, and we have done.

Pahar Singh did not long maintain his promise of
abstinence from violence.   It had become, together
with avarice, the ruling passion of his character, and

led him on, after a while, to fresh outrages ; and though
pardoned by the King again and again, in memory of
his strange services, it was impossible, in the end, to
overlook the daring character of his proceedings, and
his occupation of royal territories. Nor was it long
before Kowas Khan discovered the active share the
robber chief had taken in his father's murder ; and
though the King's acquiescence in that deed was more
surmised than ascertained, the fact of his being acquainted with Pahar Singh's part in it was not afterwards denied. On an occasion, therefore, when, by a
more than usually serious outrage, the King's pardon
had been absolutely withdrawn, his reduction and
punishment became unavoidable,—Kowas Khan led an
army against the castle of Itga, Pahar Singh was slain
in its defence, his estates confiscated, and the castle and
its walls blown up.

His nephew escaped, but returned to the village to
live as a farmer under reduced circumstances. When
Aurungzeeb conquered the country, he became again
" Hazaree," or commander of a thousand, and the title
remained with his descendants, who, however, never
abandoned lawless courses. Long afterwards, a de-
scendant, also named Pahar Singh, became a leader of
Dekhan Pindarees, or freebooters, after the Mahratta
war of 1818-19, and when that crime was no longer
practicable, took to a minor practice of it in highway
robbery. In 1828-29, the family were found to be
largely connected with Dacoity and Thuggee, and the
leading members of it were tried, convicted of both

crimes, and sentenced to various terms of imprisonment,
during which their head, Pahar Singh, died.

Persevering to the last, the other members, on their
release, again took to highway robbery on horseback,
and for a brief period were the terror of certain districts in the Dekhan, extending their operations, too,
to distant points ; but they were gradually hunted
down,* and the last six were brought to justice by the
writer of this chronicle in 1850, and sentenced to
penal servitude for life. One member only of the
family survives free, and, as late as 1860, was a private
in the police of the —— district.

Our friend the Lalla, who played a conspicuous part
in the early portion of this history, became a prosper-
ous and wealthy man ; but the question of his honesty
remained an open one. He sent for his family, and
settled at Beejapoor, and his talents gained him lucra-
tive employment in the state. He remained attached
to Kowas Khan, whom he is believed to have cor-
rupted ; and, finally, as the kingdom was on the point
of dissolution, he is said to have made peace with his old
master, the Emperor Aurungzeeb, by materially assisting his designs, and tampering with the nobility and
officers of the state previous to the last investment of
the city. He probably returned to Dehli with the
royal camp, for no traces of his family are to be found
in Beejapoor.

Bulwunt Rao remained as he was, the leader of a

* They were apprehended by the author, committed to the Zillah
court of Sholapoor, and there tried by the judge.

troop of his own horses in the Päigah, or household forces of Fazil Khan. When his cousin and hereditary enemy, Tannajee Maloosray, was killed in that famous escalade of Singhur, near Poona, which has furnished the subject of many a Mahratta ballad, Bulwunt Rao went to Sivaji, and the circumstances he related being well remembered, he obtained substantial justice in the restoration of his hereditary property. Sivaji offered him service, which was respectfully declined, and the motives for refusal being appreciated, he was honourably dismissed. He married among his kinsfolk, and his wife, a practical woman, kept his house well. It is questionable, however, whether his habits were ever reclaimed, and he died before the dissolution of the Beejapoor kingdom. His wife, finding the care of the troop-horses irksome, sold them, returned with her children to the family estate, and settled there, and their descendants are now connected with many of the noble families of the Dekhan.

The hunchback, Lukshmun, after his return home, took to Itga all that he had saved, together with a heavy purse of gold which Fazil Khan had given him, which he buried immediately on his arrival. Somehow or other, however, the fact of this gold being possessed by him, got wind, and the idea of a mere retainer possessing gold at all, was too much to be endured by his avaricious master, who demanded to see it. We are sorry to record, that the poor fellow was obliged to submit to some rough torture, which was more than he could bear, ere he would surrender it ; but Lukshmun always supposed that it was by the desertion of his master at Tooljapoor, rather than by the possession of the gold, that evil eyes fell upon him; and perhaps he was right. The gold was given up to his chief, and by it the last link between them was broken ; and profiting by Pahar Singh's temporary absence, Lukshmun, taking his wife and children with him, left Itga one day, and returned to Afzoolpoor, where Fazil Khan's retainers were stationed, and was protected by them. Pahar Singh threatened to burn the town if he were not given up ; but Fazil Khan paid what was demanded for him, and he remained.

Years afterwards, and as his lord's children grew up, the hunchback was their especial favourite. He taught the eldest boys athletic exercises, the use of their weapons, and riding ; and as long as any girl was allowed to go out of the private apartments, he carried her about in his arms, told charming fairy stories, and manufactured playthings—his dolls, being of all, the most hideous, and most delightful. Nor was there any greater treat to the children possible, than when their mother sometimes, and especially on certain anniversaries, sent for the hunchback and Ashruf, now a stout cavalier in the household troop, and having seated them outside a screen, made them sing ballads again as they did once long ago; and of all their store, "The Vow of the Necklace," was ever the greatest favourite with the children, because their mother's name was mentioned in it. With her, because—well no matter : we know why, long since, and 'tis now an old story.

Many years before them, and in all honour among her children, as she always called them, the lady Lurlee passed away. She never gave up astrology, and found perpetual occupation in discovering lucky days for her grandchildren's wants, and for all sorts of household observances. Not a tooth could be cut, or any ailment of childhood exist and pass away, without appropriate ceremonials of thanksgiving, in the discovery of proper times for which, the old lady was held to be especially skilful. Nor in these only. Was she not the authority of the neighbourhood for ascertaining lucky marriages, for deciding the proper colours for proper days of her grandchildren's dresses ; and did not she keep the cords of all their birthdays, and tie the knots in each as the anniversaries returned ? Was she not the undisputed director of all such household family matters, and the universal referee on them by all her acquaintance ?

Her affection for Zyna and her children remained to the last, though she never cordially liked Kowas Khan, or forgave him for being the son of one who had been a slave. But her love for her own child, Tara—the child whom God had sent her—transcended that for Zyna. It filled her heart, and overflowed upon her grandchildren, who loved her dearly, and did with her pretty much what they pleased. After Kowas Khan's death she went to Zyna, and lived with her till her son was old enough to protect his mother ; then she settled finally into the place she held with Tara and her children ; and when she breathed her last, her head lay on Tara's bosom—resting peacefully.

With her outward conversion to a strange faith, did Tara forget the old ? No, it was impossible. Though her studious disposition enabled her to master enough Arabic, under her husband's teaching, to understand the daily prayers, and some simple ceremonials, yet the grand old Hindu hymns of the Védas, and other devotional portions of the Shastras, especially the Bhugwat Geeta, were never forgotten ; and when the purport of them was explained to her husband, he did not object to her reading them. She could not either, change her frugal mode of living ; and, to her death, never overcame her natural repugnance to animal food. In this respect also, her husband indulged her ; though perhaps the lady Lurlee thought it a sad dereliction of orthodox observances in general, which could only be overcome on the festivals of the Nowroz* or the Bukreed,† or other occasions of religious ceremonial.

When Tara was dying, and the Moollas without were chanting the service for her departing soul, her eyes seemed once to flash with a bright radiance, and her husband and children, who were around her, heard her say gently, " I come, O Mother," and repeat some Sanscrit words. The priests, jealous of her perfect conversion, would have it, that she alluded to Miriam,

* New year.
† Festival in commemoration of the offering up of Isaac by Abraham.

the Mother of Jesus of Nazareth, for there could be no
other Mother.   It might, indeed, be so, for she seemed
of late to have taken a peculiar delight and interest
in this history, especially since some Christian monks
from Goa, who had established a mission* at the town
of Chittapoor, only a few miles distant, had come to
beg alms of her, and had told her of the purer faith of
Christ, and his loving mother Mary.   It might have
been that she spoke of this; or, more probable perhaps, that her spirit, trembling on the brink of the
unknown world, had wandered back into the old days
of her trials and deliverances, once, ere it departed.

* The mission still exists, and is visited periodically by priests
from Goa.   There are, or were, about seventy Christians in it who,
with an affecting simplicity, preserve their faith in purity.   They
are shepherds, weavers, and distillers.

THE END.

PRINTED BY WILLIAM BLACKWOOD AND SONS, EDINBURGH.

www.ingramcontent.com/pod-product-compliance
Lightning Source LLC
Chambersburg PA
CBHW031336070726
47496CB00017B/1145